Fake PERFECT Me

Two Harbors Press

*Jennifer —
Discover your
TRUTH!*

Fake PERFECT Me

Cari Kamm

Two Harbors Press

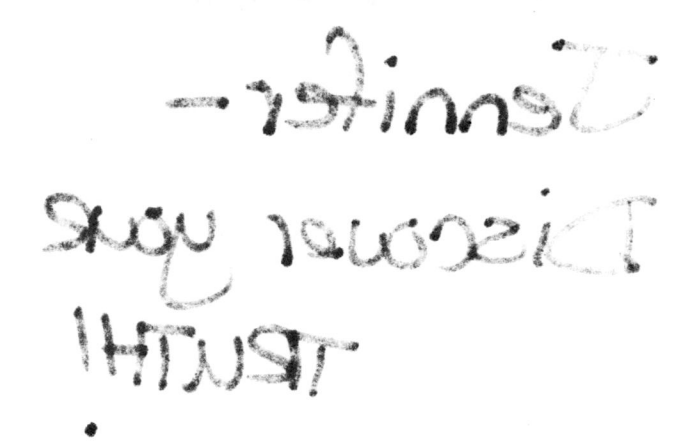

Copyright © 2010 by Cari Kamm.

TWOHARBORS
WWW.TWOHARBORSPRESS.COM

Two Harbors Press
212 3rd Avenue North, Suite 290
Minneapolis, MN 55401
612.455.2293
www.TwoHarborsPress.com

All rights reserved. No part of this publication may be reproduced, stored in a retrieval system, or transmitted, in any form or by any means, electronic, mechanical, photocopying, recording, or otherwise, without the prior written permission of the author.

Fake Perfect Me is a work of fiction. Characters, places, and incidents are a product of the author's imagination and are used fictitiously. Any resemblance to actual events or people, living or dead, is coincidental.

ISBN - 978-1-936198-88-7
ISBN - 1-936198-88-6
LCCN - 2010932942

Cover Design and Typeset by Wendy Arakawa

Printed in the United States of America

In loving memory of Jonathan

Acknowledgments

A HUGE THANK YOU TO my parents for everything, both the pretty and the ugly, especially those times when you grounded me and I wasn't completely fond of you. Every moment of my life has placed me directly in this spot, and I wouldn't have it any other way. Your hardest decisions were my strongest moments. Thank you, Mom, for keeping me in your daily prayers—for all the ones that were answered and for all the ones that weren't. Thank you, Dad, for allowing me to carry out every possible dream, or what you refer to as "always having to go big." I always know you are standing on the sidelines, cheering me on. Thank you to my little brother for making me want to be my best every day, as being your mentor is one of the most important jobs to me … well, until you actually grow up or I have my own children. You are such a wonderful young man, and I'm truly blessed to be your sister. Thank you, Debra Davis, for being a passionate publicist and, most important, a supportive friend through all my endeavors. A million thank-yous would not be enough to my mentor and aunt, Aimee Caudle. Having you in my life is a blessing and I am thankful every day. You have given me unconditional love and support through my most beautiful moments and helped to guide me through the roughest of storms. It has been the greatest joy to dance in the rain with you. You define the term "role model." Thanks to my closest friends, who have supported me through thick and thin. Also, a very special thank you to RJF. You are that true light that helps me shine even brighter. Your support is a gift.

1

Journal entry—May 14
Three days ago, I was officially dumped by my boyfriend of two years. And two months ago, my own skin care company crashed and burned. And just one month ago, my precious dog, Potato, died. What more can happen? What has happened to my perfectly perfect life?
I. R.

ALTHOUGH I WAS HEADED OUT the door, I was in no condition for Friday night. Emotionally, I was a disaster, but physically, I was blown-out, manicured, and dressed in black Dolce & Gabbana from head to toe, with my black Chanel clutch. It all looked so effortless. This evening, however, D&G stood for "Doom & Gloom."

"Isabella. C'mon ... just pull yourself together. Christ!" I whispered to myself as the elevator descended to the lobby of my building. Looking at my reflection in the elevator doors, I thought I looked like I was ready for my own funeral. I could feel the tears forming for the tenth time this evening. *Does anything last forever?* I wondered once more. *Does believing in fairy tales only cause someone to end up a heartbroken, sentimental fool?*

To keep the ugly cry-face on lock down, I directed my attention to my polished gold Krugerrand coin, which hung against my chest by a thin, twisted gold chain and flashed against my black blouse. It was my Batman signal, alerting the universe that I was in crisis and in desperate need of being rescued immediately, if not sooner. The coin's weight was also a reminder of the reason I'd moved to Gotham City. After all, it was a result of my great-aunt and her one-ounce gold-coin collection that afforded me the opportunity of the life I was leading.

By the time I reached the street, it was 7:43 p.m., and I had just enough time to catch a cab and head up to Nobu 57 for my biweekly dinner with my best friend, Pia, aka "the Czar." She would be there exactly on time, as she was privileged to have a driver at her beck and call. These dinners always lasted three hours, took place at one of our favorites—like Café Boulud, Nello's, or Cipriani's downtown—and were followed by a bill the price of a new pair of Manolos.

Pia and I had met at Columbia University seven years ago, during our graduate study-abroad trip to Italy; we were each completing a thesis on the Mediterranean diet. Pia's family was in the restaurant business and owned a historic and famous Cuban restaurant in Manhattan. We loved to talk about food, look at food, order food, and eat food. A few years ago, we both had gotten addicted to the Zone meal daily delivery program, as every socialite was swearing it was the easiest method of being a size two—if you did not want to develop a cocaine habit to curb your appetite. At the time, this threatened to affect our lavish dinners, until we realized we could still enjoy the restaurant scene with a nice bottle of wine and remain in the Zone. Back then, I would bring my meal bag to Pia's restaurant, and the chef would heat it, plate it, and serve it. We had the best of both worlds: the restaurant scene and a legal diet. I clearly remembered the moment I saw Pia and knew we would be best friends. I had just left the Vatican in Rome and was walking to the Sistine Chapel to stand in line for what I figured would probably be ten hours. While in line, I overheard Pia and another student mention that they were going to get blowouts and shop before heading to dinner at Obika, which means "here it is," a mozzarella bar and the newest restaurant trend in Rome. The setup was similar to a sushi bar except there was no raw fish, just pyramids of cheese from different regions, such as Campagnia and Puglia. I thought it would be a more pleasant experience to dine with people who actually liked to eat, as my roommate, another nutrition student, seemed to strongly believe in anorexia. People were always surprised by how much food I could "put away" and not gain four hundred pounds. What was so terrible about wanting to have my cake, eat it, and then make sure it never counted? Though I had my methods for staying thin, I was never strong enough to be anorexic; I loved dining too much to rob myself of the experience of the taste and smell of cuisine from all over the world and from the best chefs in every country.

As it turned out, Pia's crowd was my type of crowd, and that night we became best friends, as I knew we would. Going to dinner at all the "must-be-seen-at" hot spots was an event in itself. For Pia and me, getting ready was a whole process that would take, literally, half a day. We got manicures, pedicures, blowouts, and new outfits, which just made dining together more of our special thing.

Once we were looking and feeling fabulous, we headed over to whichever restaurant we had reserved for that night. As soon as we were seated, usually at the best table in the house, the first task was to order drinks. Sipping and looking is what we did for the first twenty minutes. Of course, the bottle of wine was selected first to ensure it would be perfectly chilled and ready to serve as we studied and discussed the menu selections. We liked to order and eat, then order and eat some more, always keeping a menu at the table. We knew, no matter what we did or said, we would never call each other ridiculous. We were just ourselves, no matter how extreme and over the top we might be.

Tonight's dinner was going to be a bit different. Although the dinner chat usually meandered over topics like the hardest restaurant reservation to score that month, the most intriguing *Us Weekly* headliner, that Bergdorf's had remodeled their fifth floor again, or our ongoing argument over which shoe was worth the price (Choo or Blahnik), I had bigger issues on my mind tonight.

Pia had no idea of the most recent tragedy in my life. For the past two months, disaster after disaster had played out; it was as if I was living in a screenplay titled *The Rise and Fall of Isabella Reynolds*.

Tonight, I needed more than my journal. Writing to myself helped me acknowledge events and feelings that occurred in my life, but saying something aloud, anything coming from my heart (especially when it was a broken one) was more than acknowledging it; it was owning it. In that I'd arrived without my consent at my third tragedy, I needed to hear the words come out of my mouth—to stain the air with my feelings, even though it was convenient and much easier to simply tear pages out and flush them. Purging and flushing my journal entries had become quite the habit. I'd remove the entries, just like the people, places, and things that didn't fit into my perfect world.

My most recent tragedy, this week, would not seem devastating to Pia, as I knew she disapproved of my Italian—I'm not referring to my ability to speak the language but to my Italian boyfriend, Santo, whom Pia referred to as Saint Santo.

Arriving at the restaurant with one minute to spare, I walked up to the usual hostess, who recognized me right away. "Hello, Ms. Reynolds. She has checked in and is already seated upstairs."

I hesitated, taking one last deep breath. *Cool, calm, and collected*, I reminded myself. *No tears tonight.* I prayed that things would go accordingly to plan.

"Isabella, you look stunning. I see the great-aunt is joining us for dinner as well," Pia said with a smirk. She knew that the physical weight of my Krugerrand coin was more than its actual one-ounce weight, as did I, and as a result, I wore it to remind myself to get myself together.

When I was eight years old, my great-aunt passed away, leaving me her South African Krugerrand coin collection. "Collection" is an understatement; investment was more like it. Each coin was a bit over an ounce of solid gold and engraved with the profile of Mr. Paul Kruger himself, the four-term president of the old South African Republic. Today, each coin is valued at roughly $1,200 a pop. At the reading of the will, I was informed that I would be receiving one thousand pieces of the metallic cash. I did the math and understood that my path of opportunity had been paved with choice—choices that were up to me to make. My thoughtful great-aunt had given me the means to succeed and afforded me the education of my choosing. The "K" was a reminder to me of not only the gift itself but also the pressure to succeed, as I had been given opportunity. The "K" was my reminder to be somebody, to do something, to only succeed. Failure was not an option.

"Pia, I am so relieved to see you. I really need to vent tonight." I slid in to the other side of the table and adjusted my shoulders, as the coin felt like a lump of lead tied around my neck.

"Oh, dear, this can't be good. What are you beating yourself up about this time?" She briefly glimpsed at my chest, and I knew she wasn't looking at my broken heart, as I hadn't yet revealed the third tragedy. "Isabella, you don't look so great. Tell me now," Pia said, focusing in on my face while signaling to the waiter for drinks.

I could feel a tidal wave of emotion erupt from my gut, move through my chest, and feel as if it was about to explode from my mouth. "Three strikes, and I'm out. I'm completely out," I said, feeling defeated. I covered my face with my hands to hide the shame.

"Hold on, Miss Reynolds, for one damn second. You are not out. What does that even mean? Is it that new job of yours that you rushed into? Sweetie, you are a smart, sophisticated, stunning, and a snappy young woman. The thing about you, Reynolds, is you think you have to be everyone's perfect something—the perfect girlfriend, the perfect employee, the perfect daughter, the perfect friend. You put this pressure on yourself that makes you a different someone—different for everyone, this person you thought they need or want you to be. What happened now?"

Even though Pia and I were the same age, she was always able to take a step away and offer that motherly advice. "Pia, Santo and I are over. I have lost something again!" I said hysterically. Our food arrived—the yellowtail jalapeño, miso cod, and two orders of spicy tuna roll (light on the rice, of course) with an extra side of spicy mayo sauce; that was how we always started our Nobu experience.

"I don't want to say I told you so," she said, trying to disguise relief at my news. "Italians are known to be romantic and passionate people. Your Italian was broken, completely defective, and he came with no warrantee or guarantee. He was not romantic and never even spoke the language to you. He was only passionate about that job that made him miserable."

I knew she was right. Santo and I were not the same Isabella and Santo that we had been during our first year of dating. Some good and some very bad changes had occurred, especially for me.

I met the Italian just as I was beginning my skin care company. He was living in Manhattan, working as a corporate attorney at a cream-of-the-crop firm. He was a small, handsome man, with dark hair and periwinkle eyes and clothes that were tailor-made to fit his muscular frame.

It didn't take me long to realize that all the other things in the Italian's life—his job, his BlackBerry, even his shopping obsession ranked higher than I did on the totem pole of his life priorities. Now, looking back, I see that we never had passion. Santo was mean to people and had no patience for anyone. I could not quite put my finger on it why he behaved this way, but even at restaurants, he was mean to waiters. To be honest, he seemed capable of being rude to a little girl at a lemonade stand.

"I wanted everyone to be wrong," I said, attempting to swallow a piece of spicy tuna. I missed my ritual step of adding extra-spicy mayo—I was such a mess—and hoped she wouldn't notice. I never took a bite of my favorite roll without an extra dip of the orange concoction. I still wanted to seem to be somewhat holding it together.

"Okay, Isabella, I can tell you are completely distracted," Pia said, putting down her chopsticks and picking up her sakitini. "So, how did this go down? I need details."

I took my napkin, dabbed under my eyes, and took a deep breath.

"I'm so proud of you for finally taking control," Pia added, "but let's sip through this so our sushi doesn't stick in our throats."

I nodded, swallowing my roll with more difficulty as well. "One day during one of our strolls, we decided to sit and relax on a bench along the Hudson River. We sat there in silence, and I could not help but look at his shoes. He loved his Tod's brown leather ankle boots. As I sat there, I began to think how those boots resembled him in so many ways. I mean, have you ever thought how your favorite pair of shoes can resemble you?"

"Is this a trick question, Reynolds?"

"Anyway, his shoes were short, tan, with a thick, hard sole for stability. At first glance, the boots seemed warm, safe, and comfy. Over the years, whatever mistakes he made, he tried to cover, but the imperfections were still visible on the surface.

Well, with such a history, the Tod's boots would seem to be broken in, but if you looked carefully, they actually were as cold as a mother-in-law's kiss. The boots could be paired with any outfit and most occasions, but now that I think about it, something never seemed to quite fit."

"Only you could bring shoes into the situation." Pia began to giggle, but I knew from the nervous sound of it that she was wondering whether I was going to redirect the shoe question to her. Pia loved to dish out the advice but didn't care for the "what goes around comes around" system of life. "I tried telling you, darling, but sometimes even when our closest people are trying to protect us, our stubborn heads need to get through it all on our own. It doesn't matter which side you come out on, but you got to go through it yourself," Pia said, trying to hide a look of pride for knowing this and telling me so.

"So I interrupted our silence by initiating a talk about the relationship, which he tried to avoid. I wanted to know what he was thinking about us."

"Sweetie, that is the first sign that something is lacking in a relationship. When it's there, it's there. The heart cannot hide behind anything. Our eyes are the windows into our souls, and the fact you didn't know how he truly felt about you after years is a clear sign that something was not right."

"Well, he was not happy with my curiosity; he wanted to relax and avoid discussing my question. He stared in the other direction, casually sitting there with his legs crossed as he pulled out a cigar to smoke."

"Typical Italian."

Pia wanted me to end up with a Cuban—that was clear. She found something weak about every boyfriend I ever had, whether it was his religion, passport country, diet, or even his last name.

"I could feel myself tearing up," I continued, "which made me even more insecure and uncomfortable. He was making me feel like such a nuisance, but I stared at him so intensely, trying to force him to look at me."

"Isabella, do not take this the wrong way, but thank you, God, for your putting it out there. It has to be so exhausting, pretending to be so happy on the outside when you are tormented like this on the inside. You are lucky you got out of this before you became bitter. Being almost thirty, successful, and effortlessly beautiful, not to mention put together gorgeously from head to toe is the angle you need to be working. Add bitterness into that, and you should just remove yourself from the social scene, single with a cat, and eating Lean Cuisines every night for dinner."

"Fabulous, Pia, thanks for reminding me of the success part as well."

"You just lost your company, so that doesn't count, and you have a new career. Now, if you remain in a job just to have a job, then yes, you have a problemo."

I'm not sure why, but I suddenly got a flash of myself in sweats, hair in bun on top my head, and eating peanut butter out of a jar with a spoon—the Jif kind, not even organic. "Anyway, in his annoyed tone he finally asked me what I was getting at. He said he was really hungry and was focused on plans for dinner. He just kept repeating 'Cipriani's or Mr. Chow?'"

"Mr. Chow is ridiculous. I went there the other night for an event. They have a fabulous—"

"Pia, focus, please. I have not even gotten down into the trenches yet," I said.

She raised her hand in the air, motioning with her fingers only to get a move on the next round of drinks, pronto.

"So, I just came out and asked where he saw his life going. Just like that. He started saying he didn't know, and how his job was killing him, and he didn't know what to do about anything, and that he thinks Mr. Chow was the best choice for dinner. My blood was boiling at that point. I mean, seriously, when you ask a man where his life is going, and he *doesn't* think you are talking about your relationship—"

"Isabella, save yourself the trouble, and don't put yourself in his head," she said, raising her eyebrows and grinning as the drinks arrived from behind me. "Ah, yes, thank you, and the champagne is for her. Do you need a martini for this?"

She knew me very well, enough to know that I was acting much stronger than I was feeling. I knew that Pia knew that I had probably given myself a pep talk before entering the restaurant. "Actually, yes," I answered. "While I'm sipping this, bring me a Kettle One martini with a twist."

"Anything for you, miss?" the slick waiter asked with a wink.

"See? Why can't all men be like that?"

"Focus, Isabella, because we are going to enjoy our sushi, as Italian is not on the menu. Let's get this over with."

"I continued the conversation by asking him if that included us also."

"Like the directness," she said with a stern nod, but all I could think about was being proud, not of my question but my holding back tears, as I hadn't wanted him to see me cry.

"Right. Well, after years of being the perfect girlfriend, he threw his hands up in the air and gave me a 'for fuck sake.'"

"Well, darling, his stomach most likely was growling by then. How rude of you to be talking about your absurd feelings and heart," Pia said, while sipping and giggling.

"Can you believe him? Obviously, he had other worries on his mind, and he wanted to make me feel guilty for bothering him about such a meaningless topic—us. I mean, it does not require a genius. I felt like I was on a hideous episode of *The Bachelor*."

Pia interrupted, "No, but it requires a heart. To him, it was just another conversation; he couldn't multi-task. I will pretend you don't even know what that show is about. Sweetie, reality shows—"

"True, dat," I said, laughing with my "I can be tough Gangster Reynolds" accent. "So, I told him to listen to me.

I demanded that he tell me, after two years of dating, one answer, right then and there."

"Ah, Isabella, yes, the beauty in the number one. Sometimes it just comes down to one. One yes or one no. That's all we need."

"I understood about his career stress, as I just had lost my damn company, but I informed him that I do want to be married one day, with kids, and I needed to know if he saw his future with me. I didn't need to know soon, but right now."

"You said that?"

"Yes, just like that. I already knew the answer, but I needed to hear it from him. Love, to me, is a true emotion that can't be analyzed; you just feel it. It's there, and once it is, don't you just want to embrace it? Wouldn't you just fight for it and protect it with all that you have? Is there a choice with true love?"

"Darling, this is about you, not me. My life is not on the chopping block this evening."

"Fine, save it for your mental doctor."

"Sweetie, you realize that for you to demand an answer, that this was not about love, right?"

"He told me my behavior was ridiculous and that this was not simple," I said, feeling tears form—being called ridiculous hurt me deeply.

"Isabella, answer me. You are you, and you come with a very special guarantee, my dear—your honest heart. Did you ever sit back and ask yourself if you truly loved him?"

"Pia, how can you ask such a thing?"

"I can and I will. I'm calling you out, Reynolds. This is about your being rejected and things not playing like you were directing your own little movie called 'My Life.' Are you going to sit there and tell me, with your great-aunt present, that this is how you see the love of your life discussing your lives together?"

"Maybe you're right, but that doesn't mean it doesn't hurt. I mean, to be avoided like that. For him to make me feel like some unstable Bridezilla for no reason."

"That little cannoli was aware of this and avoided the topic for months. Sorry, but do you mean Singlezilla?"

Hysterical now, I said, "Yes, I can't believe that I wasted two years of my life with a selfish jerk. Talk about trying to push a round peg through a square hole."

"Isabella, you don't see yourself as you are. He didn't want to lose you. That cannoli was all about his job, his space, and his little precious things all to himself. His dilemma was that who wouldn't want you, and maybe, deep down inside, he knew he would never have a chance with someone like you again. He loved you, but he loved himself a lot more. I mean, what do you expect when you give your heart to someone who doesn't even know how to use his own? Miss Reynolds, you finally got your answers—the ones you did not want to hear but knew it was the truth all this time."

"Ah, my martini." I sat back, raised my glass to my lips slowly, and then quickly sipped half of it down. It was like pouring peroxide on an open wound. It stung at first but made it feel better.

Pia stared at me intensely, encouraging me to go on.

"I noticed I was not talking to the Italian that I had so desperately loved," I continued. I was now feeling uncomfortable using "love" and him in the same sentence without Pia's judging me. "His eyes were cold and dry, and I knew he didn't want to share his life with me. At least he was kind enough not to blow smoke in my face." I finished off my drink. "Pia, I got up from the bench that day and walked away. I had no idea when I sat down an hour prior that I would be walking away and leaving the Italian still sitting behind me. As I walked off, I thought of our dinner the night before at one of the city's newest restaurants. Just like Potato and our last night of Chinese on the couch, I didn't know that would be my last dinner with the Italian. If I had, I would have eaten everything on the menu that night, drowning my sorrow like a fat girl."

"Sweetie, I'm so sorry that you are having such a tragic couple of months. But trust me, the loss of the man who thinks he is a saint is a blessing in disguise," Pia said, raising her hand to signal for another round of cocktails. "Why didn't you call me?"

"To be honest, I didn't even know what to say." I swallowed my drink as if it was going to give me a boost of life. "Even when I go home, I'm forced to feel another void with Potato gone."

Pia was fighting her own tears. "I know. I know," she said. She picked up her chopsticks and suggested we should begin eating, as our courses were beginning to cover every inch of the table.

"You know, Potato loved my bed, probably because it resembled a huge white cloud, covered as it was with a duvet and six fluffy pillows. He was clever and quick enough to jump down and go back to his own bed at the sound of my key in the door. Of course, he didn't know that he shed, and I could be gone for hours and know exactly where he had been in the apartment from the traces of hair and drool. Somehow, he managed to leave me feeling guilty for screaming 'bad dog' at him, especially when he was already lying on his own bed, feigning innocence. I miss his morning wake-up calls. Every morning, he would come into my room and put his slobbering face on the side of my bed and bark to wake me up."

Pia placed her hand on my shoulder. "Isabella, you are not alone. I know it feels like you have lost everything, but you haven't. You have yourself. You have all of us. You can't isolate yourself like this. What did you do that evening after you left the saint on the bench?" she asked in a concerned, motherly tone.

"I went home alone, and I continued to analyze our relationship and why I played this game, knowing that no matter what, I was going to lose. I tried to figure out how I missed all of these losses as they occurred and if there was any way I could have prevented it from unraveling."

The waiter placed our drinks on the table. "Thank you," Pia said, startling me, as I had drifted into another place for a second. My mind had wandered and was trying to follow the void in my heart. "Isabella, you should have called me."

"I was so scared to stay home, only to cry while trying to figure out the easiest way to glue all the tiny bits and pieces of my broken heart back together. I called some friends, went to a private Jay-Z concert at the Roseland, and danced for hours. I danced and danced, song after song, until exhaustion. We ended up at the Rose Bar in the Gramercy Park Hotel, where I drank martini after martini and ate the olives for a source of nutrients—I had forgotten to eat that day and was famished. I adore the Rose Bar for its edgy sophistication."

"I love the Rose Bar." Pia nodded and raised her glass to mine.

"I finally made it home by five in the morning. I was home alone for the first time on a weekend, in bed with neither the Italian nor Potato beside me. I slept in the middle of my bed that night and this was when the breakdown began. The next day, I stayed in bed and cried like the pathetic heartbroken single girl I never wanted to be." Tears sprinkled like raindrops off my cheeks. I would not admit it to Pia, but the deep, hollow pain in my chest took on a life of its own, and there was no stopping it.

With the kind of insight only several martinis could bring, Pia knew that a thirty-minute consultation with her

Dr. Goldstein was needed immediately. I hesitantly agreed and took the good doctor's phone number.

Pia was a big fan of psychiatry; she went to a therapist every week, just for direction. As much as I resisted the idea of seeing a head doctor, I had no problem getting free advice from Pia over dinner. Once, she explained the hidden meaning of shopping addictions—how the need for new Manolos or the latest from Chanel could be related to a void in one's life. She also emphasized the importance of never letting your boyfriend be aware of your addiction, especially if you ever wanted him to marry you.

Despite the emotional turmoil I'd been living in, I felt silly making an appointment to see a shrink. I mean, what was she going to find wrong? She would probably just say, "What a fabulous life you have, Ms. Reynolds."

After all, I did have a glamorous lifestyle in Manhattan, with a closet full of designer labels, a Manolo Blahnik collection, a must-have social circuit, the most important maître d's in my pocket and, until recently, a career as president of a skin care company, an adorable doggy, and a handsome Italian boyfriend who was a successful lawyer at one of Manhattan's top firms and whom I had been expecting to propose. Until recently, I had been looking forward to my upcoming thirtieth birthday.

Now, I was not really in the mood to hear a lecture from a stranger about how I should have seen this coming.

2

SLOWLY OPENING MY RIGHT EYE—my left was comfortably shoved into my fluffy pillow—I officially knew it was Saturday morning by the massive martini blow to my head.

Almost as painful was that I had been too drunk to remember to rid myself of last night's Nobu experience after dinner. Typically, my routine was less obvious, as I would make trips throughout the meal, rather than one long trip to the ladies room toward the end. However, this was decided on a case-by-case basis, and my hysterical breakdowns last night had been a bit distracting.

Although it was extremely painful, I was able to reach under my stomach and grab my Pinkberry (my pink BlackBerry, which I often slept on, as I would pass out at some point during my drunk-dialing) to see how much time I had until I made the big call.

At sixteen minutes until noon, until I ordered my Chinese "for four." I passed the time by moving my white down comforter and two pillows from my bed to the stiff chestnut Pottery Barn leather couch in the living room, directly in front of the flat screen. Next was a shower to help ease some of my drunkenness and exfoliate my body from face to feet. These days, I always seemed to forget to wash my face before passing out into a sleep coma, only to wake up looking like an owl or—as Bobby, my other best friend, would say—a street walker.

It felt good to scrub my skin, as if I was removing everything that felt dead about me. I was the "queen of skin care." Who knew that simply exfoliating my skin until raw (which I knew better than to do but now couldn't resist) would one day be what was left of my skin care regimen? My daily cleansing and moisturizing, weekly hydrating and purifying masks, along with monthly photo facials, glycolic peels, or microdermabrasion, was down to "super-scrub Saturdays." Pampering was a thing of the past. No more sunscreen applications to guard against the "UVAging" rays that were out to get me 365 days a year. No more weekly Epsom salts hot baths to detox my body, or lathering up with my favorite vanilla-scented moisturizing cream. No more applications of extra virgin olive oil to the ends of my hair to prevent splitting. I didn't even treat myself to my bedtime chamomile tea. All that had been replaced by a new nightly ritual of passing out on the bed, face down, which went against my cardinal rule of youth maintenance. Before the deep hollow pain was born inside me, I slept on my back, at the perfect thirty-degree angle to ensure proper circulation and prevention of any unnecessary creasing or wrinkling.

Even though my high alcohol consumption, as of late, was taking a toll on my skin, dehydrating me to the bone, at least I wasn't waking up to any "stress bumps," or what sane people would refer to as pimples—this despite the fact that on most days, I was actually removing my makeup just in time to apply everything again.

But not today. Today, I threw on my oversized light gray Columbia University sweatshirt that, in addition to the navy letters printed across my chest, was covered with food stains from all the previous Chinese episodes. Oh, the memories. It was important to be as comfy as possible and to wear clothes that would not be tight around my stomach, especially once it expanded. After putting on my Victoria's Secret Pink label boxers and big white socks, I was back on the couch, waiting patiently. Switching channels to Lifetime, I felt anticipation as the clock displayed 11:59 a.m. One minute until I could place the order.

This was becoming my typical weekend schedule lately, but of course if anyone would ask, "Where were you Sunday for brunch? Shopping? A movie? Pilates?" I always had an excuse. To be honest, I liked the isolation. After nights of vodka martinis, all I could do was lie all day on the couch, eat my Chinese buffet, and wait until I had no choice but to force myself up to get ready to go out and do it all over again.

Fake Perfect Me

As painful as it was at times, I had to do this. I had to put myself out there and be the single Manhattanite that I was unfortunately forced to be. Grazie, Santo.

Noon! That was exactly when they opened. I hit voice recognition "Home's Kitchen." It rang and rang and rang; then I heard "Home's Kitchen. Please hold."

While on hold, I thought about my Chinese order for "four." After each binge, I made a mental note to work on getting the number down to two or three, but then I didn't think it was fair to me to have so few options. Life was about choices, right?

No one knew about my take-out indulgences. When Potato was alive, he was the only witness to this dark secret. He could not tell and even if he could, he wouldn't have. The trade-off meant I shared my BBQ spare ribs and half my fried cream cheese and crabmeat wonton order.

The whole process repulsed me. These days, I never binged on junk food, as it was such a waste of time. My thing included long lunches, lavish dinners, and home cooked Southern meals when I went home to see the family and, of course, my Chinese orders on the weekends. My habit didn't seem so deceitful, until Bobby confided to me about his own deep dark secret that would also occur after a night (well, sometimes a day) of drinking.

I clearly remember the first time we graced each other's presence three years ago at Desi's Christmas party. I was actually anticipating meeting the infamous man, as the hostess promised that he and I would get along like vodka and vermouth.

As I walked up to the bar, I overheard this character talking to a handful of people. "It's my curse; it truly is. I have learned to live with it, as difficult as it can be sometimes. I mean, seriously, with my gorgeous lashes and beautiful neck movements, I am constantly looked at and have no privacy, as normal people do."

People began nodding their heads in agreement, like he was a ringleader of the cult that formed in the corner. I couldn't help but stare. His voice distracted me again, and we looked at each other as he continued. "It doesn't matter if you're not smart, as long as you're extremely pretty." He sent me a wink, one that was meant just for me. Rather than smile, I dismissed his attempt at a compliment by rolling my eyes, letting him know I was thinking "That's all you got?" I could tell by the spiked movement in his right eyebrow that he now realized I was smart and pretty. Perhaps Desi was right; we were a match.

As I turned my attention to the bartender, I could hear him speaking fluent French, which added to his superior attitude and which appealed to me in the way water would appeal to people living in hell. I didn't speak the language, but I knew he was trying to impress me. I knew that I was one of the few for whom Mr. Bobby made the effort.

As I carefully grabbed my 'tini, I felt an abrupt sharp tap on my right shoulder and heard someone clearing his throat.

"You must be Isabella Reynolds."

Trying to control my smirk, I turned around to make direct eye contact and hold my ground. Looking him in the eye and holding contact demonstrated my level of confidence, in a way where we were both trying to prove that who was, in fact, Desi's best friend.

"That is correct, and you are …?"

"That's cute, sugar. I think you know exactly who I am. I know Desi has mentioned me."

"Yes, I believe she has, perhaps," I said with my prettiest pensive expression, while glancing over his shoulder with a pensive look.

"Again, cute. Desi warned me you were stubborn. So, you are from one of the Carolinas, I hear."

"Yes, South. Why do you ask?"

"Just wondering which side of the tracks you come from."

"Excuse me?"

"Just a joke, sugar—well, maybe," he said with the most glamorous giggle I had ever heard. "I'm originally from California but moved to Paris as a teenager and was a model during the whole up-and-coming waif phase. I used to run with the Moss crowd."

"Sounds lovely. I'm glad I asked," I responded, trying to knock him off his stage, as I didn't remember buying a ticket to his performance. "Desi described you perfectly, I must say."

"How was that? Tall, dark, and tremendously lean and attractive?"

"Sure, of course."

"And do you agree, Miss Reynolds?"

"Hmm ... I would have said ..." I paused, trying to test if what I thought even mattered to him.

"Sugar, go on. Please—you can tell me."

"I would have said theatrical, loud-mouthed, no-nonsense conversationalist with a twist of exceptional pretentiousness."

"Let's get a 'tini, beautiful," he said, wrapping his arm around my waist and turning me toward the bar.

"A 'tini?"

"Yes, your new drink is a Kettle 'tini with a twist. Accept it. Love it. You are a 'tini girl."

"Well, you are just in luck, as that is my drink, but I adore 'tini, because I hear 'tiny'!"

We became so close that people often assumed we were a couple. We could be separated and across the room but talk through our eyes and be exactly on the same page. That's what made us so dangerous, but no desire existed between us—none whatsoever.

After years of being such close friends, it was during one of our long afternoon lunches, which normally included several rounds of 'tinis and a salad or some sort of pureed soup, he confessed that he needed to get something horrible off his chest. I remember being frightened, wondering if my best friend accidentally killed someone and if would I turn him in. "Bobby, you can tell me anything. I'm here for you always."

"Isabella, please don't be ashamed of me. Just listen. I want to stop, but I can't. It has control over me."

"What, Bobby? Tell me."

"I'm addicted … to … um …"

"What? You can tell me anything, but please don't say heroin!"

"The double cheeseburger value meal at McDonald's."

Gasping for air, I asked, "What do you mean? How do you get the food? They deliver?" This was the first thing that crossed my mind, as Manhattan did not have drive-throughs, and I knew it was not possible for him to actually walk in there. Was it? I laughed, realizing I actually was worried about him bumping into someone he knew at a fast-food restaurant. It was impossible. It was also impossible for him to blend in at McDonald's, as he was tall, model thin, and most likely dressed head to toe in Costume Nationale.

"Isabella, stop … there's more. I also get the chicken nuggets, but just the four pieces. Um … and a strawberry shake."

"Dear God, Bobby, how did this happen? What do you carry the food home in? I'm mean, it's not like you walk down the street sporting an 'M' bag."

"What do you mean?" he asked, confused.

"Well, how do you take the food home to eat it? It's not like you sit in there."

"Um, well ... yes, I do," he said, shamefully looking down at the floor. "But ..." he continued, his head jerking back up hopefully. "I don't sit by the window. There's a place in the back."

"Um ... okay, that makes everything all better, I suppose."

There—my best friend was telling me of his five-dollar dirty secret, which did not compare to my average sixty-dollar order that took place sometimes once per week on a Saturday or a Sunday. And I was not willing to share my secret to make him feel better. I could not bear for him to know that I did that to myself, even within the boundaries of my own home; that I had no self-control; that rather than having weekend brunches at fabulous restaurants, sipping champagne and eating steak tartare, I preferred to binge on greasy, fatty Chinese takeout in a stained sweatshirt ... alone. This was a step up, considering that back in the day it used to be sugar or what I liked to refer to as "hitting the cane"—cake, cookies, doughnuts, anything rich and sweet. I soon learned that MSG withdrawals were more tolerable to get through than sugar, as the headaches were not as lethal.

"Hi, give me address," the accent said—the controller of this chaos.

"Hi, 480 West 20th Street, PH A," I said, slightly annoyed, thinking after my weekly calls that I would be noted as a familiar and loyal customer.

"Order?"

"I need one order of BBQ spareribs, one order of fried cream cheese with crabmeat wontons, one order of General Tso's chicken with white rice, one order of pork lo mein, and one order of chicken with spiced walnuts. And a side of fried rice, one spring roll, and four Diet Cokes."

"Your total is $58.43."

"Hold on. ... Do you want anything else?" I asked my imaginary person so the woman would not think this was all for me. I even cared what the voice on the other end thought of me. "Okay, that will be all," I confidently said.

"Be there twenty minutes."

"Thank you!"

I went to the kitchen and grabbed a plate and a glass with ice and set up on the coffee table. Some Lifetime for Women movie was on. This channel annoyed me, as all the stories portrayed weak and pathetic women who could not even dress fashionably. Why I even watched this mess, I had no idea. Switching to the movies-on-demand channel, I sadly noticed I had seen everything else.

Lying back on the couch, I look at the other end, toward my feet. Potato should have been sitting there, watching my every move and occasionally glancing into my eyes. I will never forget the first time I saw him in the store window. He was all one big fat wrinkle, which meant his small frame still had plenty of room for growing. In fact, he had so many wrinkles that the skin hanging from under his chest looked like cow udders, and his paws were pretty big for a puppy. *Perfect*, I'd thought.

He loved our Chinese delivery orders. He had coffee table manners, at least, as he would look at my eyes, waiting for me to say, "Potato, come on; get over here." For every bite I ate, he took one, so I split half the guilt. Now that he was gone, I was here alone, eating my buffet for four. No witness to the binge or the purge. He didn't like listening to the latter much, anyway.

It's amazing how people go through life, struggling, working, loving, and attaching themselves to situations, whether it is a person or a pet. As comfortable as we become, things can change, and we are forced to face a new path to walk on, to adapt to the change, whether it is a result of death or an end of a relationship. If we don't, we just end up stuck in a dead end, eventually realizing that the reverse is not an option. It's peculiar—no, absolutely outrageous—to me to think that at points in our life, we are supposed to live as if the people and pets we loved and lost had never existed. How can someone who was once so present in our lives, in our thoughts, end up being just distant memories from our past?

Twenty minutes later, the doorbell rang: it was time. I brought the delivery bag to the coffee table and took oversized portions from each container, organizing a section for each dish on my plate, placing a spring roll topped with a line of duck sauce and a couple of fried wontons on each side. I poured a Diet Coke and switched Lifetime to *America's Next Top Model* reruns, which reminded me not to get too comfortable with myself. *Platinum Weddings* on the WE channel was also good, as it literally made me sick to my stomach. If only people could see me now.

After the purge part of the routine, it was the three-point checklist to thin reassurance: scapula bones on back, legs together with no thigh-touch, and slightly gaunt in the cheeks. Check, check, and check. As familiar as I was with this part of the two- step process, the tension never went away, and I could not ignore that eating like this and then sticking my two fingers down my throat was not absolutely disgusting and horribly wrong.

Journal entry—May 15

I'm really not sure how the binge & purge (B & P) routine became a part of me. I occasionally recall instances from childhood that may have been a clear sign that an obsession was starting—things I will never tell anyone, like being twelve and sleeping in one of those plastic sweat suits to lose water weight or plastering the back of my bedroom door with Kate Moss and Claudia Schiffer ads from magazines to remind myself each morning before school to strive, each day, to be beautiful and thin. How did I, at age twelve, even come to know about water weight?

Is this my disease? Contagious? Simply a learned behavior? A result of a traumatic event or a rough transitional period? Did my mother or father judge me too much based on my body? Is it all about control? Is it a result of my endless efforts to try to please everyone? Do I have low self-esteem or am I addicted to perfectionism? Is my "nothing ever is good enough" and "please everyone so they will like me" attitude doing this to me? Is it because I believe that if I can re-create myself into something different, even better than who I am, my life will be better? Maybe, just maybe, if I could just have the perfect body, would everything else would be okay?

The routine has recently popped back into my life, and I can't help but wonder how I still persist. The worse off I become, the more I have to pretend to be great.

I know I use it to occupy myself when it all becomes too much. It always slowly creeps back into my life and now, looking back, I can see how my relationship with him caused me to want it as well, on a regular basis. I got away with it on a weekly routine with closing my company, but with Potato gone, I needed it daily. These days, it seems it's the only thing I can control. I know I use it as a negative means of coping with stress. It is my self-destructive way of dealing with my defective Italian, my company closing, and the loss of my dog. This I know, yet who am I without it?

One of the reasons I can't share my Chinese for "four" secret with Bobby is that he is not stupid; he would be able to calculate the caloric intake of these episodes and what he came up with would not add up to my figure. He knows what I am capable of doing to maintain certain aspects of my life, especially my sleek physique. And my B&P routine is something I can't afford to share with anyone—not even my best friend.

Being thin isn't the most amazing dream. I only relish it when I am out and feeling beautiful in my designer clothes and have envious eyes on me. Thin is beautiful, right? The truth of it all is that the thinner I get, the more miserable I am. It means more pressure and each time a harder struggle to maintain. It means more obsessing about it throughout the day, hardly leaving time for anything else. There truly was a grand illusion to glamour.

The root of this evil is the positive reinforcement I receive for being thin, which traps me in this vicious cycle, over and over. Dieting is an obsession that started at such an early age. As I sit here and write, I am disgusted when I think of every diet I have tried: the "10 fat grams per day" diet, the "hot lemon water" diet, the "no carbs diet," Weight Watchers, LA Weight Loss, Zone Delivery, and the "high protein with more shakes than food" diet.

I can't really recall how I learned to purge. After doing it for so long, it just gets easier. All I need is copious amounts of water and my two little fingers. Out of all the weight-loss options, in the end, I still sit here and vote bulimia for beauty.

I. R.

3

ON A SLIGHTLY CHILLY SATURDAY morning in June, I walked home from the gym, looking forward to the change in seasons. Maybe I would be able to let go of the painful events of late and move on. It had been about a month since the breakup. It was time for a new me. Well, so I thought.

I felt satisfied after the one-hour cardio session that I had burned away any leftover calories from the Chinese takeout I had consumed the day before. Also, it helped calm my nerves for my appointment with Dr. Goldstein, which was in a couple of hours. I guess I should have felt fortunate that Pia got me to finally call Dr. Goldstein, but something about seeing a shrink did not make me feel fortunate. Besides, I was feeling better today—for the moment anyway.

While walking down Ninth Avenue, I admired the width of the freshly cemented block and how the meatpacking district looked at 9:00 a.m. It was peaceful watching the city wake up after a long night's sleep. As I approached my block, I decided to sneak into my favorite neighborhood café, Le Bergamot, for a large bowl of cappuccino.

I entered the tiny French café and glanced at the pastry display up front, eyeing every imaginable temptation possible—specifically, the tall creamy Napoleon topped with a perfectly ripe raspberry, which haunted me every time I passed by the window. The woman at the register always had such a welcoming smile and recognition in her eyes, even when I hid behind my large black Gucci shades, which overwhelmed my face. The glasses allowed me to feel invisible, which was perfect for when I felt a mess or when I was ordering something I shouldn't have been. Distracting myself from the pastry case, I asked for my nonfat, extra-hot cappuccino and waited patiently as the milk was being frothed. I was hoping to bolt out pastry-free, but the ham and cheese croissants with perfectly crispy, crunchy, cheesy edges were calling my name. *Iss-aaa-bellla.* After all, I did work out and would need some protein to maintain any lean body mass, right? "I'll take one of those, to go."

Satisfied, I headed home. This was typical thinking for me. After two academic degrees, years of reading clinical nutrition journals, and being a past member of the American Dietetic Association, I was still capable of allowing myself to believe that this greasy ham and cheese would aid in the protection of my lean body mass, which I'd killed myself to maintain during this morning's workout. Of course, I had also forgotten my post-Chinese buffet binge resolution to start a healthy diet. However, I would not purge this before my appointment. If Dr. Goldstein asked anything regarding an eating issue, I could at least be honest and say no. None of my friends had ever picked up on it. How could she? Yesterday and all the times before was the past. Today was a brand new day.

As much as I always laughed it off, I believed there was something to the statistic that indicated that most nutritionists have eating and food "issues." I mean, if I wanted to see any of the conditions I learned about in graduate school, all I had to do was look around the classroom. My own experiences aside, I only needed to look to either side of me to observe that we were all "mental." I spent a total of six years of my life studying clinical nutrition, a subject that really taught the tricks of the trade but in no way was my true calling.

Ever since I could remember, when I was not playing with my Barbie doll kingdom, I was in my mother's bathroom, playing with her skin care creams and potions. I loved mixing the consistencies and making my own formulas. She did not care for this so much. When the brain light bulb went off and said, "Isabella, create a skin care company," I thought, *What a brilliant idea, Ms. Reynolds.* People search their entire lives for their passion. *I was lucky*, I thought. *I found mine at age twenty-five.* Also, I could still incorporate my educational background into the mix. My parents could not say I wasted years of study and their money. I didn't have to live as a hypocrite and counsel people on well-balanced meals and portion control while I was on my own maintenance program. I don't think the American Dietetic Association would approve of my methods.

Over the course of four years, I developed ingredients and created formulas, as well as brainstorming marketing ideas and package designs. I was interviewed by major editors and the press. My pictures and products were in window displays along Madison and Fifth avenues. What more could I have asked for? Well, making more money is the only thing that comes to mind. In reality, I ended up rushing into a senior-level position in public relations after I lost my dream company. Hello, corporate America. Say hello to Monday morning status meetings; scheduled, daily 1:00 p.m. lunches; and cubicles in which I'd eat lunch. This was not why I had moved to Manhattan. This was not what I had set out to be. This is not what "if you can make it here, you can make it anywhere" stood for.

As I opened the front door to my apartment, I scrolled through my iPod to Bic Runga, then got undressed and stepped into the shower. I was more self-conscious than I'd expected about meeting Dr. Goldstein. As I applied a Bumble & Bumble deep conditioning mask to my hair, I wondered what her first impression of me would be. I wondered how one should dress for one's first appointment with an Upper East Side shrink.

It was then I could not forget to apply my Shiseido eye gel pads. This would reduce the puffiness and bags from all the crying jags and sleeplessness, as well as the dryness from all the Chinese food episodes.

Standing in my narrow walk-in closet, one of the few features I liked about my New York apartment, I contemplated my clothing options. "What do mentally healthy people with just a couple of issues wear to therapy?" I decided to play it casual yet trendy-conservative. I threw on a pair of black denim Seven brand jeans, a Rolling Stones tee, and a black Theory velvet blazer. As I stared at myself in the mirror, I realized it was going to be an okay day. The way my clothes fit always determined if it was going to be a good or bad day for Isabella Reynolds. Though my jeans did feel a bit tight as a result of that damn ham-and-cheese monster, I still felt pretty good.

Last but not least, I slipped on my favorite pair of shoes—a must for my ensemble—classic four-inch-heel black Manolos. These shoes were a staple in my wardrobe. I went through two pairs a year, as I wore them with everything. Even though I was five foot seven, the four-inch heel was always a must. I always wanted to be taller and never got over the fact that I did not inherit the model-height gene from my father's German side. Still, I was happy to have passed the five foot five benchmark of my Italian mother's side. Sometimes, it would have been easier just to throw on a pair of Uggs and call it an outfit, but my Manolos elevated me—and my life—in so many ways. I felt sexy yet casual, taller, and therefore thinner. At the same time, they were surprisingly comfortable. After many late nights and way-too-early mornings, these shoes helped me glamorously sprint after that impossible cab. I adored my Manolos and considered them an investment, although some would say the price was over the top. Well, they helped me look at the tops of other people's heads, so sue me.

With twenty-five minutes to spare, I quickly blew out my hair, added Cle de Peau concealer under my now not-so-puffy eyes, a bit of cream blush, and a couple swipes of Christian Dior burgundy mascara. I had just enough time to hop in a cab and shoot up Tenth Avenue, crossing Central Park to the Upper East Side, for my 10:15 a.m. mental session with Dr. Goldstein.

While in the cab, I started to think about what the hell I would even discuss with this complete stranger. I mean, how do people sit down and share all their problems or even their deep dark secrets with someone they don't know. I had my journal for that. I suppose it was similar to confession—not that I had been to confession since I received confirmation, so I really had any idea what I was talking about. I wondered if the couch would be comfy. Wait ... was I supposed to sit or lie down on the couch? Would she tell me what to do?

I took a deep breath. I was a normal, mentally healthy person with a couple of issues, I reminded myself. Then I began to outline the discussion I would have with Dr. Goldstein. Would I start with the closing of my dream company, the sudden death of my dog, or the break up with my Italian ex? Perhaps I should begin with my obsession with perfection or the fact that I needed approval from others to feel significant. And what about my parents? Christ, would they come up? Maybe I would simply start with my likes and dislikes. I could tell Dr. Goldstein these things and then she could see inside my soul and fix everything without having any kind of bad impression of me.

Yes, starting with my likes would get things off on a positive note. I liked traveling, going to the movies, reading memoirs, long lunches, champagne, dogs, cupcakes with sprinkles, and surprising people. Now, for the dislikes. I hated feeling fat, getting a "stress bump," people who did not listen, bad skin and teeth, and men who called themselves men but who were really little selfish boys.

Or maybe I should start with a more creative conversation. For instance, during one Saturday afternoon of crying and not being able to pull myself from bed, I was amazed at all the things I accomplished. Who says depression can't be productive? Without leaving my apartment, I ordered three blockbuster hits from On-Demand, made spa appointments for my "tomorrow I will pull myself together" program, ordered Chinese for four, some apartment décor from Shabby Chic, set up a dry cleaning pickup (as my housekeeper was out sick), and looked at some "potentials" on various dating websites to replace the Italian ex.

Then there was the possibility of my Saint Valentine curse. At this point, I was not even sure he truly existed, but where else would the curse be coming from? Throughout my life I have felt cursed by Saint Valentine, always dreading my birthday. It was the curse of being brought into the world on a day associated with love, heart-shaped symbols, red roses, and winged cupids, thanks to a man who some respected as a saint—it was not easy to live with.

Valentine's Day, which can be traced back to the ancient Roman Empire, was named after two Christian martyrs, Valentine of Rome and Valentine of Terni. Some believed that these two men were originally the same person. There are several legends on the origin of the day. During the reign of Emperor Claudius II, Rome was involved in several murderous and rejected crusades. Claudius thought that the recruitment of soldiers was difficult because men did not wish to desert their wives and loved ones. Because of this, all marriages and engagements in Rome were canceled during this time. A passionate and noble priest, Valentine defied the emperor by secretly marrying couples. This was eventually discovered, resulting in Valentine's death on February 14. From this day, he was named a saint for his courage and devotion to love.

Another legend told is that Saint Valentine's life ended as a result of helping Christians escape torture in Roman prisons. An additional version is that while imprisoned, Valentine fell deeply in love with the jailer's daughter, who would often visit him while he was confined. Before his life was taken, he sent a final good-bye letter to her from jail and signed "Love, your Valentine."

Which version of the legend was the truth was not so important to the meaning of Valentine's Day or my saint. He honored his beliefs; he fought for love—love between others, love for one's beliefs, love for his own sweetheart, no matter who judged him.

I could not help but ask why I was born on this cursed day. Was I to be held responsible for loving too much and wanting to simply be loved by people in return?

I have never spoken to another soul about this. I wanted my world, myself, my life to be perfect; to seem perfect, even as a child. I kept the pain in, never showing my melancholy, disillusionment, or dysfunctional roots. The acting—or in my case, the pretending—had become my existence and was definitely deserving of an Oscar.

The cab dropped me off in front of a three-story brownstone. I entered through the black iron gate and looked over the list of names on the buzzer. Dr Goldstein, buzzer number three. Immediately after pressing the button, the door clicked, and I walked into a small waiting area with five chairs that faced three doors, each labeled with a letter: "A," "B," and "C." There was no reception area; no one to ask if I needed a glass of water or to announce my arrival. Not knowing which door to knock on—or for that matter, if I should even knock—I took a seat and waited nervously. The sound of Mozart playing on a classical radio station grew more annoying with each second. I could understand that it was to protect the conversation of the person in the session, but being in the tiny box that was supposed to be a waiting room with this overwhelming noise made me want to make a run for it.

I studied the doors, remembering an experiment that I had read about in an Introduction to Psychology textbook in college. Which letter door would she choose, and would that unveil her character or type of personality? I started to wonder if there was even a separate room behind each door or if all the doors opened into the same room. Maybe I was too smart for this. Again, I contemplated making an escape. Lately, my hesitation had been getting me into trouble. *Maybe I just need to get up and—*

Suddenly, door B opened abruptly, and a young, petite brunette girl walked out. I immediately pushed my face into *New York* magazine, as I was sure that there was some secret rule that two crazypants were not to acknowledge each other in the name of privacy. As the other patient exited the office, an older petite woman, casually dressed and wearing sneakers, came out to greet me.

"Hello there. You must be Isabella."

"Yes, nice to meet you." I followed her into another small room and sank into the leather sofa as she took the chair directly across from me—I felt like I was practically sitting on her lap. Smiling nervously, I studied her. Dr. Goldstein looked to be in her mid-sixties and was a bit fragile-looking. The office itself, however, was in desperate need of some decorating. I had imagined one of those wall waterfalls or little sandbox dishes with stones and a little rake for me to play with as I cried. However, there wasn't much in the room; just the three of us—her, me, and the deep, hollow pain in my chest.

I didn't know where to begin or if I should even embark on one of my pre-planned conversations. I began regretting this whole situation and made an oath to myself that I would never drink so many lychee martinis again. Still smiling, I watched the shrink get situated and quickly thought about how much I should reveal. After a brief introduction and discussion about insurance policies, Dr. Goldstein asked, "So, what brings you here today, Isabella?"

For shits and giggles, I wanted to respond, but I became overwhelmed with emotion instead. My neatly positioned body fell into a slump, and my big pearly white smile quickly disappeared. I dissolved into tears, my hands immediately covering my face.

"Has this been happening a lot?" Dr. Goldstein asked.

I could only nod my head.

"Isabella, let that pain out when it hurts you. When you are sad, cry out all those tears. When you feel angry, release all the pain. I strongly believe that when people's problems continue to occur, it's a result of never dealing with certain issues. In some way, shape, or form, these lessons always come back and confront us. One thing that won't apologize to us is life."

I then realized the shrink session was long overdue. Finally, removing my hands from my face, I gently dabbed my eyes with a tissue.

Dr. Goldstein tried initiating the conversation once again. "What has happened recently in your life that brings you here today? Let's try putting things into perspective, shall we?"

I took a deep breath and got down to business. Something came over me and suddenly, I forgot about my pre-planned outline. I grabbed another tissue and took a couple of small breaths. As I looked at Dr. Goldstein, I felt more desperate for the answers to make this deep, hollow pain in my chest go away. I refused to cry like a crazypants over one more nice dinner. Hoping she would understand what I was about to say, I opened my mouth and the words just started spilling out. "Recently, my life disappeared, and I don't know who I am."

"What do you mean, your life disappeared?"

Almost annoyed with having to repeat this entirely again, I continued. "Well, let's see. Over the past couple of months I have lost my dream company, to which I'd dedicated four years of my life, to a trademark lawsuit—I'm not sure what the hell I was paying a legal team for. Then my healthy English bulldog of four years went from having a loss of appetite to dying of undetected brain disease. And my two-year relationship just ended with the man I thought I was spending the rest of my life with. Just a month ago, we were talking about real estate in Gramercy Park and now, suddenly, I'm contemplating online dating."

Dr. Goldstein leaned closer to me. "What was your dog's name, and how did he die?"

"His name was Potato, and his illness started early one Monday morning and ended that same night around nine o'clock." My quivering lip was shutting out my ugly cry-face.

"Isabella, please continue when you're ready."

"I panicked that morning as I threw on clothes to take him to the vet. As we stood on the corner, trying to catch a cab, I realized that my dog and my happiness were at the mercy of a New York City rush hour—hailing a cab was nearly impossible. Finally, a cab picked me up and we headed toward the Upper East Side, where my vet was located. As we sat in traffic for the next twenty minutes, Potato began to foam at the mouth, lying in my arms almost lifeless. Though my Potato was not present so much anymore, the only thing I did recognize in his big eyes was that he was scared. Once the cab pulled to the block where the vet's office was located, I hopped out to save time and put Potato on the sidewalk, where he fell over and lay limp on the ground. I quickly prayed to God to give me the strength to pick him up and run as fast as I could. When I finally made it to the office, the vet and an aide met me at the door with an oxygen tank and I handed him over. If I'd only known then that it would be the last time I would see him alive …"

"It's okay; take care time. Do you need another tissue?" Dr. Goldstein asked.

I responded by clearing my throat and trying to improve my posture a bit. "That night, at dinner with the Italian, I got the phone call. Potato did not make it. That was the first moment I felt the deep, hollow pain in my chest. I remember not feeling my core or having the strength to hold myself up. I looked at the Italian from across the table and simply said, "He's gone." I stood up and walked out to the street corner, falling to my knees in my sorrow, hating myself for not staying with Potato that day.

"This must have been extremely hard for you, Isabella," she said, sitting back in her chair.

"The next morning we headed back to the vet to make the arrangements and for me to say my final good-bye. As I walked into the cold, sterile room, there he was, lying on the table so peacefully. He was on his side with his front legs crossed, eyes barely open, and the tip of his tongue sticking out, as it was always too long for his mouth. This was exactly how he slept on the couch every night. I thought that maybe, just maybe, this was all a bad dream. I slowly touched his ear and moved my hand down his body. My nose pressed to his cheek. I whispered "I'm so sorry" three times. Then I gave him one last huggie and walked away."

As my face fell into my lap, I heard Dr. Goldstein ask, with a peculiar curiosity in her tone, "And do you recall what you did after?"

"It's odd, but I can't recall what the Italian and I did after we left the vet. The rest is a blur and only causes a burning in my head when trying to evoke it. I do remember him saying, 'We must get you something to eat; you are too thin.'"

As I said that to Dr. Goldstein, I recalled feeling hopeless and desperate that day, and being told I was thin only disgusted me. What did he think I looked like the rest of the time when I was not eating and was starving myself for the previous year and a half? But that was my defective Italian.

"I still thank God every day that the night before Potato tragically passed away, I decided to stay in instead of going to dinner with the Italian. I ordered Chinese and lay on the couch with him for hours, feeding him. I let him lie on me that night, as uncomfortable as it was. I had no idea that this would be the last time I would ever spend the night on the couch with him."

For a second, I thought maybe this was a good time to go into all the things I could accomplish during my Saturdays in bed. "Finally, I believe I have developed an addiction to Chinese food takeout and I should mention that I order for four, and this is getting in the way of fitting into my skinny jeans with the size 26 waist."

Dr. Goldstein tilted her head slightly. "For four?"

"I can't commit to one dish. Who knows what I will actually feel like eating twenty minutes later when the food arrives? It's like having my own personal buffet." I paused before I went on. She was not going to trick me into discussing B&P.

"Isabella, let's go back to your 'being too thin' comment that you recalled after losing your dog and the Chinese for four that night before he passed. You give off this very confident persona. Are you confident, Isabella?"

"Is this a trick question?"

"No. Please just answer the question."

"Yes, I believe I am."

"I think you are, but the fact that you are not comfortable with yourself is the underlying issue. How often do you choose to stay at home and binge alone?"

"Binge? I don't binge, Dr. Goldstein," I responded confidently.

"Okay, Isabella. Let me ask you this: How do you cope?"

"Cope?"

"Yes, cope with stress, your daily problems, or even when you are emotional."

"Well, I guess I talk to my friends or I write in my journal," I responded confidently again.

"I want you to consider something for me. Next time you are craving your Chinese for four, pay attention to what you are feeling at that moment when ordering. Perhaps you use food as a way to block out your feelings or painful emotions."

"Dr. Goldstein, I have lost the most important things in my life, and I don't know who I am without them. I feel so alone. I feel like a nobody. I am no longer the president of a company but am in corporate America hell. I'm no longer a dog owner or a soon-to-be-engaged twenty-nine-year-old woman. I mentioned that I'm single now, right?"

Dr. Goldstein nodded slightly.

"These are my problems," I said, trying to get her away from binge theory.

I could feel what seemed like two-pound tears beginning to fill my eyes, making my lids so heavy that I could do nothing but close them. As the tears rolled down my cheeks, they burned much in the same way that the deep, hollow pain in my chest did. "I have been stripped of everything."

"What is your relationship with your parents? What are they like?"

"My parents?" Here we go, of course—classic textbook psychology. "Well, they are divorced, but both are in my life."

"Okay, Isabella, what are some of your earliest memories of your childhood?"

Where was she going with this? Why were we not talking about my failed dreams, my precious Potato, the Italian ex I wasted two years of my life with?

"Well, I remember my family around our swimming pool a lot. My parents always had parties and well-planned parties for the holidays. Perfect Christmas trees, everything decorated in detail, with tons of presents."

I waited for a response, and she just stared at me. "And when did your parents get divorced?"

"When I was a kid."

"How old were you, Isabella?"

My mouth opened, but nothing came out. I sat there a bit puzzled, as I did not know what age to tell her. I know that in the past I'd told people I was seven or eight, but I always said that without ever really thinking about it. I quickly glanced at her; she was still waiting on my answer. How the hell could I not know the answer? I was the most detail-oriented person I knew. This was a skill listed on my résumé, for Christsake. "I don't know."

"Why did your parents divorce?"

"I don't really have the answer to that."

"Where you a heavy child?"

"Excuse me? No, I was not." I could feel the boiling of my blood in my chest rising up to my face.

"Were you obsessed with thinness, growing up?"

I just ignored her with what I could feel with the most unattractive, pensive face.

"Isabella, it seems that you have never allowed yourself to really mourn over any of these losses. The past couple of months you have had one loss after another, and your grief for those are tied into the major loss of your parents. Think back to how you coped as a child with this; all these things you had no control over. I'm sure you were not ordering Chinese for four."

I ignored her remark. "But Dr. Goldstein, my parents aren't dead." The divorced-child syndrome was her answer, and this was beginning to feel more like a Psychology 101 lecture than a mental session.

"You have not mourned any of this and have buried it all in your subconscious. These most recent events have triggered something inside you, and you have reached your breaking point. It was inevitable. You cannot change any of the past. I can't help you predict your future. You can only live your best today."

"Sure. Okay," I responded, still confused.

"I guarantee you that the relationship you had with the Italian was similar to your parents' marriage. I'm also guessing he mirrored a lot of the same characteristics of your father and your issues with him. Perhaps you were trying to fix issues with this man, rather than dig up any memories and confront your parents." Then, finally, she asked the question I'd been waiting for. "Please tell me about your relationship with your ex."

Once I began speaking, I began purging everything and could not stop, only allowing her to fit a word or two into our conversation.

"Dr. Goldstein, the whole time I was so consumed with making him happy, with making sure he loved me, that I forgot about me. I don't think I loved myself. I am always so much happier when someone else loves me."

"Red flag you ignored," she interrupted.

"His high-demanding job would leave him no time for me, and for the majority of our relationship, we would go all week without seeing each other, even though we lived a five-minute cab ride apart."

"Isabella, that was another red flag you ignored."

Fake Perfect Me

"Though I was often sleeping alone and didn't have him to talk to when I needed him, I still continued with the relationship and continued to give more and more. I was unhappy. I was crying all the time. I was drinking all the time—at times, even alone. Not that he knew any of that. No one did."

She nodded. "Isabella, please continue."

"It was like the stupid stargazer lilies he would send me time after time. Dozens of stargazer lilies right before his Italy departures. I would have that orange dust from the buds all over my apartment and myself, and it stains! Just like those damn lilies, he was everywhere, embedded and stuck on me. I can't seem to wash him away. As careful as I tried to be with him, I was always a mess. We were completely a mess, and now I am left with this stain on my heart."

"Good, Isabella, very good. Now, why did you feel everything had to be perfect? Did you think that somehow by doing these things you could make him love you?"

As soon as she said "make him love you," I thought about chocolate chip cookies. I pretended to be a fabulous baker, and he believed I was. He loved chocolate chip cookies and being the resourceful person I am, I found the best bakery, City Bakery. I purchased cookies and then would neatly wrap them in waxed paper and put them in Tupperware. These cookies were a bit sizeable, and no one in his right mind would think someone actually baked them at home. But he did. I was the perfect girlfriend—the PG—and if I said I baked cookies, I baked the cookies. I even prepared myself for any doubts on his part. My kitchen had all the baking necessities—flour and baking soda. I was too ashamed to admit this to her. I could only look at my knees as I said, "Um ... all my efforts to please him, and I now realize none of it mattered."

"Isabella, how do you know?"

"I had already entered the phase of self-medicating before we'd even ended things."

Suddenly, the room was uncomfortably silent. The way she glanced at my chest, I contemplated for a moment if she could see the deep, hollow pain. She was a mental doctor, so her glance most likely was that she could see right through me. I hesitantly turned my attention back to her, but she just sat there with a blank expression. I knew she was waiting for me to speak. "Where do I go from here?" I asked.

"You must learn how to cope and mourn, Isabella. You must let yourself mourn the loss of your company, the loss of Potato, the loss of a boyfriend. You must move on. Crying is just as important as giggling, and bingeing is not a solution. You are being so cruel to your body with the bingeing and drinking."

She was right. I needed to move on, to get the Italian out of my life in a real way. The first thing that came to mind was my hall closet. I needed to purge myself of all the skin care boxes and Italian memories but minus Potato's belongings. I need to clean out my closet, literally.

Fake Perfect Me

"Isabella, when something like this ends, it's always easier to remember the perfect times and highest moments, rather than all the reasons that led to the ending. The problem with that is that it feeds that deep feeling of loss. Your heart does not want to remember all the sadness and loneliness with your boyfriend, but it remembers instead your fondest times. This is why the hurt is so deep. All of this has a purpose, Isabella, as does everyone and everything that enters and exits your life. The way you handle it, the outcome, is all in your hands."

"I see."

"If you don't control your destiny, then someone else will. One of my favorite doctors said that."

"Wise," I responded, unsure of how much I was taking from all this, if I was absorbing anything.

"Why on earth would you want to compromise your own expectations of yourself, your dreams, your needs, and even those selfish wants? In work, in friendship, in love, there can be thousands to one hundred to ten possibilities. But in all these equations of life, you are one."

"What is the name of the doctor?"

She started to giggle. "That would be Dr. Seuss. Well, our time is up for today. Let's pick up from here next week."

I knew I would never return to the shrink, but since I could not face the inevitable Q&A of "Why not?" I pulled out my Pinkberry and pretended to look at available dates and times for the following week. "How about next Thursday at 1 p.m.?" I asked.

Dr. Goldstein replied, "See you then, Isabella. Please remember I have a twenty-four-hour cancellation notice. If you need to reschedule, please call. Just hold on, and hang in there long enough to see these lessons through. Some of your tragedies and pain will add structure to your foundation for the rest of your life, while some of this will only affect you briefly."

"You really make it sound so simple. So, what do you suggest we attack next week? The broken heart, the flawed self-image, or the misplaced emotions?" I asked with a smile.

"Enjoy your day, Ms. Reynolds," she said as she pointed at the door with her eyes.

I eagerly jotted down in my Pinkberry for tomorrow, Monday, at 8:30 a.m.: "Call shrink to cancel appointment." Dr. Goldstein's office hours did not begin until 9:30 a.m., so I knew the earlier I called, the safer it would be for me to make a clean getaway. I stood up, shook the shrink's hand, and said, "Dr. Goldstein, thank you. I already feel better. See you next week." I flashed her what would be my last large pearly white smile behind door B.

"And remember, Isabella, when you don't allow yourself to deal with all of these circumstances, they will continue to revisit, only to fight you again."

"Of course. You are exactly right."

This time around, I was not going to ignore any red flags. I had ignored so many at this point, the red flags had become giant banners, with fireworks.

I did not need a head doctor at $200 per hour to tell me that.

4

ONCE OUTSIDE OF DR. GOLDSTEIN'S office, I grabbed my Pinkberry and noticed I'd missed one call and a text message from Bobby.

I went directly to the text and opened it up. It read: "Hey, babe, let's go to church, say 11:15-ish?" I was worn out from the therapy session, so I could not help but think *Perr-fect!* Church was what I really needed this morning, not the shrink attack that I'd just experienced. I hailed a cab and headed back downtown to Chelsea. "Nineteenth and Seventh, please," I said with an uncontrollable smirk. As the cab headed to the West Side, I put down the window and lowered my oversized shades, letting the cool breeze refresh me.

Recapitulating my first therapy session, I wanted to pinpoint where she could be wrong. To imagine that I had never mourned any of my losses was quite confusing. I was detail-oriented and could recall most things in my life, but I was unable to recall many details of my parents' divorce. I remembered memories before and after but not the divorce itself. Somehow, the middle got lost in my mind but was still affecting and hurting my heart. This was the shrink's answer? This was her solution to this deep, hollow pain that was turning me inside out?

Was this the reason that I feared rejection? Did this explain why, for the first time in my life, I fell deeply in love with the Italian—because I knew he would never want me? I knew he had commitment issues. As much as I thought I wanted commitment, love, marriage, and a family one day, was I terrified of living the life of my parents and getting divorced?

Dr. Goldstein was right, I realized. My relationship with the Italian was my parents' relationship—the fighting, the lack of communication, the coldness, the lies. The pain of losing the Italian brought up feelings of abandonment by my parents. This relationship, in my mind, had been a second chance to win, as I had lost the battle with my mother and father. I tried my entire life to be the perfect daughter, living in the box everyone thought I belonged in.

I knew Bobby would make me feel better, as would Jesus; church was just what I needed. As the cab turned the corner onto Eighteenth and Seventh, I saw that Bobby was standing in front of the building. I hopped out of the cab and skipped up the block, giving Bobby a big squeeze and a kiss on each cheek. We walked in and shuffled directly to our usual seats. At the same time, we both belted out, "Hey, Jesus!"

Jesus, a thirty-six-year-old bartender with tightly braided dreads and a hippie-like vibe, quickly turned to look down the bar at us. "Hey, trouble! What brings you two in so early?"

"Isabella needs serious therapy today," Bobby responded in a devilish tone. I shot him a quick look. "Um ... I mean she needs a lot of attention today!"

"Well, then, how do watermelon martinis sound to you both?"

I looked at my Pinkberry and noticed that it was barely noon. I thought that a mimosa or Bellini would seem more appropriate at this hour, as both at least contained fruit juice, but Bobby had already responded "Perr-fect," and Jesus was already shaking the special light-pink cocktail. He poured it into two martini glasses that had been set on the table in front of us. For a final touch, he placed a large watermelon wedge on the side of the frosted glass. Bobby went straight for the watermelon wedge and I rolled my eyes, knowing that was probably his first meal today. I removed my wedge and took a large sip, slowing down as the chilled cocktail numbed the nerves in my teeth. I gently set the glass on the table, feeling a bit guilty for drinking vodka so early. But then I decided that if Isabella Reynolds wanted to drink vodka today, before noon, then that's what she was going to do.

"Church" was what Bobby and I called the bar/restaurant that others referred to as Ernie's, a local spot we used to frequent on Sunday afternoons. Now, we came whenever the need arose.

Jesus was shaking another cocktail and heading in my direction.

"Jesus, my glass is still half-full, and it's only noon," I said in shock, but secretly, I was dying for him to fill me up. As he poured more of the light-pink substance into my martini glass, he stared at me with a boyish grin and said, "Beautiful, a lady is always on her first drink."

Bobby and I laughed, leaning into each other.

"My family would be so proud; I finally found a church where I enjoy the mass," I whispered.

Whenever we came to church, we'd drink ourselves silly, and there was no stopping what came out of our mouths. I also liked coming here because it was more of a gay scene, and all the boys loved me. Whenever I sat at the bar, I was surrounded by men who wanted nothing more than to know my hair color or the secret to my porcelain skin. Of course, I gave out the name of my colorist but as far as my skin was concerned, I professed a strict daily sunscreen regimen, leaving out the details of monthly photo rejuvenation laser treatments and, of course, my stocked closet of a previous skin care line that had crashed and burned.

If I wasn't at the bar but at a table, as I was today, Jesus would often make loud announcements, such as, "Isabella Reynolds, please come to the bar! Attention! Miss Isabella Reynolds, please come to the bar." Any lingering insecurities

I was experiencing after the Italian ex drama were wiped away during church.

After a long day of watermelon therapy, I called it an evening and left Bobby with a new circle of acquaintances. I entered my apartment and headed straight to the couch. Sitting there, I realized I was indeed sitting alone in the dark as the intensity of the moonlight lit up the room. I felt alone and restless, not knowing what to do with myself. Usually, I would be at dinner with the Italian, with a group of friends, or on the couch with Potato, eating Chinese. I began to feel more of the deep, hollow pain in my chest, which brought me to tears, as it sometimes felt so deep, so overwhelming.

Struggling to get up from the couch, I walked into the bathroom to wash the day off my face and then slipped into an oversized T-shirt. My cell phone's ringing startled me. It was Pia, of course, wanting to get the scoop on my first therapy session. Considering my watermelon therapy had lasted seven hours, I was in no position to discuss anything. Plus, I was in no mood for a lecture; Pia always had a concerned tone in her voice lately when she spoke of my unconventional therapy. The fact was that over the previous couple of months, my drinking had taken on a life of its own. But not only did drinking make me feel better, it also caused a loss of appetite so that I was as skinny as I had ever been. I clicked "ignore" on my cell and placed it under one of the couch pillows.

The couch smelled of Potato, and I could only lie my head down where he used to sleep. I missed him, but what I missed most about him were our "huggies." Whenever I needed him, I would sit down on the floor and spread my arms and legs out. "Potato, huggies," I would say, and he always came to me and sat down between my arms and legs. As I hugged and squeezed him, he would just lay his face on my shoulder, waiting until I was okay. I would have done anything for one of those right now.

Still crying, I grabbed my journal and walked to the hall closet. I slowly opened the closet door and sat on the floor, staring at what I referred to as my past—the boxes that contained what remained of my company—some leftover bottles of product and a stack of business files.

Journal entry—June 6

I am desperate to pull down boxes and submerge myself in memories; I simply sit here and stare into the closet, paralyzed by pain and sadness. I wonder how everything from my previous life could fit so easily in these boxes; how my life could look organized and neat but be such a devastating mess at the same time. Crying hysterically, I yelled out, "What am I supposed to do now?"

I did not get an answer. The boxes did not respond, of course.

Resting my head on the floor, I wondered where I went wrong and how I ended up down this path. Somewhere, there was a crossroad and, of course, I took a left instead of making a right. Why was I following this a habit lately of lying around for hours on the floor, just staring at the boxes at what used to my life?

Who would have thought that I would wind up in this state of despair when I moved here seven years ago, full of dreams, from my small hometown in South Carolina? I had come to attend a graduate program at Columbia University, but I had been thinking of getting out of South Carolina since my freshman year of college and had applied to six out-of-state graduate programs. I always felt bigger than the town in which I was raised. I knew there was more in the world, beyond my hometown, and I wanted access to all of it.

I can still recall that late night, while studying for an exam in front of the TV, when my favorite show at the time, Law and Order, *was interrupted by the news. There had been a plane accident and a search for the Kennedy plane that disappeared close to Martha's Vineyard. All night long, the news discussed the lives of JFK Jr. and Carolyn Bessette, their Tribeca apartment, their accomplishments, and their hardships. I was intrigued by how dynamic their lives were in every aspect. If you could make it in New York ... you could make it anywhere, right?*

I remember always being told I lived in a fantasy world. I'm not sure how I started thinking that if I dreamed big and fell short, I would at least still fall above average. Being average was my biggest fear, and this applied to every aspect of my life—living average, dressing average, studying average, dating average, pretty much doing anything average. Manhattan seemed anything but average. Although the horrible crimes from my favorite show took place in the New York City, I was starving for change, a new beginning and a bigger life.

As I write, it seems like a week ago that I was quickly going online, submitting an application to a clinical nutrition program at Columbia, my seventh application for admission to a graduate program. A month later, I received my acceptance letter in the mail. I can't believe how I did not even wait to hear from the other schools. I took this as a sign. My life was to be in Manhattan, and I could feel it in every cell in my body. I can still recall that presence in my heart and the eagerness to start my new unbelievable life.

Lying there on the floor in front of the closet, I thought about my first night alone in my new city.

The small town girl that I was quickly grew up into the city girl, faster than I ever expected. My personality, my wardrobe, my manners changed. It was only natural.

Soon after, at age twenty-five, I thought building a skin care company was my purpose. I had the education, the dream, the connections and, most important, the investors. I aspired to be something remarkable.

And then, after four years, my company was forced to close its doors, and UPS delivered the boxes to my door. All that remained of my dream were some leftover products, business files, press releases, and headshots from the PR blitz. It was over.

All I could do was start sending out résumés ASAP. It was not about money. Money was not important to me; success was important. The Krugerrand afforded me that place to chase after every dream I gave life to in my heart. As a result, the thought of the "I told you so" or having no answer to "What do you do?" or "How is the skin care business?" made the losing of my company feel more like a failure than a dream that ended early. What would my affluent Southern family think of me?

I glanced back to my journal, the pages filled with pain and my deepest fears.

I write this, so I am only saying everything aloud to myself. Once I say anything aloud to others, it means I have to own it. I'm confident, I think, in a fake perfect way. But to answer Dr. Goldstein's question, "No, I am not comfortable with myself." I can't say I am and mean it.

I. R.

I leaned against the wall. My breath was stuck in my throat, and I could not fully relax to completely exhale. I thought about all the hard work that sat in this closet. I remembered so well the official day my company was over; I could still feel it. It was a beautiful afternoon and after I had tucked everything into boxes, I figured a celebration was in order. Don't get me wrong—I was devastated. But I was trying to lift my spirits. After all, there was only one way to go after such an ending and that was up—or so I thought.

I called my friend Desi and told her to meet me at Pastis for a champagne lunch. I first met Desi while shopping at Bergdorf's. We both were alone and trying on clothes, so we asked for each other's opinions. I remember thinking that Desi was sort of ridiculous for asking me if she looked fat in something because she was under a size zero. She had the kind of beauty most women would hate her for. Originally from Chile, Desi had that extremely exotic look that men gravitated to. Still, I knew we would be friends—how could we not be, dressed as we were that day in a matching uniforms of velvet sweat suits, oversized glasses, and thousands of dollars worth of jewelry? And not a stitch of makeup on either one of us. Clearly, we made no sense from a fashion point of view, and we laughed at the idea that this was what we would look like fifty years from now, barring a couple nips and tucks.

Now, after two bottles of champagne and two orders of steak tartare and French fries, Desi confronted me with the big questions. "What happened with the company?"

"A big fish kicked me out of the small pond."

"Come again?" Desi squinted elegantly, jerking her head.

"This multi-million-dollar West Coast company contacted my lawyers and filed a lawsuit against me for trademark infringement. It is ridiculous. Our names were different and not even in the same category of business. They claimed my name could be understood as taking possession of their own name."

"So, what happened? Why didn't you fight them?"

"Desi, I'm a beginner fish who got into a small pond successfully and was learning how to swim. They are the big fish who could chase me, cause me to swim in fear, and waste my time and energy—and my money—trying to secure ground in this small pond. It was either sink or swim. Let's just say swimming was sinking me financially and the smartest thing to do was let them win. It was a lose/lose situation," I said, getting lost in the wet ring my flute was leaving on the table.

"So, Isabella, what are you going to do now? Are you going to start another company, or does this mean we can have fun?" Work for Desi meant taking care of her amazing self by living at the city's best spas, going to fabulous restaurants for amazing meals, and shopping at fabulous places for amazing things. Desi's favorite word was "amazzzzzing." I didn't tell her that day, but the God-awful truth was that I was going to have to start submitting résumés the following week and begin the next phase of my life. I wasn't sure Desi would understand, seeing as she had no need of a job, having come from a multi-million-dollar textile empire. She also had just married Vito, a CFO at a record label.

I, on the other hand, later accepted a senior position in PR at a skin care laboratory on Park Avenue, managing their beauty clients. This was not my dream job, and I knew that during the interview. The company, the job, the position was not glamorous enough for me. Going from the president of a skin care company and developing and creating formulas, interviewing with editors, and having my product shots featured in *Gotham* and *Vogue* to working in a cubicle and eating tossed salads in front of my computer was not what I had in mind for my life. This was not why I had moved to New York City; this was not what I was meant to do. Even though it was a step back for me, I accepted the direction with my head held high. I just told myself that obviously there were lessons I must have skipped in my life, and I needed to learn. At least now, when someone asked about my skin care company, I could easily change the subject by talking about my new job. It saved me from feeling less than perfect and like a failure.

But when I lost my Potato, and then the Italian, I knew this was only the beginning of the life lessons I would have to learn.

I pushed myself off the floor, popped two Ambien, and crawled into bed. As I began to give in to the Ambien, calmness came over me. I finally stopped crying and the deep pain began to go numb.

During the night, I woke up when I felt something run across my hand. As I sat up in bed, I could see in the moonlight small, dark, shadowy spots on my bed and walls. The shadows moved from corner to corner on the floor, then scurried cross the bottom of the bed. Screaming, I jumped out of bed and flipped on the light. Roaches were scattering simultaneously. I ran into the bathroom and slammed the door behind me, causing a small picture frame to fall off the wall and smash, with tiny glass pieces exploding everywhere. The sound of breaking glass woke me up from the nightmare of roaches invading my bedroom.

My reaction may have seemed dramatic, but anyone who has ever seen the size of a New York City roach would understand. Even though I knew it was just a dream, I still could not shake off the feeling of things moving in my room, so I decided to sleep on the couch. It smelled like Potato, and I found it comforting to lie there and pretend he was sleeping on top of me.

While trying to hold on to my peace of mind, I reminded myself that there were no roaches in my apartment. Then, I did what any rational person would do next. I shut my bedroom door and lined the bottom of the door with a towel, safeguarding myself in the living room. Picking up my laptop, I strategically positioned my body on the couch so I could see anything coming. Then Google'd "meanings of dreams" and typed in "roaches."

Roaches in dreams, according to one site I happened upon, represented an undesirable aspect of myself that I needed to confront. Now, I was even more puzzled. "An undesirable aspect" of myself? Of course there was no mention of failed companies, dead dogs, or defective Italians. Maybe it was time to face the one person who I did not want to deal with—myself. For the first time in my life, I felt exposed and raw. Lying back on the couch and closing my eyes, I prayed that the Ambien would still have some effect and just let me go to sleep.

5

Journal entry—June 8

I STEPPED ON A PIECE OF glass from my little disaster the other night. I knew I would miss a piece.

I realize my life is not only stored away in boxes but also that I live in a box. I need to stop living in the box that everyone puts me in. I have been doing it for so long, sometimes I can't even tell where the lies end and the truth begins. This is preventing me from ever learning how to accept myself or even to discover who the hell Isabella Reynolds is. I just want to be loved by everyone and need to stop trying so hard to be who I think they need and want me to be.

I realize I have been spiraling out of control for a while and the past couple of months have caused everything to explode. My eating disorder and obsession with looking perfect popped back into my life. Rather than nourish myself with the nutrients and love that I so desperately need and want, I distract myself in other ways that help ease the pain and sadness, while still maintaining the smallest size I have ever been. This was the only upside from all the loss that has been occurring—weight loss.

I. R.

I returned Pia's call from Saturday evening. I knew she would be at her Monday morning spin class, so I would be able to just leave a voicemail and avoid the Q&A. I was working on a plan to fix everything, and I did not need Dr. Goldstein or Jesus (the bartender) to do so. I would face everyone once I had the answers and the perfect plan of action.

I walked into work an hour early and headed straight to my cubicle. First task of the day was to cancel Dr. Goldstein before her office hours. The phone rang four times, then voicemail. "Good morning, Dr. Goldstein, it is Isabella Reynolds. I was hoping to catch you before my meeting. I need to cancel our next appointment and will call back to reschedule. I am leaving on an unexpected business trip. Thank you so much."

Most important, I wanted to think and work on my plan of action before the partners came in and started bothering me. Every time I walked into the lab, my life felt a bit less glamorous. The nightly dinners with the Italian at some trendy restaurants had kept me alive during the week. I was living a double life, like Clark Kent. During the week, I was in creative strategy meetings or sitting in my cubicle, eating a salad, in front of the computer. Once Thursday came along, however, I would reveal my designer costume and have amazing drinks at fabulous scenes that some people only knew from reading "Page Six" or *Us Weekly*.

A Rolling Stones song played throughout the office: "You can't always get what you want, but if you try sometimes, you might find you get what you need." I closed my eyes and began to think: *What is it that Isabella Reynolds needs?* Okay, maybe I was jumping the gun a bit and should focus on my new life as a single woman in New York. I thought how wonderful it would be for my needs and my wants to be the same thing. Was that what true fulfillment was?

First, plan a fabulous weekend. Next, call Desi and see if she and Vito would be going to their Hamptons house, as beautiful weather was forecast for this weekend. They owned a home in Southampton on the ocean; a weekend with them would definitely set the right tone for my new life.

"Buon giorno, Isabella," Desi answered. Desi spoke Spanish, Italian, and French and often sprinkled the various languages into her speech.

"Hola, Desi! So, I wanted to see what you and Vito were up to this weekend."

Immediately Desi's tone became excited. "Isabella, you must come to the Hamptons this weekend. We are attending the most *amazing* party; well, actually it's a benefit for a Save the Children organization. We can help save kids, and you can wear one of your Cavalli dresses and even have one of the bedrooms. I have already called Bobby, and he is coming!"

"Perfect, Desi! Bobby and I can take a car out Friday afternoon."

"Perfecto. Mark it down for June 13." Desi giggled devilishly.

We exchanged "ciaos," and I quickly marked the plan of a fabulous weekend as a newly single woman off my checklist of things to do.

Desi and Vito were a party in themselves. She always attended the best events and had a wardrobe that fit her social circle. Not only that, Vito's job as the CFO of a record label—one owned by a historic rap artist who was married to one of the top recording R&B females—ensured that I'd get all the up-to-date gossip before *Us Weekly* even got a whiff of it. Sometimes I even annoyed Pia, when she was discussing a headliner over dinner, and I would tell her how that was so passé.

The second thing on my list was to start on a die-hard workout regimen immediately after work. Now that I was back on the market and going to the Hamptons this weekend, this was a crucial step. My great aunt always taught me that I could never be too educated, too rich, or too thin.

Third, no more Chinese takeout for four. I would delete the number from my cell and pray every night that the place would burn down. Maybe I would try to become a vegetarian or do that crazy raw-foods diet. Because breakfast usually consisted of a grande skim extra-hot soy latte, I could still start today, so Googling "raw food diet tips" today was still an option.

Fourth, find a new boyfriend. All the previous goals would result in obtaining goal four and most importantly help me permanently erase the Italian from my mind and mute that deep hollow pain in my heart. Since Chinese takeout was out of the question, I needed something and at least a new man would be sodium free.

Later that night, after a two-hour workout and a twenty-minute steam session, I called up a neighborhood vegetarian restaurant and ordered an organic hummus and cucumber sandwich on Ezekiel bread with a mesclun salad and a side of brown rice. I was already feeling the disappointment of opening the door and not seeing the Chinese delivery guy with my ten-pound bag of food.

I began to brainstorm on other ways to work on my list. As *Access Hollywood* went to break, a fifteen-second spot ran for an online dating site. When had online dating become so acceptable? Of course, I knew of people who met or hooked up from online networking sites, which were thought to be just an added benefit of being a member. It was a more chic and subtle way of meeting people. However, being a member of Asmallworld.net clearly proved how small the world truly was and how few good men existed in Manhattan.

I thought that seeing the commercial for Findyourperson.com—the dating site—was a sign, as it was convenient for me at this point. As I typed in the website address, I was scared that someone would see what I was up to, but then I reminded myself that I was alone in my apartment. Hitting enter, I sat frozen in front of the screen.

Was I really going to do this? Was I about to become an online serial dater? Focusing on the profile section for what seemed like an hour, I eventually began to write in the "About Me" section, typing whatever words came to mind, allowing the process to be natural.

"Former entrepreneur, recently forced into a corporate America rabbit hole, who cries herself to sleep every night because she was abandoned by the most defective Italian man in the world. On a positive note, I'm not thirty yet and not living with a dog. He died last month from an undetectable brain disease, according to the vet."

Maybe this isn't exactly the best approach, Isabella. I held the backspace button down; erasing what had first come to mind. Taking a deep breath, I called on the Hollywood actress inside me. *Let's try again, Reynolds.*

"I have made my life what it is today. Great! I am a highly educated, ambitious, former entrepreneur now working in advertising. I love to laugh and seriously enjoy life. Family and friends are my foundation. My range of interests is unlimited. I can go from ponytail and a DVD to a night out, beginning at a great restaurant or a weekend getaway from the city. Conversations can go from intelligent to talk about shoe trends in an instant. I have been told I am quick-witted with a side of fun sarcasm (but only if you have it coming). Each day is an adventure, whether I am networking for business, wine tasting, traveling, learning a new language, previewing a new art gallery, or spending time with my amazing family and friends. I am looking for a male version of me but with less attitude. I'm interested in a strong, confident, ambitious, and genuinely "good" guy who can embrace a girl who knows who she is and what she wants out of life and the people she spends time with. I am looking for someone who I look forward to seeing."

Next section, some of my favorite things. Well, let's see ...

"Cupcakes with sprinkles, giggles, surprises and shopping—there is no room for discrimination in that category."

Thirty minutes and three glasses of Gavi later, all that was left was to create a user name, write a physical description, and add some photos. "Height: five foot seven inches tall. Body type: athletic and toned." This was always a safe answer, rather than "slender." Just my luck, I would meet some male psycho who thought that at my height, anything over one hundred pounds was a big girl. Last: *Blonde hair and light blue eyes.* I added a couple photos that included a serious pose, a laughing one, and a more natural one to capture a couple of sides of me. Completo finito, IR214 (Isabella Reynolds February 14) was now a member of the Findyourperson.com cult. I clicked "show profile" and signed off. *Come and get me, boys.*

6

OVERWHELMED WITH ANTICIPATION, I WOKE up two hours early for work on Tuesday morning to go online and see if anyone had looked at my profile. I had received forty-three e-mails and fifteen winks. This was cost-effective, as I didn't have to buy a blowout, manicure, and pedicure or a new outfit. The downside was that it seemed I had attracted everything and everyone. This was going to be a full-time job in itself. Some were handsome, some sweet, and some very scary men, who were mature enough to be my grandfather. The "interested in" section of my profile was created for a reason, and it seemed that some men were already demonstrating poor effort. I was sure an online dating code had been broken. *Do not contact profiles that are clearly NOT wanting to be contacted by you.* Here I was opening myself up in such a widespread manner for all of the site to see, including the creepies. Why did we learn the honor system as kids if we were only going to ignore it as adults? Perhaps, the honor code was just like geometry. You have to learn it, but no one in the real world actually applies it. I quickly deleted the convict-looking and Daddy types and left the honorable, literate ones to read when I got home from work that day.

What I didn't expect was that e-mails and winks would come in all day long. By the time I got home, I had fourteen more e-mails and eight more winks.

I was going to have to create a more specific checklist to sort through these connections. My idea was to quickly scan the profile. First, I'd look over the pictures. If the guy was attractive and not Italian, I would then check whether his location was New York City. I was not interested in going on dates with guys from the bridge-and-tunnel crowd, who would inevitably try to take me like each time was their first big night out in the city.

Next, I checked the height for six feet or taller. I also checked "baggage" status (for example, never married, no children but wants them). Last, income and occupation. I was getting older and was not going to waste any time with guy who was still trying to find himself or lived with roommates.

Of course, all of these potential dates would have to somehow match up to my "favorite five men" list:

1. The talent of Christian Bale
2. The voice and charm of Ed Burns

3. The husband skills of Andy Garcia's character in *When a Man Loves a Woman*
4. The boyishness of Hayden Christensen
5. The beauty and sex appeal of David Gandy (a D&G model)

After using this screening method (and what seemed about 30 percent of the qualities from my favorite five men list, as I didn't want to end up with zero potentials), I was left with only eight profiles:

Chef Julian, thirty-five, lived in Gramercy Park with a French bulldog named Bugsy. Real estate investor Brady, thirty, athletic, and in the meat-packing district. Architect Mason, who was thirty-eight, looked a bit crazy but handsome, and was on the Upper West Side. Forty-two-year-old Kirk from Scandinavia, who now lived in Chelsea (a little too close for comfort) and was a corporate lawyer. Two thirtysomething Germans, Klaus from Hamburg, now living in Midtown East, and Tanner from Munich, who lived in Midtown West. Conner, a twenty-six-year-old Irishman who was an established artist on the Lower East Side. Last, there was Alan (boring name), a forty-five-year-old Wall Street guy who lived in the West Village.

It was time to live a little and finally find what I needed in a person, I decided. Actually, it was quite convenient that they each had their own neighborhood, just in case I wanted to date them all.

Finally, after responding to all their e-mails in my uniquely charming and witty manner, I crawled into bed and prayed that at least one of these guys would pique my interest enough to meet. I hoped this Internet dating would not become the full-time job it looked like it could become.

Days were becoming hell at the office. Annoyingly long meetings were often a result of the partners' having nothing to do all day long and our not wanting to feel guilty for our client's hefty retainer fees. Going from running my own company to having to sit around a boardroom was so frustrating, particularly as I was there with eight men and one other woman, who clearly had never heard of or used an eye cream. All I could think about was how to put myself into the nearest hospital emergency room during these so-called brainstorming meetings.

I refused to eat in my rabbit hole in front of the computer and headed to Madison Square Park to enjoy the beautiful sunny day. I grabbed a salad and sat on a bench, one that didn't face the Shake Shack (as a burger and milkshake were not on my new vegetarian and raw-foods diet). On the other side of the water fountain, a stunning fifty-something brunette with the perfect blowout and a Tocca two-piece suit was staring at me. I wondered why she was sitting in Madison Square Park, as she was more of a Central Park and Madison Avenue restaurant kind of woman. She seemed so familiar, but I could not place her. She was also making me uncomfortable, and she did not care about being obvious at all. Eating my salad felt like I was swallowing pins and needles, so I tossed it in the trash bin and then walked back to hell.

"Excuse me. Excuse me!" I heard a woman's voice calling from behind me and turned around to see Tocca woman. "Do you remember me?"

I wished I did, as I loved her sense of style. "I'm sorry. I don't think I do."

"We met about two years ago at the Equinox Gym on the Upper East Side. My name is Sylvie Rousseau, I approached you before a spinning class."

How could I forget that day? I'd never stepped foot in a spinning room after that, as I could not walk or sit down for a week—I'd refused to where padded shorts. The sound of it made my mind wander to territory where I did not want to travel. "Yes. So nice seeing you again, Ms. Rousseau. My name is Isabella."

"Darling, I have been looking for you at that gym every day since I met you. You never called me, and it's raining men right now."

A couple of years ago, Sylvie was covered in *New York* magazine as the premier matchmaker for the rich and famous. Her clients included everyone from multi-millionaires to actors, athletes, and politicians who were too busy to date and just wanted to meet the one who was worthy of being spouse material. The problem was, I had just met Saint Santo and was head over heels.

"Are you seeing anyone now, Isabella?"

"No, I'm newly single," I said, as if "newly" made a difference; it only reflected my insecurity about it by the use of the word.

"Well, I'm not sorry to hear that! You must call me first thing tomorrow morning to set up a consultation. I need to know what you want in a man."

The sad thing was, at this point, I just wanted to find one who knew what love meant and the weight of the meaning; one who, when he said "I love you," meant he wanted to spend the rest of his life with me. Not one who used those three significant words in a way such as "I love you, man," "I love Wii," or "I love my dog"; a man who used those words and meant them and did not use them out of convenience, like the newest iPhone application. I did not think that was too much to ask.

I took Sylvie's business card and promised I would ring her first thing. As I walked back up the busy streets of Park Avenue South, I looked up at the sky and thanked fate for stepping in. Maybe the universe was on my side. I mean, what were the chances that a matchmaker would approach me within a day of my deciding to find a new boyfriend?

The rest of my day in the land of cubicle was smooth sailing. It was already Wednesday, and this meant I was in the middle of the week and closer to freedom once again. When I got back to the office, I secretly logged on to Findyourperson.com, and my eight potentials had all responded and were all asking to have drinks or dinner. Because I was leaving for my fab weekend in the Hamptons, I only had Thursday evening of this week. Of course, there was always next week to book the rest of them.

I chose Chef Julian and Bugsy for date one on Thursday at restaurant A Voce. Monday was drinks at 6:30 p.m. with Upper West Side Mason, the architect, at Sushi of Gari; then downtown at 8:30 p.m. with athletic Brady for drinks at La Bottega in the Maritime Hotel. Tuesday was drinks with the Irishman, Conner, at the Bowery Hotel at 6:30 p.m., and dinner with Midtown West Tanner, the Munich German, at A. O. C. Wednesday night at nine o'clock. Even though I would run late in my work schedule on Thursday due to my matchmaker consultation, which I planned to schedule with Sylvie for that morning, I went ahead and scheduled lunch that afternoon with the Midtown East German, Klaus, at Haru. Friday night was dinner at 8:00 with Scandinavian Kirk at Olives in the W Hotel Union Square (no way I was about to risk meeting in my own neighborhood), followed by 10:15 p.m. drinks with Wall Street Alan at Turks and Frogs in the West Village. It was a lot for one week, but I had already wasted two years of my life with Saint Santo, and I was not about to waste the final few months of my twenties. I would give all of these eight potentials my five- to fifteen-minute rule—five minutes for me to scan them from head to toe and the remaining ten for them to charm me into believing they deserved my time. *In and out, Reynolds!*

First thing the next morning, I called, as promised, and scheduled a consultation with my new matchmaker for the following Thursday. Thank God that it was a slow workweek, as it allowed me to leave for lunch and make a quick stop at Intermix for a new dating wardrobe and anything worthy of wearing in the Hamptons this weekend. With Desi and Vito, it was a given that the press would be covering any of the events or parties we would be attending. *Hamptons* magazine would be there, for sure.

At Intermix, I did a quick run-through of the store and went back to the middle rack. I picked up a Missoni blouse, a couple of Alice and Olivia tops, a Diane von Furstenberg wrap dress, and a couple of staples from Theory that could be mixed and matched.

After work and my pre-Hampton two-hour Equinox boot camp session, it was straight to Bliss 49 spa to get a mani and pedi. The vegetarian and raw food program on which I had so regretfully put myself was working, and I was feeling great. I hoped that the restaurant had some selection of carpaccio or tartare, but I had a feeling that Chef Julian would not approve of my choosing those as main entrée selections.

From Bliss spa, it was straight home to quickly change into a purple bubble mini-dress to meet my first blind date at eight o'clock. I arrived at 8:07 p.m., ensuring that Julian would be there before me to secure a seat at the bar. I began to think that maybe agreeing to dinner on a first date was not such a genius idea. How would I escape if he was a total nightmare?

When I walked in, I saw him right away—he was hard to miss at six foot three; he towered over the crowd. I found myself seriously attracted to his stature. Julian was handsome and conservatively dressed, and I was very happy to have dinner with him.

I hated to admit it, but several appetizers, entrées, a bottle of Barolo, and tons of giggles later, I realized that I was having a fabulous time. He was charming, attentive, and stuffed me with food, as he loved eating. *This might be the only negative to dating a chef.* He was originally from Marseille, and I felt like he might slap me if I ever said the "D" word—diet.

Dating a chef was inconvenient for my new healthy diet. Even worse, it meant the B&P cycle had to take place on our date. I was uncomfortable in my skin, feeling so full, and I knew that I would seem preoccupied to him if I didn't purge. After dinner, I excused myself to the ladies room to rid myself of the delicious meal. I had to stick to a strict regimen as well. I rinsed my mouth out with cold water several times, popped in three one-and-a-half calorie TicTacs, and swiped some gloss across my lips. *Voila!* Good as new; the "P" never happened.

Later, as we stood outside saying our good-byes, he leaned in and kissed my cheek, and we both agreed to do it again soon. While in the cab, the deep, hollow pain in my chest began to overwhelm me, and I broke out into a silent cry. I put my head on my knees, not wanting the cab driver to witness my crazypants breakdown. It was then I realized that

I had just been at dinner with a man who was not my Italian. I decided that I had to use this weekend to help me purge myself of Santo. I just needed new and better memories, and the Hamptons was the best place to create them.

I pulled myself together so I could pack for my first newly single weekend in the Hamptons with my misfit crew (Bobby, Desi, and me). Tomorrow, I would escape the concrete jungle and lie in a hammock overlooking the water. I would numb myself with a bottle of my favorite rosé, *Domaines Ott Clos de Mireille*. After stuffing my Louis Vuitton duffle bag with a weekend's worth of clothes, I crawled into bed and cried myself to sleep. The only time I could not feel the pain was when I was sleeping.

7

THE HOURS I SPENT AT work on Friday morning were about as interesting as watching paint dry. Noon finally came, and all I had to do was pop into a liquor store, buy a nice bottle of Sancerre (it was Bobby's favorite), and then go back to the office, as the car service was picking us up there. Desi and Vito had left Thursday night, so Bobby and I were taking a car, which wasn't a bad deal; we would be able to enjoy a nice bottle during the two-hour drive to our weekend escape from reality.

When I returned to my office building, Bobby was already by the car, waiting for me with open arms. Judging from his expression, I must have looked bad. His mouth went from a puckered "Oh" in surprise, to a furrowed brow, and straight to a fake smile. Without making a sound, he grabbed me with a bruising squeeze like he was going to spontaneously spring an intervention on me.

After we got cozy in the back seat, we opened up a bottle of perfectly chilled wine, but I had forgotten the glasses. I took the first sip directly out of the bottle, and I felt like I had reached another low point. But as the driver pulled on to Park Avenue, I felt a little free.

I took full advantage of the Sancerre. As I poured, I said, "Do you find it hard to meet people in this city?"

"Um,... how about no Isabella." He turned his body toward me, seeming completely confused. "Spit it out, missy. We only have two hours, so no time for charades."

"Charades? You are such a pill, Bobby. Can't we just have a conversation?"

He dropped his shoulders a bit, and I could tell he felt a bit guilty for jumping to conclusions.

I rephrased my question. "Why is it so hard to meet nice people in a city of eight million people?"

"Sugar, you mean 1.6 million?"

"Bobby, there are a bit more than 1.6 million people in New York City."

"Yes, I am fully aware of that, missy, but when do the borough boys count?"

"Good point. Let me rephrase again. Why is it so hard to meet a nice guy in a city of 1.6 million people?" I hoped I would get a solid answer from him that would be the missing piece of my puzzle.

"A nice guy or your soul mate? Reynolds, you are setting me up for something. Don't give me a headache; spit it out already. Why is it when you have a 'tini you can't shut up, and now we have to play tug-of-war with your tongue? Get on with it, will you?"

"Fine. I—"

He started giggling. "Oh, my God, you're doing online dating, aren't you."

"What? What makes you think that?"

He raised his right eyebrow—his infamous response.

"I joined findyourperson.com," I said in a rush then went into turtle mode, trying to force my head as far down to my shoulders as possible.

He asked who I was looking for, and I explained to him that it was to find my soul mate—or at least to regain a social life.

"Findyourperson.com," he said. "I haven't heard of that one."

"It is not like those hook-up sites," I insisted. "It is to truly find ... wait—what do you mean, you haven't heard of 'that one'?"

He snapped at me. "I'm a man! It's different, Isabella. This is about you, not me."

Why do all my friends keep saying that to me? I wondered.

"I disagree; it just depends on how you want to put yourself out there. You get what you give," the driver said, adding his two cents and proving that we were all in the same "car."

Bobby and I slowly turned toward each other and tightened our mouths in disbelief.

"Sir, how about a beautiful, five-foot-seven, smart blonde?" Bobby asked, pinching me.

The driver looked at him in the rearview mirror. "She is quite beautiful," he said with a wink.

"Yes, a beautiful mess," Bobby responded. "Look at me; now I'm a matchmaker. I'm ridiculously talented."

I pulled my sunglasses down and focused my entire self out the window. I was replaying it all in my head, the conversation that just had taken place. Would he or wouldn't he use this as material during one of his weekend drunken rants? I couldn't tell, but I knew not to bring up the topic, as that would only remind him of my insecurity. Sometimes, my shyness and insecurities were his favorite toys.

By the time we arrived in Southampton, I was drunk. The driver pulled into the circular driveway in front of the two-story house, parked the car, and brought our bags to the door, where I saw a note for us: "Went to the market for tonight's barbeque bash. Be back in a couple of hours." We let ourselves in and walked directly upstairs to the second largest bedroom. Bobby and I would be sharing a room, but I knew we'd hardly sleep all weekend anyway. We tossed our bags on the bed, slipped into our bathing suits (and I applied SPF), and headed toward the kitchen.

Bobby opened and iced my bottle of rosé, and I grabbed some sliced cantaloupe that was in the refrigerator. We went outdoors to situate ourselves comfortably by the heated pool, as we did not plan on leaving that spot for the rest of the day. Thirty minutes later, another bottle was down, and Bobby headed back in to grab another. With the brief period of silence, I began to feel the deep, hollow pain in my chest again and broke down into another silent cry. Despite my oversized Gucci shades to hide my eyes, Bobby could tell that I was sad, probably because my body had gone limp and lifeless beside him; he knew I was having another crazypants breakdown. Here I was in Hampton heaven, sipping rosé and rocking the cutest baby-doll bathing suit. I looked great, as I had not eaten anything in two days (well, nothing that I actually let digest) other than a couple of crackers, yet all I could feel was pain.

Only four hours into my first single-girl weekend, and I was already a mess. The Italian was not even in my life, but he was still making me unhappy. He was still holding me back. During the two years we had dated, the only time we did not spend a weekend together was if we went home to see our families. I could not stop wondering what he was doing or if he was even thinking of me.

"Isabella! Stop it. Stop it right now, crazypants!" Bobby had never really raised his voice to me before. "Sugar, you just have to cut the cord. You were never happy with him. I know it's hard, darlin', but just let it out and stop trying to hold everything in." Even though Bobby spent many years in Paris as a model and spoke fluent French, when he was drunk, his Southern accent came out. He had not grown up in the South, but his grandmother had, and he had picked her accent, probably from his tendency to mock her at times. He really could be too dramatic, but at times I felt like my life was my own movie as well.

Annoyed by having to balance the wine bottle between my legs, I could only look at him and gesture with my hands. "And … scene."

We both lay back down, not looking at each other. The perfect breeze came in at our toes and rolled up to our chins like an ocean tide. It was a stunning sunny day, and we both inhaled to take our deepest breaths. Watching the calmness of the pool water soothed me and gave me a refreshing peaceful feeling. Getting into the pool would probably be even more rewarding.

Twenty minutes later, we both were startled by the sound of voices approaching. "Hola!" It was Desi, Vito, and the chef they had hired for tonight's extravaganza. Because tomorrow would be a long night out, we were having a night in. However, a night in at Desi and Vito's meant a hired chef and a dinner party for ten. The back of the house had the most gorgeous wraparound porch and dining table that seated twelve. This is where we would dine, drink and watch the sunset over the ocean. I sometimes wondered what it would be like to have the ability, at the end of the day, to just disappear like that—to sink like the sun.

To be a smart ass, Bobby blasted some Bob Marley ("Don't worry; be happy"), and we all started dancing around the pool while the chef and servers began to prepare for the barbeque. We still had two hours until the arrival of the others, so we did what misfits do best: opened bottle after bottle of rosé and danced around like no one was watching.

During one of my dance moves I began to see the world spin, literally. I excused myself to get ready for the evening and ran upstairs quickly. I was drunk. I was sick. I had not even noticed, but I was crying again. The pain and sadness was out of control, but I could not even tell it was happening until I looked at my reflection in the bathroom mirror. I turned on the shower so my friends could not hear me, as I did not want them to think I did not appreciate my weekend invitation. Stripping out of my clothes, I stepped into the shower and sat down on the cold stone floor, letting the hot water run over my head and down my back. I just let myself cry, releasing as much pain as I could, as I knew that I only had so much time alone upstairs in the bathroom before the others became suspicious.

I pulled my hair back into a ballerina bun and slipped into a black Juicy Couture cotton dress with some Havaianas flip-flops. I lightly brushed Lamer powder across my forehead, down along the sides of my nose, and under my eyes. I touched my cheeks with blush, swiped my lashes with brown Bobbi Brown mascara, and tapped my lips with Smith's Rosebud Salve before heading back downstairs. Guests had arrived and champagne was being served. I grabbed a flute and headed to an empty hammock in the backyard. Closing my eyes, I took a couple deep breaths and swallowed the entire flute of champagne. *Cool, calm, and collected.* Minutes later, I forced a full-sized pearly white smile on my face and headed back inside to join the misfits and the rest of the party.

We had a fabulous and leisurely dinner of ribs, lobster, squid salad, and pears poached in Port with cranberries. By the time we finished, it was 2:30 a.m. and time for me to call it a night. I headed upstairs and pulled five of the twenty down pillows from the bed to build a barricade in the middle to separate Bobby and me. I popped an Ambien and watched the moon from the window slowly disappear.

The next morning a breakfast buffet was waiting for us. The chef handed me a mimosa, and I returned to the hammock to take a morning nap. We planned to attend a benefit this evening for a children's foundation. It would be a celebrity-filled and press-covered event. A car was scheduled to pick up Desi and me to take us to get blowouts, as well as a brow wax at Eliza's Eyes. The woman charged a hundred bucks to wax eyebrows, which I thought was absurd, but Desi's using another of her "it's the most amazing" speeches could sell ice to Eskimos.

Groomed and ready to go, I slipped on a Roberto Cavalli halter dress and my metallic gold Jimmy Choo strappy sandals with matching clutch. I tried to get back into the bathroom, as Bobby pretty much had taken over our room. I could hear him freaking out about something. "Hey, are you okay in there?" I asked. The door flew open; there stood Bobby, and I could see the worry in his eyes. His allergies were acting up, leaving him puffy, nasally, and with bloodshot eyes. The thought of his being photographed pushed him over the edge of panic.

"Isabella, oh, my God, I think I have an upper respiratory infection!"

This was typical drama. "Silly, you are not suffering from any infection; it's just your allergies. I think I saw some Benadryl in here." I searched through all the meds and reached for the children's Benadryl. I gave him double the dosage and promised him it would all be okay, as we had a twenty-minute drive to the event.

The black Mercedes SUV pulled up, and the driver beeped the horn. The four of us <u>harmoniously</u> loaded into the car and were off. During the drive, Bobby became extremely loud, crazy, and a bit delusional. He kept shouting, "You are trying to sabotage me, Isabella! She is trying to poison me!" Vito asked if everything was all right, but Bobby had passed out with his face smashed up against the window. *Thank God for tinted windows*, I thought.

Vito turned around in the front passenger seat. "What the hell is wrong with him?"

"He wasn't feeling well, so I gave him some children's Benadryl. I thought he could take a double dose, but I guess with all the alcohol, maybe it wasn't such a great idea. Honestly, is the silence really so bad?"

We all looked at each other, shrugged, and enjoyed the remainder of the trip in silence. We had no idea what we would do with Bobby once we reached the event; we could not ask the driver to babysit him. The driver did not speak English, and only Desi could communicate with him in Spanish. We all imagined Bobby waking up in the car with a complete stranger and having a total freak-out. What chaos it would be—the driver would speak Spanish, and Bobby would respond in French and then most likely go into his Southern accent.

As we pulled up to the event, I shook and slapped Bobby as gently as possible, trying not to abuse him since he'd already accused me of poisoning him. "Hey, wake up. *Hamptons* magazine is right outside the car. You are about to miss your chance to be photographed." I knew that would bring out the ex-model in this crazypants as he was already paranoid that we would take any of his "lights, camera, and action" moments.

Instantly wired up and on alert, he ran his fingers through his hair and looked at all of us with a sharp, spirited, and watchful eye. "I am not missing anything!" The driver rolled his eyes as though he had determined during the past twenty minutes that he had been stuck in the car with a group of lunatics.

We walked into the event tent, posing here and there for photos. No one suspected the drama that had just occurred seconds ago. The tent was filled with celebrities, models, fashionistas, and hot, rich, single Manhattan men. We floated around and drank champagne for the next five hours. Desi and I avoided the dinner by socializing, as it would be a sin to eat in our Cavalli dresses. Some clothes were not meant to be worn while eating. That actually included the majority of my wardrobe. I somehow always went shopping on days when I felt super-thin, which mean I had not eaten in a day or two. If I ate in clothes I had purchased on those days, they wouldn't fit properly for the rest of the evening. It didn't matter. Tonight I was more concerned with obtaining the "I haven't eaten in days" feeling. I accepted a fresh flute of bubbly, swallowed the last drop from the glass I was already holding, and then handed that empty glass to a waiter.

Here I was at a charity event in the Hamptons and totally was not flirting. What a waste of Cavalli. Why I was not taking full advantage of the menu of men, I had no idea. Maybe the champagne was easing my mind about finding a new boyfriend. Or maybe it was because I had my secret eight potentials in my pocket.

The after-party was at a new spot in Southampton, so we grabbed our must-have gift bags, organized by Scoop, and piled back into the SUV. The gift bag was loaded with fragrances, skin care, cosmetics, and vodka. I opened up the mini-bottle and soon had consumed the entire thing—it had started as a sip on the way, but I'd finished it by the time we exited the parking area of the charity. I was officially beyond my misfit crowd's usual mode.

The car pulled up outside the club, and we quickly bypassed the herd of people trying to pass the red velvet rope. I actually felt sorry for them for a half a second, but then the sound of "Love Generation" by Bob Sinclair caught my attention, and I focused on the party inside. We were escorted to a large corner booth, where we downed more champagne. The night flew by—we danced until three in the morning—and I did not even focus on any of the handsome Manhattan men who surrounded me. This was the first time that the deep, hollow pain did not interrupt me, and I felt free and fabulous.

The next afternoon, our last day of the weekend, we all woke up out of our comas and decided to head down to Sag Harbor, grab a lobster roll, and lay on Vito's friend's yacht all day. A certain little shack on the harbor had the best lobster roll in all of the Hamptons, in my opinion. We climbed on board the yacht, devoured the rolls like fat little kids, and washed them down with glasses of Dom Perignon. I truly enjoyed meals like this. I hadn't eaten, so I was having a very skinny day, which meant no purging. A very skinny day was a result of at least two days of depriving myself and resulted in a feeling of needing to eat, rather than just wanting.

As I lay there in my Missoni bikini, I wondered what I would have been doing if the Italian and I were still together. At that moment, I wanted one of his tight-squeezing hugs, just for one minute. Maybe Dr Goldstein was right about one thing: I was in denial and just kept remembering the good times. I knew better. We would have been stuck in the city. He would have been working at the office all day, apologizing for ruining the weekend and promising dinner later, except that I would wait for him and eventually be disappointed. No dinner. No Santo.

Now, I was on a yacht with a crew of gorgeous Australian men who waited on me hand and foot. My only concern should have been watching their every move and remembering to reapply my sunblock every fifteen minutes.

After a day on the yacht, Bobby and I headed back home that night. As exhausted and partied-out as I was, I was surprisingly eager for the new week and my online potentials. I quickly stripped down, popped an Ambien (as a preventive method to guarantee sleep), and crawled into bed. I was not going to allow the deep, hollow pain to show up tonight.

8

WHEN I WALKED INTO WORK the next morning, everyone was discussing his or her weekend. I had already learned that this was a routine thing that people in corporate America did on Mondays. I always down played my weekend by saying, "Oh, I rested, read a book, went to dinner, and caught a movie," as my co-workers most likely would watch the events I attended on Monday night's *Access Hollywood*.

The responsibility of having a job was such a hassle with my new single life. I had to come to work dressed for my date but had no time for a blowout or manicure. This required waking up extra early to make myself as perfect as possible for online date number two. I flat ironed my hair to the best of my ability so at least it would last throughout the day. Then I packed my makeup bag to touch up my face later in the firm's bathroom. I dressed in one of my favorite Theory ensembles, which included a knee-length black satin skirt, a white cap-sleeve blouse, and a tweed vest. Of course, I paired it with my black Manolos but with the three-inch rather than the four-inch heel. I was at work and thought the extra inch was a bit too dramatic.

At 6:00 p.m., sharp, I jumped in a cab and headed to the Upper West Side to Sushi of Gari. I saw Mason the architect waiting at the sushi bar, sipping sake. He was tall, dark, and handsome in a bit of a nerdy way, and he dressed in an expensive pinstriped black suit with a light blue, custom-tailored shirt. At first, I thought his shirt was covered in mini lint balls, but after investigating it more closely, I realized it had a hideous pattern of raised white dots. The black patent leather shoes were not in his favor either. I let them go for the moment, as I found his shiny, slicked-back black hair attractive and his small glasses with the clear frames intellectually adorable. He sort of had the whole Christian Bale *American Psycho* theme going. Thank God I was obsessed with Mr. Bale. As I walked toward him with recognition in my eyes, I reminded myself I could do this again. "I'm in the game. Play the game."

"Hello, Isabella, so very nice to meet you."

I just flashed a pearly white smile, wondering why he'd forgotten to stand up while greeting me.

"What would you like to drink?" he asked.

"I'll have some sake, thank you." I was already bored, and we had not even had a convo yet. Granted, I was new at this, but they say you will *know* when you know, and after one Mason minute, I knew—I knew there was nothing. While he was ordering more sake, I scanned him again and noticed that his sterling silver cufflinks happened to be tiny skulls. We gave a brief bio of ourselves to each other, and while he was speaking, I zoned out and remembered *American Psycho* scenes.

"Honey, are you all right?" he asked as he touched my hand on my lap.

"Yes, of course. Why do you ask?"

"You just had a painful look on your face."

"Not painful but pensive. I'm just really listening to you and learning about you."

"Wonderful, honey." He tugged at the little heads on his cuffs.

I was completely freaked out, and every time I looked at him, I could not separate Mason from the movie. It was completely disturbing. He was the type who would have memorized my profile, word for word, and would pretend otherwise. He had "neurotic" and "routine" written all over him.

"So I forget—are you thirty-three or thirty-four?"

"Excuse me. I'm twenty-nine, to be exact."

"Oh, well, you act so much older."

I was stunned that this asshole thought he was going to play this mind game with me. I laughed to myself. I did not have one hyper-pigmentation spot on my face because I wore sunscreen 365 days a year, and yes, monthly zapping treatments had erased everything. Who was he kidding?

Now that psycho Mason was on my die list, it was time for my exit. "Well, it was lovely—"

"Oh, Isabella, I hope you don't mind, but I took the liberty of ordering the omakase for us."

"Oh, I thought we were just meeting for drinks." A hot flash moved down my body, similar to the flight-or-fight reaction. I was new to this online octo-dating club, but he'd said drinks. Not dinner, but drinks. I had a schedule!

He seemed surprised that I would say this, as if I should feel honored that he wanted to have dinner with me. "Well, I saw you checking your coat, and I thought you must be hungry." What he meant to say was that he saw me, confirmed that I looked like the girl on my online profile bio, and thought *Approved*.

Before I could say thanks, but no thanks, the first course was placed before me. *Shit. Shit. Shit.* I had to call Brady and reschedule. "Excuse me for one second; I'm just going to visit the ladies room."

Behind the bathroom door, I quickly dialed Brady's number. "Hi, Brady, it's Isabella."

"Well, this is a nice surprise."

"Actually, it isn't. It seems a meeting has just been scheduled tonight, and I'm not going to be able to meet you at La Bottega."

"I understand—well, as long as you are planning to reschedule. What about tomorrow evening?"

My week flashed before my eyes, and I realized I was

booked until Saturday. "Actually, Saturday night is supposed to be a gorgeous evening to be outside, and La Bottega's patio would be perfect. Does that work for you? Same time, 8:00 p.m.?"

"Anything for you, Isabella."

"Perfect. See you then. Have a great week." I tucked my phone back in my bag and went back to Mr. Patrick Bateman, aka Mason. This was going to most likely hurt. "Sorry about that. Shall we order more sake?"

As the omakase continued; so did the sake. All I really cared about was the good-bye and good riddance. "Let's do this again sometime," I said, but I didn't give him time to respond. I waved as I left in a cab.

The next morning I woke up looking forward to my next online potential, the twenty-six-year-old Irishman, Conner. We were to meet after work at the Bowery Hotel bar for a martini. I'd agreed to meet him primarily because he was *not* still living with roommates. He was younger than I was, which was a first for me, so I decided to play it less conservative and more hip and trendy. My after-work date bag contained my skinny Rock and Republic jeans, a black silk camisole, Chanel clutch and, of course, the four-inch Manolos.

After entering the dimly lit lobby of the Bowery hotel, I walked through the back area to the bar scene. As I entered the lounge, Conner turned around; we were facing each other. He was tall with brown hair and crystal blue eyes and dressed down in jeans, with an untucked shirt. He had a boyish look about him (more like twenty-two), and the whole artist edge, which made him seem a bit risky. When someone said he was an artist, in this city that usually translated to "I'm a bartender or waiter waiting for my big break."

"Hey, you," he said, grinning while standing up to greet me.

"Hi, there," I responded, leaning in to accept his warm cheek kiss. I felt his sweetness and was waiting for his charm to begin.

"Did it hurt when you fell?" he asked.

"Fell?" I asked, confused.

"From heaven," he said with a confident chuckle.

"That's cute." I flashed a fake smile.

"What's your poison, Miss Reynolds?"

"Kettle martini with olives, please." I was actually hungry, but the olives would be sufficient for now.

He ordered my 'tini, along with a Guinness and a shot of Jameson. I tried not to seem scared of the young Irishman. "Would you like a shot of Jameson?" he asked.

"Oh, no, thank you."

"Sweetheart, I'm a lot easier to look at if you do one. I can be Brad Pitt tonight, baby."

"Conner' will be just fine for tonight, but thank you." Okay, this was getting weird, and I was anxious for my 'tini. Was he messing with me, or was he for real? I took a quick glance around the room to find any sign of a hidden camera moment. Nope, he was not so much a charming Irishman as a complete idiot.

"Is your dad still in prison?" he asked.

"My father is not in prison. What are you talking about?"

"For stealing the stars and putting them in your eyes, gorgeous."

"Why don't we cut the jokes for a bit?" I asked hopefully.

"I have a better idea—why don't we get out of here, grab a slice of pizza, and go back to my place and make out?"

"Excuse me?

"What? You don't eat pizza?"

"Sure. Let me run to the ladies room first."

It's crazy how we can look into another human being's eyes and know in a split second if there will ever be a chance for a connection, if the person could possibly be "the" person. As soon as we made eye contact, I thought we would have a fun night, sipping and socializing (I'd totally overestimated even that), but this would be the first and last time I would listen at the Irishman's jokes, which were not even funny. I walked right past the powder room and right out of the Bowery Hotel.

I was starving when I got home that night but decided to just go to bed. I had not had the energy to purge the omakase the night before, due to the abundance of sake I'd consumed.

So tonight, starvation was the only way to counteract the effects of my seven-course meal last night.

I woke up on Wednesday morning, exhausted and still with a sake headache. I wouldn't have known that I cried myself to sleep last night except that it was obvious—I'd forgotten to take off my makeup. The black mascara stains all over my twelve-hundred-count Egyptian-cotton white pillowcases gave me emotional distress. I was thankful I did not remember crying or how long it lasted.

I was seriously starting to rethink my week of online potential boyfriends. Tonight, was Midtown West German, Tanner, at A. O. C. Wine Bar in the West Village. I was trying to push for a meeting location in the neighborhood where he lived, as it helped me keep all of these men straight without actually creating a chart. I remained in my rabbit hole at the office most of the day. My puffy eyes were out of control, along with my dehydrated skin.

Thank God that Tanner and I were not meeting until 9:00 p.m., leaving me sufficient time to pull myself together with a nap, long shower, and some serious exfoliation.

Walking into A. O. C., I immediately spotted the tall, blond, blue-eyed German at the bar, sipping what looked like an Amstel Light. "Hello, Tanner," I said, extending my hand. "Isabella."

"Wow, you are so beautiful."

I smiled and prayed this would not be another project;

perhaps it would be a nice time. I took a seat and thought, *What would one drink hurt?*

"So ... I recently moved to this amazing place called New York City," he said. "It's very nice. I don't have many friends yet, but you seem really nice. I hope we can be friends. What would you like to drink?" I smiled as he continued, "I am a volunteer with the organization Big Brothers. It's so rewarding. I'm a big brother to a young boy ..."

Wow, what kind of batteries is this guy running on? I wondered. "Excuse me, Tanner," I said, and then turned my attention to the bartender. "A glass of champagne, please."

Tanner continued to speak, and I completely zoned out. This guy was in love with himself and most likely rambling on about his good will and deeds because that was what he thought that silly American girls like to hear in order to bed them. He didn't ask me one question but continued to talk about his volunteer work for the next twenty minutes. I finished my glass of champagne and politely interrupted Mr. Deeds.

"I'm so sorry. I'm truly having a lovely time, but unfortunately, I have a bit of a headache."

He eyed my glass and shot me a grin.

"I think I should go home and lie down."

"Are you sure? We are really getting to know each other."

"Wow, that's amazing that you are able to know me without asking me one question. That is a real talent. Do you have an agent?" I realized I was being a bit snarky and it was indeed time for me to go. I stood up abruptly. "Thank you again." I walked out of the restaurant and turned the corner. Taking my Pinkberry out, I noticed it was only 9:12 p.m. Dear God, I'd only been there for twenty-five minutes! It was too early, and after all the effort of getting ready, I could not just go home.

What the hell—I called Brady to see if he wanted to meet now rather than on Saturday. Did I really have anything to lose at this point? I was an online serial dater. Seriously? Seriously now?

Two rings later and after a "Hello, beautiful," I had fifteen minutes to get to La Bottega to meet Brady. I walked up the steps of the Maritime Hotel, enjoying the beautiful spring night with its crisp breeze. All the side panel doors of the restaurant were opened, allowing the patio and indoor restaurant to be one room. It was extremely crowded, and I didn't see anyone resembling Brady. Suddenly, a text message popped in my inbox—it was from him: "Have a table outside behind the large tree." I walked through the crowds of people in the outdoor patio section and did a 360-degree turn. There were eight large trees on the outdoor patio. Was this guy playing a mind game with me or something? Out of the corner of my eye, I could see someone motioning with his arm.

As the thirty-year-old real estate investor stood up to greet me, I took in his athletic Abercrombie & Fitch model-like body. His checkered button-down shirt, jeans, and Gucci loafers were a plus. We ordered a bottle of Pinot Grigio and an antipasti plate to nibble on.

I was laughing and smiling—I was excited about Brady. He was sweet and shy, and he twirled a small strand of his curly blond hair behind his right ear, never taking his baby blues off me. He also chewed on his water straw, which I assumed was a nervous habit, and he seemed to stare at the freckles on my arm that peeked out from under my capped sleeve. The candlelit tables and gentle breeze were working for me; I could not have been happier. During our three-hour date, however, he went to the bathroom several times. I thought, *Great, I'm dealing with a great potential who might have a slight habit.* But then I went to the bathroom myself, and I noticed the TV above the bar was showing a baseball game. I soon realized he wasn't powdering his nose. For a split second, I could not decide which was worse—that this was the "catch" about an eligible thirty-year-old, or that he watched a sporting event on TV while on a date.

Afterward, as we stood outside the Maritime, he held my hand and said, "Isabella, I really had an amazing time. I would love to do this again soon, like next week."

"Me, too," I said, smiling. After a sweet kiss good night on the cheek, we walked our separate ways. Tonight, although a double feature, had been a nice night. I would look forward to his call.

Once in my bed, I fell asleep, smiling and Ambien-free.

9

I WAS SCHEDULED FOR MY consultation with Sylvie Rosseau, the matchmaker who was going to marry me off, at 8:15 a.m. on Thursday. I quickly jumped into my pre-therapist routine of using a conditioning hair mask and Shiseido eye gels to reduce all the puffiness from partying and crying. I dressed conservatively, as I was going to the Upper East Side. I already had one strike against me, as I had moved out of the 10021 ZIP code and near the meat packing district. I selected the perfect ensemble—high-waisted dark denim jeans; a tucked-in, white buttoned shirt; my chestnut velvet Gucci blazer; and my four-inch-heel black Manolos. The four-inch heels were a must, as I had learned from researching Sylvie that she worked with a lot of models. I slipped on my diamond-encrusted gold bangle bracelets and my smoky topaz David Yurman cocktail ring, grabbed my brown Fendi spy bag, and headed out the door.

Butterflies flooded my stomach, and I began to feel nauseated in the cab while we crossed to the East Side through Central Park. I arrived at East 81st and Third Avenue. The white-gloved doorman greeted me eagerly. "Good morning, miss. You must be here to see Mrs. Rosseau. She mentioned that a gorgeous, tall blonde would be coming this morning. She is expecting you; please take the elevator to the penthouse."

Smiling, I quickly escaped into the elevator. I felt ashamed that I was going to see a matchmaker. What happened if she secretly ran an escort service for old geezers, and I was fresh meat? The cops could come barreling in during my consultation and next thing I knew, I would see my face on the cover of tomorrow's *New York Post*: "Isabella Reynolds, call girl, busted in Upper East Side sting at French brothel."

Maybe I was being a bit dramatic. But I could see my father's face when he received his copies of the *New York Times* in South Carolina.

I knocked three times on the door and a small, fragile-looking woman dressed in a maid's uniform greeted me.

"Welcome, Ms. Reynolds. Please follow me."

I walked through the antique-cluttered foyer into the seating area, where Sylvie was sipping tea.

"Ah, darling, so happy to see you. Would you like something to drink?"

"Water would be lovely," I hesitantly responded, not able to get the image of my mug shot out of my mind.

"Flat or sparkling, darling?"

"Sparkling would be great. Thank you, Sylvie."

I sat down directly across from her in one of the most uncomfortable chairs my ass had ever met. I positioned myself with perfect posture—crossed legs with my hands folded gently on my lap.

"Are you comfortable?"

"Very much so," I said, smiling though feeling ridiculous. How comfortable could it be to take your heart on an interview for love? As the maid was pouring my water, I took the opportunity to quickly take in the room. Everything had its place and seemed un-lived in. The couch was untouched, and I wondered why we were not sitting on it. I hoped this process was not going to be as painful as these chairs. How could she be an expert on love when there was no heart in her own home? She lived in an *Architectural Digest* magazine ad. I took a sip of my water and relaxed a bit. *Perhaps it would be similar to the therapy session with Dr. Goldstein*, I thought.

I had underestimated Sylvie Rosseau.

"Let's get down to business, Isabella. I have married twenty-four couples this year and over five hundred in the past sixteen years. I have been the premier matchmaker for the elite. I'm going to ask you a series of questions to get to know you better. That way, I'll discover who your perfect husband will be.

Perfect? I thought.

"My clients are all men and are ready to meet 'the one' and settle down. They pay mean fees for me to do the dirty work for them. They find me, or maybe I discover them. We discuss how my process works, and then I have them go on a fake date with me to a restaurant of their choice.

Fake?

"I also do background checks on them and even visit their homes to see how they live. So, let's begin." Sylvie's questions came rapidly and from every direction. "Where do you live in Manhattan? How long have you lived here? Where were you born? Are your parents divorced? What do they do? Do you have any siblings? How tall are you? How much do you weigh? What size do you wear in designer clothing? Do you go to the Hamptons in the summer? Have you ever traveled on a private jet? What happened with your last relationship? What do you find attractive in a man? Do you have any pets? What do you do for a living? Did you go to college? How often do you see an herbalist and acupuncturist? What type of skin care regimen are you following? Oh, dear, I almost forgot—how many times have you been to St. Bart's in ... let's say the past five years?"

My head was spinning from the twenty-minute consultation, and I already knew I was going to be late for work. After the grueling interview, Sylvie was assured that one of her clients and I would hit it off, as long as I didn't mind dating from a different ethnic background. His name was Clay. He was originally from Chicago, went to an Ivy League business school, and was part Indian and Buddhist. Right then, I thought about cow worshipping and a big hamburger and wondered if he would have any beef about that.

"Is something funny, Miss Reynolds?"

"Oh, excuse me. It is just everything you are saying sounds so perfect," I explained. I couldn't believe I'd been laughing at my own joke.

"Clay is a thirty-nine-year-old who developed three companies, sold them, and now is one of Manhattan's billionaires. He lives in a fabulous brownstone on one of Greenwich Village's exquisite tree-lined streets. He is looking for a woman to finally call it home."

I know they say true love is not a choice. It unconditionally and naturally exists. There seemed to be nothing natural about Sylvie's idea of love and from her interview process, it sounded very "under conditions." I could see a prenuptial in which "weight fluctuation" or a "change in hair color" would be grounds for an annulment.

"Where did you meet him?" I asked. I wondered where she hunted for her clientele.

"Well, darling, I was at Barney's picking up a Tocca candle for my T-Mobile gal, as she is always such a dear when my BlackBerry is down. Really, it's the least I could do. All of a sudden, the Barney's girl gasped, which caused me to turn around, and there he was. We thought he had to be someone, but we didn't know who. Even though he is only five foot eight, his beautifully toned skin, slicked-back jet-black hair, and perfectly defined facial features took our breath away. I must have him call you right away!"

Despite my hesitation, I agreed. After all, I'd gone through the interview and was accepted into the mate-matching world. She was convincing, and he sounded accomplished. The upside to this was that I knew going in that he was not a convict and his "fake date" must have been perfect. "I'm in; sign me up."

With findyourperson.com and Rosseau playing for my team, my chances had to be good.

Now, I was running twenty-three minutes late for work.

Sneaking into my rabbit hole, I could not believe what I had just done. I called Desi to give her the scoop. As expected, she loved hearing about how I had met "the most *amazing*" matchmaker in Manhattan. However, she had no idea about the profile I put on Findyourperson.com. When she asked me how I was meeting all the men I had gone out with this week, I just made up stories. "Oh, at a bookstore." "Oh, while walking along the West Side highway." "Oh, at the gym." "Oh, through a coworker." Keeping all my stories straight was going to be another full-time job. It had only been a week, and I was exhausted from the singles scene. I knew that online dating was popular, and everyone seemed to put themselves out in cyberspace to find love, but I just didn't want to accept that I was doing it—not that I was ashamed, but it wasn't the fairy tale I wanted for myself. I preferred Romeo and Juliet's style, although they died, so perhaps *The Notebook* was how I envisioned meeting my soul mate.

I could not get too caught up in my call with Desi, as my lunch date with Midtown East German Klaus was at 1:15 p.m. Haru was close to both of our offices, but I was not too excited to eat sushi again for a first date. The thought of having to delicately place an entire piece of fish in my mouth with a complete stranger watching me freaked me out a bit and I felt slightly traumatized from the last experience. It had been hard enough being forced to eat sushi with Mason, the *American Psycho* guy, against my will. What if I actually liked this guy?

We decided to meet outside on one of the benches directly in front of the restaurant. It seemed that I had arrived first, so I took a seat in the sun. The heat on my face felt nice, sending me into a deep relaxation. Soon, I leaned my head back and closed my eyes.

"Isabella?"

My eyes popped open. "Hi, sorry, just enjoying the weather." I stood up to a more appropriate position. "Hi, Klaus, nice to meet you."

"The pleasure is all mine. Would you like to go in?"

"Sure." As he opened the door to the restaurant, he placed his hand on the small of my back.

Klaus was over six feet tall with salt-and-pepper hair, light blue eyes, and strong features. Nice build, but I could tell by the way that his neatly pressed shirt would not remain so neatly tucked in that the stomach might be his problem area.

Fake Perfect Me

We took a table by the window and ordered immediately, as it was lunchtime and all the Park Avenue suits were quickly eating.

He ordered sushi, and I opted for the chicken bento box, ensuring I could take all the small bites I wanted and still have the ability to carry on a conversation. This second German was definitely better than the first, but there was something about Klaus that I couldn't put my finger on. He had a great personality, was highly educated, held a PhD in architecture, and was the president of an architect firm on Fifth Avenue. I couldn't help looking at my reflection in his translucent blue eyes.

"You are a breath of fresh air. A real stellar girl," he said, his gaze fixed on me.

"Klaus, you are sweet. Thank you." I smiled while my eyes slowly moved down his nose, to his lips, then his shirt and suit-clad shoulders. What was with the material of his suit? It almost had sheen to it.

"So, why are you on findyourperson.com?" he asked. "I'm on there to find the girl of my dreams. My brother recently got married and is expecting his first child. I can't wait to have a family one day. You know, Isabella, we would make beautiful babies." He said, smirking while anticipating my response.

"Oh, my God," I said, and I could feel a horrified expression form on my face. He was wearing a cheap suit! How could I not have noticed this? Dammit! The sun must have blinded me when he approached me. Then I must have been so worried about what to order that I had been too distracted to notice.

"Dear, what is it? Sorry—am I being too forward?" he asked.

Trying to regain my composure, I said, "Sorry. I just ate something very spicy."

"Really? I thought the chicken bento box was quite bland," he said, confused.

"Well, um ... I'm extremely sensitive to spice."

"Aren't you half Italian? Why are you not drinking your water?"

Geez, this guy was pushy. "Great idea, Klaus." I took the largest sip possible while wondering how much longer until lunchtime was over.

And there you go. The successful Park Avenue architect who wore a cheap suit and was talking of babies clearly had mental problems. I knew I was overreacting a bit, but this was the crazy perfectionist in me. What was the point of being with an imperfect man when I put my blood, sweat, and tears into being perfect? Although, where did trying to be perfect get me? Maybe he seemed pushy, or maybe I just wasn't used to being around a man who knew what he wanted and wasn't scared to voice it. *Dear God, maybe I am the mental one.* Here I was, having a fine lunch with a nice guy who likes communication, and I was picking on him for his suit and talk of having babies. Was I that pathetic and scared to allow anyone to get close to me now after Santo? Why was I pushing people away, based on such superficial things? I felt like damaged goods and had no idea how to begin dating again. I needed to leave—I did not want to have a crazypants breakdown over sushi again. I immediately eyed the waiter for the check.

I was sure that he would pick up that lunch bill, although I noticed he allowed the bill to sit there for a couple of seconds while he studied my reaction. *Gosh, the guy wants to have my kids but is hesitant to pick up the check?* What he didn't know was that I was aware of this and would not make a move. I would make him feel uncomfortable for making this an issue. They say the man makes the suit; the suit doesn't make the man. Well, in this case, it didn't really matter. They were both cheap.

Thursday afternoon at Haru was the end of Klaus, the Midtown East German.

10

I RETURNED TO MY RABBIT hole and refreshed my inbox. I was sitting in front of my computer and, in a non-stop robot mode, was responding to the client e-mails when it happened—he popped up in my inbox between the creative brief and a request from Paramount. It was the Italian ex's name, with the subject line "From Me." I'm not sure how the whole referring to each other as "Me" started, but it was our personal thing with signing our e-mails.

I was shaking and could feel the deep, hollow pain trying to creep up on me. This could not be happening at work, for Christsake. I was in a cubicle. I clicked on the e-mail and just stared at the words, not even reading them at first. My heart was racing so much that all the noise from surrounding office faded as I read.

Hope you are well, Isabella. This past week has been particularly hard and so crazy for me. So many things have gone unnoticed and undone. My work schedule and my own issues have prevented me from seeing so many things about myself. It's like the mist is starting to lift a bit, and I'm seeing my life for the first time in such a long time. I would like to know if you would join me for dinner at Mr. Chow in Tribeca. I would hate to leave things like we did. Love, Me."

He was just now seeing his life for the first time in such a long time? What was he doing during the past two years with me? My entire body started to feel hot, and I could feel my eyes welling up, but I responded to the e-mail immediately, even though I told myself not to. However, I did need to settle one very important issue with him, as this city was not big enough for both of us.

I wrote: "Santo, nice to hear from you. Sure, I will see you at 9:00 p.m. at Mr. Chow. I have been craving their sweet-and-sour pork, to be honest. Love, Me."

Of all places to meet, it had to be one of our favorites, where we did not even need a menu as we ordered the same thing every time. Actually, at Mr. Chow, the thing to do was to not even ask for a menu; it was purely tacky.

This would also be the ideal opportunity to discuss my restaurant and post-breakup plan. There was no getting around that fact that we dined out four times per week and that we had "our" places with a fair share of maître d's in our pockets and any perks that came along. I had already strategically written out my suggestions, hoping that Santo would gently follow along. The upside for me was that I was more into the scene, while he was locked away in his office. I could easily give him a restaurant that he would be excited about and distracted, as I had the new up-and-coming in my back pocket. Once agreed, he would not be able to touch it.

The list went as follows:

"The Restaurant Plan"

He is on his own to figure it out (Santo)   Cipriani's Downtown (Isabella) *

* Could not think of a comparison for him, so his loss. This was not up for discussion.

Nobu Tribeca (Santo)   Nobu 57 (Isabella) **

** Pia introduced me to my hook-up at our last gathering, before my crazypants breakdown, of course.

Waverly Inn (Santo)   The Lion (Isabella)

Pastis (Santo)   Balthazar (Isabella)

Da Silvano (Santo)   Gemma at Bowery Hotel (Isabella)

Gold Bar (Santo)   1 Oak (Isabella)

Per Se (Santo)   Daniel (Isabella) ***

*** Daniel was my place, and he knew it. There would be no discussion on this one.

That night, as I headed downtown in a cab, I thought about two years prior to my meeting Santo, when Dorthea, Alexa's psychic, revealed that I would fall deeply in love and marry a man soon. The man would be very good-looking, a lawyer, nice dresser, hilarious, dark hair, with light eyes. We were to meet at a place surrounded by a body of water, which we did. She constantly visited Dorthea for answers and insight into her own life. Of course, she was incapable of asking me about my own future, my career, my dreams, and my future husband. She never thought for a second to just ask me what I thought I wanted or needed. Did I need all these details about my future? Now that I had them, this annoying little voice whispered in my ear at times, reminding me of what Dorthea supposedly saw for me.

I allowed Dorthea's predictions to distract me from seeing the red flags, and it kept me from seeing what was really going on in my life and heart with Santo. I thought he was the dark haired, light-eyed lawyer she saw, but we were no perfect couple.

As I stepped out of the cab, my heart felt heavy, and "anxious" was an understatement. I walked around the corner of Franklin and Greenwich, and I could see him seated at an outside table, waiting. He looked up in my direction. This was the first time we had made eye contact in over a week, and it was uncomfortable. How was it that I could spend over two years of my life with someone, share my life, my family, my problems, and my tears and, with a week of distance, we became two strangers again? We both seemed nervous and avoided eye contact as much as possible throughout dinner. He ordered for both of us, as there was no question about what I was eating.

He looked tragic. He looked miserable. I was dying for him to say he had made a mistake, that he could not live without me. Instead, he did what the Italian did best—talked around the situation, avoiding mentioning anything true and especially anything involving me. I had no idea why I was sitting across from him at that very moment.

During his monologue, I thought about our first encounter. Pia had finally forced me to meet up for drinks after I had refused to come out for hours, not wanting to leave the safety of my apartment as a monsoon was taking place. Of course, Pia couldn't understand my reluctance—she had the luxury of a personal driver who would also escort her, her blowout, her $3000 handbag, and her new Jimmy Choo's to the front door. But when her driver showed up at my own door to escort me to the Tribeca Grand Hotel for cocktails, I couldn't refuse any longer.

I was blown out, manicured, and wearing jeans topped with a diamond-studded white tank and a blue pinstripe D&G blazer. Once we arrived at the hotel, I quickly rushed inside and got my bearings once more, as the fear of getting wet had made me frantic. Proceeding through the crowd to the bar, I found Pia eagerly awaiting my arrival. I felt warm, almost flushed. Then, I saw him—he was alone, sipping what seemed like a glass of Pinot Grigio. As I turned my head slightly in his direction, my stomach filled with butterflies.

"Pia! I'm here. I'm here. Thanks for sending the escort," I said while twirling around, showing her I not only had arrived in one piece but without getting soaked.

"How could you turn down champagne with me? Sometimes, Ms. Reynolds, you do not make sense."

"Well, I …" Suddenly, I stopped speaking as I looked in mirror over the bar and saw him standing behind me.

"*Buona sera.* Hello there."

Licking my lips, I slowly turned around and shyly smiled.

"I wanted to introduce myself and wish you a nice evening. My name is Santo. And you are … besides *bella*?"

I could feel Pia rolling her eyes behind my back. I extended my hand. "Hi, I'm Isabella." That is how I met my Roman Saint Santo.

The sweet-and-sour pork was stuck in my throat. After dinner and before we took our stroll—a regular after-dinner routine—I excused myself to the ladies room. The B&P was even more familiar and painful tonight. This dinner was a disaster and forced me to realize I had no control over the situation. I was downstairs purging pork when what I really needed to purge was still sitting upstairs. As usual, I rinsed my mouth out with cold water a couple of times, popped a one-and-a-half calorie mint, and dabbed on some gloss. I took one last glimpse in the mirror and felt relieved. Perfecto.

We ended up walking by Magnolia Bakery and getting a box with four cupcakes to eat on our bench in the park across the street. It seemed that we were Santo and Isabella, but we weren't. In one week, too much had changed. We were two strangers pretending to be a couple, and he was pretending to know that he knew more about himself and possibly us since last week. I didn't miss the red flag this time. My heart told me that he was more confused and knew less than he had before.

In the middle of our third vanilla cupcake with butter-cream icing and sprinkles, he began to choke up and cry.

His show of emotion resonated with me, as I had cried much in the past weeks. He did not speak but kept his head low and cried like a little girl. Every so often he would blurt out, "I'm so unhappy, Isabella; I'm just so unhappy." I listened, but I refused to open up and give him any more of myself than he had already taken and thrown away.

Suddenly, he grabbed me and squeezed me so tight that I lost my breath for a second. When he let go, I rested my head on his shoulder for a moment, wondering how we ended up sitting on a bench, so unhappy, and eating cupcakes. This obviously was not the time to bring up my restaurant list. I decided I would just e-mail it to him. That was probably the polite thing to do. I also could not help but think about the night he helped me pack up Potato's belongings and promised it would all be okay. (Obviously, he lied.)

When I got home, I stood in front of the hall closet but did not have the energy to open it. I leaned against the wall and slid down to the floor. The deep, hollow pain in my chest caused me to cry. Even though I refused to show the Italian any more of my pain or tears, I could not hold back once I got home. My friends would die if they knew I'd gone to dinner with Santo, especially Bobby. I could already hear him saying, "Cut the cord, Isabella!" But even though I saw Santo, I really wondered how much trouble it could actually cause. I was moving on. I was on Findyourperson.com. I was an online serial dater. I wondered if I'd made a bad move by going to dinner with him, but I knew the answer already. I knew it from the ashamed and disgusted feeling I had.

That night I did not sleep a wink. I'd waited too long to attempt to purge on the sugar and sprinkles that felt stuck on my throat. I curled up in a fetal position and cried all night long. Everything hurt so much, my body felt numb, and I realized that heartbreak, no matter what type, was true pain. Physical pain had nothing on a tortured heart.

The next morning I pulled myself together to the best of my ability. Two rounds of my magical Shiseido eye gel masks did not even make a dent in the two large knots that were where my eyes used to sit on my face. Avoiding everyone at the firm was going to be a real doozy. *I will just have to say my allergies are acting up.* The fact was that I was an absolute mess. I had not slept, stress bumps were now strategically placed on my face so that it looked like I had adult chicken pox, and I was thinner than ever. I always went for the gaunt look and finally it was coming. Who knew there was any benefit to being bitter?

During lunch, I just hid in my cubicle, avoiding everyone. It was Friday, and I only had two time-wasting, unlikely-to-be-my-person dates, and then I could just lock myself in my apartment or maybe go to church with Bobby for some watermelon therapy. Or perhaps I could get into some real trouble with Desi and Vito. I went to weather.com to check on the weather for the weekend and was confronted with a banner ad for expedia.com.

Then it hit me. I needed to leave all of my mess, hop on a plane—alone—to another world and see everything from a different view. I needed to get myself back to the real Isabella Reynolds. I had not used any of my two weeks' vacation days, so what was I waiting for? I had always wanted to return to Italy, ever since my Columbia University thesis trip. I had always wanted to go and get lost in that country alone. Well, now I was alone.

Search, scroll, click, enter, submit, confirm, and I was on a flight leaving July 1 from JFK to Italy for nine days. I would fly into Rome for two days, take a five-hour train ride through Florence to Venice for four days, and then return to Rome for the remaining three days. I quickly ran into the partners' office and informed them that I would be taking a vacation in two weeks and apologized for giving such short notice. They did not complain; they needed me to get back to my 110 percent, "do it all" attitude.

I immediately called Desi to let her know my plan of action. Not only did I need this journey to see everything for what it truly was, but also, I knew she would throw me one hell of a going-away bash. Having excuses to have parties was never a bad thing. My friends all warned that I was on my way to a mental breakdown. It was understood that if that happened, I would not be the same. You never come back from something like that as the same person. You just never come back.

The cab dropped me off on the corner across from the Union Square W Hotel. It was Friday night at 8:00, so I wasn't surprised that it would be packed. I just prayed it would not take more than five minutes to find Chelsea Kirk from Scandinavia, as I had drinks at 10:15 p.m. with West Village Alan, originally from New Jersey

Crossing the street, I turned heads—I looked fabulous in my black-and-gold mini backless Milly dress. As I came to the opening of the revolving door on the inside, our eyes met and for a split-second, I thought about just following the door back around and making my escape.

Seriously? Seriously now, God? Kirk was most likely five foot ten, not six-two as he'd mentioned. He was a bit overweight, bland, and if it weren't for the fact that his profile said he was looking for a woman, I would have thought for sure I was playing on the wrong team. I mean, what were the odds that a single, straight man would live in Chelsea?

"Hola, Isabella."

"Hello, Kirk. You speak Spanish?" I couldn't help it; he was from Scandinavia and was as Caucasian, blond, and blue eyed as it gets. Why was he saying "hi" in Spanish to me? Ugh, dumbass.

"No, why?" He looked at me, confused. "Our table is ready. You look hungry."

Really? I thought. *Maybe crying is my new workout routine.* People kept telling me I seemed hungry, which I took to mean "thin."

Throughout dinner, I zoned out, just occasionally remembering to nod my head and say things like "Really?" and "I agree." He spoke the entire two hours about American literature, and how he loved black licorice and reindeers, never once asking much about me. Throughout our dinner, he occasionally would drop a Spanish word here and there and even said "Gracias" to our server at times. I was completely annoyed and beginning to grow nervous, worrying if Alan would turn out to be worse than this moron; I was seriously going to have a crazypants episode before I reached the West Village.

This was even more frustrating as it was a Friday night. I gave the Spanish-speaking Scandinavian reindeer lover a Friday night. This was a big no-no with online dating, I just knew it. *Think of Italy, Isabella*, I told myself. *A couple more days and you can leave all of this humiliation behind you, like it never even happened.* I was my only witness to this. I just had to make sure that I didn't become a big mouth during a watermelon therapy session so Bobby would have another tell-all.

Eventually, I was in a cab heading down to the West Village to meet Alan at Turks & Frogs. Hopefully, Manhattan had rubbed off on him a bit, and I wasn't walking into a big collared, untailored sport coat with Gotti sterling cufflinks. I ran my fingers through my hair, touched up my mascara, and swiped some pink Christian Dior gloss across my lips.

As I got out of the cab, I noticed that the wine bar was empty but could see a man sitting at the end of the bar. He had a nice head of hair that I recognized from his profile headshot.

"Alan?"

"Isabella?"

"Hello, have you been waiting long?" My initial impression, which caught me off guard a bit, was that this one might not be so dreadful. He was handsome, fit, and definitely older. But maybe it would be better if he were older. Mid-forties aren't that much older anyway. His collar was fine, but just as I expected, the sport coat was untailored, and I just pretended not to see the cufflinks.

"What can I get you to drink?"

"I will have a glass of champagne, please." As my bubbly was being poured, I asked, "What are you drinking?"

"Pinot noir. It's the only thing I drink."

A man this age most likely was set in his ways. Additional work might be required.

Four hours and five rounds later, we were still laughing and going through the usual getting-to-know-you banter. I squinted to concentrate on the movement of his lips. I couldn't tell if alcohol was impacting his speech or if he was beginning to stutter a bit.

Then it happened—the "ex" conversation. He asked about my last relationship. I created a "healthy" version of the tale. Dated for two years, Italian, workaholic, we just wanted different things, we saw living our lives differently. This sounded much better than admitting I'd been led on for two years of my life by a selfish man who worked his life away in a job he hated but neglected me and who did not want marriage or children in his future, which resulted in his not wanting me or the life I desired. Yes, I think the "healthy" version sounded much better and a bit less angry.

Then he dropped the bomb. "Well, I'm recently divorced, and I have a child who just turned eight."

Christ! He reached into his back pocket and pulled out his wallet—I assumed he was reaching for a picture. Hopefully, the kid was cute because after all these rounds of bubbly, my poker face was dead.

"Here is a picture of my son." Turned out, the kid was cute; he was wearing a bright green Polo shirt and a big smile. Still, I thought that this must be a school headshot and why was he not wearing Lacoste? That is what I would dress my kid in.

"Alan, your profile didn't mention that you were divorced and had a child."

"Is this going to be a problem, Isabella?"

"It's just I was not expecting this?"

"Expecting what?"

I wanted to say, "Not expecting a crazy ex-wife who is most likely going to see me as the young girlfriend and make your son hate me. If I were to marry you, she would be taking most of what is yours and mine and making it hers, which means there has to be a lawyer or two involved in this already established mess." Lastly, I didn't like the idea that I would be someone's second choice.

Of course, I'm not a complete crazypants and did not dare to say any of the things I was thinking. "I just didn't expect that you would have a family. That is pretty serious, and you should have included that in your profile. It's only fair to let potential dates know what they are getting into, even if it's only meeting for drinks."

"How would you like a change in scenery? Why don't we go to the Spotted Pig for one last round?"

I ignored that he ignored my point and agreed to the Pig.

We took two seats at the bar and ordered a round of drinks; Alan just looked at me.

"Is something wrong?" I asked.

"Isabella, I'm having a great time with you. I really like you. I have to be honest." "What is it?" I was terrified and already yelling at myself on the inside that I'd gone on that ridiculous website and was now on my ... Christ, I couldn't even remember what number date he was. I was a serial online dater, and he was about to tell me that he was a serial killer on the run or had time for some heinous crime. Oh, dear God! "Alan, what?"

"I have four children, not one. But the other three don't count, as they are nineteen, twenty-one, and twenty-three and away at college." I felt my head drop and saw the words, "Isabella, stepmom of four" flash before my eyes. I had the urge for my Chinese for four. I needed out of here immediately, if not sooner.

"So, what you are saying is that you lied to me before our first date and then again on our first date? Thanks for the evening, Alan, but no thanks." He looked shocked that I was about to walk out on him. I grabbed my coat and turned around but was pulled back when he grabbed my right arm.

"Please hold on."

I hate men who don't do what they say, or say what they mean. I also hate men who say something just to get what they want. "Let go of my arm; I will not repeat myself." I pushed opened the door and hailed a cab. On my way home, I realized that walking out on him was what I should have done to the Italian during his lies to keep me around. How could I have walked out though, when I had been lying to myself the entire time? Denial is such a bitch.

Four kids, yeah, right. I could see my place on that totem pole. Alan, could not afford me, emotionally or financially.

My phone began to ring. It was the village idiot. I clicked "ignore." He called back four more times before I just turned off my phone. I'd just walked out on this man and now he was harassing me. *Great, I have a soap opera star on my hands.* The next word that flashed before my eyes was "trouble." There was no room for crazypants behavior or more stupid mistakes so soon in this game called my new life. Points for Team Isabella.

11

Journal entry—June 30

TONIGHT AT 6:00, DESI AND Vito are hosting a caviar and champagne dinner in my honor to wish me safe travels to Italy. They are true friends. They are real people. They are my people.

My original plan was to get a good night's sleep last night and wake up early this morning, start packing, and order Chinese for four, as I would most likely have withdrawal during my nine-day trip. Sodium withdrawal can be a real bitch. Even though the feelings of guilt and shame fill me, I feel the anxiety this morning for my trip tomorrow. As disturbing as it is, this vicious Chinese cycle gives me comfort. It gives me a sense of control, and I am a bit nervous for this spontaneous trip. The more I think about it, the more difficult it is to fight temptation, when purging allows me to avoid the consequences. I was hoping by being out of my painful reality that the deep, hollow pain would stay in New York while I'm away, along with the B&P. I do not plan on packing any of my triggers and flying them across the ocean with me. The perfection, dieting, overeating, crying, and pain would not make it through security. This was my hope.

It is perfect timing—I woke up at 12:16 p.m. and will place my Chinese order immediately.

I. R.

While I waited for brunch for four to arrive, I made a list of some necessities I needed to purchase, including a travel book and a journal, which I could pick up at Barnes and Noble. I could not forget a map of both Venice and Rome, as I wanted to use the flight time wisely to map out my days. I never slept on planes, particularly long flights. It wasn't as much that I was scared of an emergency occurring while I was passed out (well, maybe a tad) as I simply enjoyed flying. It was the beginning of the adventure—getting cozy in first class with a blanket, reviewing the menu for the upcoming meal, ordering bubbly, and watching every movie possible. A bad movie menu could seriously ruin my flight and that of the victim who had to sit next to me. The whole point of flying first class was to feel at home, relax, and pass the time away with similar movie selections to On-Demand. At the end of it all, I would step out into another world. This time, it would be Rome.

I had much to do before I headed to my caviar and champagne party, so I decided just to call my parents from Italy at some point and let them know where in the world I was. I was not about to risk having a sane person talk me down from the crazy ledge—well, not just yet.

Of course, nothing went as planned. As soon as I received my Chinese buffet, I received a text from Brady that read: "Hey, beautiful, how about brunch at Extra Virgin on West Fourth and Perry tomorrow?" That would have been nice, but I would be jetting off to Italy. "Sorry, but I'm leaving for a trip. How about when I get back?" Brady put a smile on my face, and I actually was dying to see what his next move would be. "Beautiful, I must see you before you leave! Let's do a send-off brunch today—say, 1:30 p.m.?" Thank God I had not started the Chinese buffet event. I never went anywhere after one of these episodes, as I felt like a fat kid. I was still skinny, so I responded, "Sounds great! See you there. XOXO." I would worry about all the small details later. The trip was booked, and that's all that really mattered.

I arrived first at the restaurant, put our names down for a table, and headed to the ladies room for one last check. The six-foot-one natural blond with deep blue eyes—Brady, with his charming yet electric smile—was waiting for me by the bar as I came out. Once we were seated at an outside table, we ordered half the menu and then began the rounds of drinks. He was such a breath of fresh air. I enjoyed the way we laughed together. We were both shy, and he tended to be quiet at times, but there were no uncomfortable silences.

Then his cell rang—and he did the most unusual thing. "Sorry, Isabella, it's my mother. Do you mind if I answer?"

"Not at all, please."

"Hi, Mom, I can't really talk, I'm on a date with Isabella."

Did he just tell his mother he was on a date and say my name? This was our second date, and he had already mentioned me to his mother. Was this too soon? Was he serious? This super-speed online dating had made me hypersensitive (and a bit nuts) to all the rules and regulations of dating. It crossed my mind for a second that this was somehow a plot to win me over. Perhaps he saved his best friend's number as "Mom" in his phonebook. The friend calls, and he responds by dropping my name to make me think that he is so into me that he has already mentioned me to his mother. Was he that eager to get me into bed? It was actually quite brilliant but also evil in the most unacceptable way. I was a bit shocked that the thought had crossed my mind, but it was totally possible.

I stopped analyzing, and Brady and I ended up having a marvelous brunch. There is something about sitting on the corner of West Fourth Street and Perry that made brunch at Extra Virgin the quintessential New York experience. The noise magically disappeared from the surrounding streets, and we were left with the wind rustling through the trees and the tweeting of the birds. Great food at a hip place on a beautiful, quiet, tree-lined street with an ex-rugby player—not so bad for a Saturday afternoon.

After lunch, he escorted me to the corner for a taxi, but to my surprise, he suggested we have a send-off drink at Sant Ambroeus. We ended up ordering two glasses of bubbly and somehow, rather than sitting down beside him at the bar, I stood between his legs. We were extremely close, and he began twirling a piece of my hair.

The bartender looked at him. "Man, give me a break."

Brady flushed a bit. "What? She has beautiful hair." Brady asked for a hug, and I squeezed him gently, along with giving him some soft kisses on his cheeks—appropriate in a restaurant, as long as it did not exceed fifteen seconds. Anything after that was a make-out session, in my opinion.

Once outside, he hailed a cab for me and wished me a good journey. As he opened the door, he gently grabbed my waist, pulled me in toward him, and gave me a soft kiss goodbye. This was the first boy who had touched my lips since the Roman saint. I wasn't complaining and assured him I would call when I returned. In the cab, I received a last text: "I will miss seeing you while you are gone. I'll look forward to your return." Unsure of whether I should respond, I did, and let the champagne do the texting: "I will miss your lips."

I headed home to pack. I pulled out the Louis Vuitton duffle and began folding and eventually tossing in all my Italian essentials. I was up for anything, so I needed to make sure I was prepared for everything. I refused to check a bag and had somehow developed the method of fitting nine shirts, five skirts, three pairs of jeans, four pairs of heels, one pair of flats, and my cosmetic essentials, all in my medium-sized Louis bag. It was all about rolling the clothes into tight cylindrical shapes.

I still needed to run to the bookstore for some travel guides before heading to my fabulous farewell party. Practically skipping down the street, I could not stop thinking about the freedom of being alone in another country, with no one to judge me and my being able to embrace the world outside the box I had lived in my entire life. Maybe I'd learn how to do something other than live up to everyone's expectations—my family's, my boyfriend's, my friends', and sometimes, even those of complete strangers. I could be whoever I wanted to be on my adventure. No one would ever know the difference. I would be the only witness, and something about that seemed so dangerous to me.

Once inside the bookstore, I quickly found maps, as well as an easy-to-carry, well-summarized guide to Venice in the travel section. I had been to Rome several times, so it wasn't completely unknown territory. After making my purchase, I checked out the various tables at the front of the store that were stacked with the latest reads. I would need a novel for some brain stimulation on my Italian adventure, as I could not be distracted with Italian boys all day long. When I was taking a break from my self-discovery adventure, I would need something to do while sipping my Prosecco and foamy cappuccinos.

Leisurely circling the table that displayed the new releases, an interesting cover came into my view with a catchy title: *Don't Just Stir It Up—Mix It*. I grabbed the book, glancing at the crowd around me, as the title sounded like the book might contain soft porn. I flipped through the book and realized it was a collection of blog entries by a forty-ish woman living in Miami. *They really will publish anything these days.*

As I flipped through the book, I came across a section that described her experience of meeting and occasionally dining with a suave Italian suitor. My eyes quickly began scanning the pages of this entry. I thought, *That is my Italian.* Frantically searching for my cell in my oversized black Marc Jacobs, I dialed Pia to read her my discovery. The sentences described the way he would say, "I'm so happy we have met each other," or the way he would play with her hair while dining at Nobu. Pia reassured me, "The world does not revolve around you, Isabella. That is not Santo. By the way, we need to talk about Dr. Goldstein and how you fell off the island of Manhattan. Most important, what the hell are you doing in a bookstore on a beautiful Saturday afternoon? Should I be worried?"

"Pia, I'm leaving to go find myself, but I will have to explain later."

"Please exit the self-help section. Don't walk; run away, Reynolds."

"Just meet me at Desi's at 6 p.m. I'll tell you everything; promise." I quickly put the phone away, threw the book on the table, and headed out of that bookstore, suddenly feeling overwhelmed by the vast selection.

I still needed reading material for my trip. Even though it was out of the way, I recalled a neighborhood bookstore, a quaint shop on the corner of West Tenth Street that I'd always wanted to check out.

I arrived at Three Lives & Company, and it was not only the literary gem that I had imagined but also a sweet surprise. As I entered, the bell above the door announced my arrival. I took in every bit of the ambiance. It intimate, cozy, romantic, and intelligent, all at the same time. Still, the scent of all the literary treasures filled the air, like a library. As I navigated the store, I couldn't stop myself from touching everything. The floor to ceiling shelves were meticulously filled with books. I had not a clue what I was searching for—not in life, in my heart, or in this small bookstore in the West Village.

The place was empty. I continued to wander around, running my fingertips along everything before coming to a stop before a somewhat hidden nook to my right. I turned around to glance at the storeowner, wondering if he minded that I was touching everything. I proceeded to the nook; it was then my body was dumbstruck.

A man stood there, his back to me. He was tall—at least six foot two—with dark hair and a tan. I could not see his face, so "handsome" could not be confirmed at this point. His olive-toned body was mannish and chiseled in all the right places. His hair was black and slicked back, from what I could tell. I could not stop looking at him, but I didn't want to be caught in the act, so I began moving my eyes around the room, glancing back every so often to watch him. Dear God, why was I sweating?

This captivating stranger was dressed in dark denim jeans, a gray cotton T-shirt with a large green number eight stamped on the back, and Nike cross trainers. What did that number stand for? I was overwhelmed with curiosity to see what was on the front of his shirt and to see his face. Dear God, just turn around, for Christsake. I was on a timing deadline, as I still had a list of things to handle before my send-off extravaganza. I didn't have all day to wait to see his face and the front of his shirt. *Please!*

And then the universe finally gave me a break. Just then, one of the bookstore staff passed between us. "Sir, do you need some help?" *Look at her flirting with him, using her "I'm part of the knowledgeable staff" to interfere with my moment. Did she not see me standing here?* I rolled my eyes and looked away. Then, chills rolled up my spine and every little hair raised on my body (which should have been impossible, as I had lasered everything off).

Mr. No. 8 spoke. "Erm, yes. I'm looking for a boouuk."

Had he just said *boouuk*? Where was he from? Everything about his voice sent my body into a frenzy, which was immediately followed by an overwhelmingly calm state. It was a feeling that was similar going somewhere new, yet it seems so familiar—like home. It was soothing and unseen, and it melted every part of my body. At that very moment, it was like I had found what I had been searching for within me; something that I didn't even know was missing. And it had happened here, in Three Lives & Company, the most perfect place ever.

Returning from my out-of-body experience and my "you complete me" scene, I realized I had completely missed out on some of the conversation. Actually, the staff member wasn't really having a conversation with him. She was trying to have her way but getting nowhere fast. "Well, Konstantino, let me know if I can help you with anything else."

Konstantino was his name. "N-T-I-N-O, and Konstantino was his name-oh." Just as I directed my attention back to Mr. No. 8, I noticed he had turned around and was now staring at me, most likely because he heard me singing my new version of "B-I-N-G-O." His face told me he heard his name slip from my lips.

There I stood, staring into his emerald eyes, like a deer caught in headlights. I had been hit by something bigger than myself. I could no longer control myself or be discreet, and I needed to do damage control, pronto. I studied all the minute details about him. I noticed an adorable freckle under his right eye, then followed his nose down to his chiseled jaw line and then to the unforgettable and strategically placed dimple on his chin. He resembled my D&G model, David Gandy.

Immediately, I headed for the door and knew I was out safe with the jingle of that damn bell above the door. Rushing home at a pace that caused my side to cramp, I remembered the front of his shirt. In green letters, "Florida," was spelled across his perfect chest.

I was flustered; I was a nervous mess. I was being a crazypants over a complete stranger. Did he even exist? Had anyone else seen him? Was it possible that I'd invented an imaginary man now? Then, I remembered the bookstore girl. It definitely was not a dream; it just felt like one.

Finally home, I ran past my doorman, Miguel, into the elevator and pushed the button, desperately wanting to splash my face with freezing water.

But when I stuck my key in my front door, it didn't work. *What the hell?* I could feel someone behind me. My neighbor, a petite elderly woman, opened her door. "You're not my neighbor, are you?" she asked. She stared at me through her oversized Chanel glasses.

I looked at her door and noticed the number was 8B. "I don't live on this floor."

"No kidding, sweetheart. I'm in the middle of my soap opera. Keep it down," she added, slamming her door.

I took the stairs one flight up to my actual apartment. "Isabella, pull yourself together, you foolish girl!"

Well, hell, I didn't even get a novel.

12

I HAD TO PULL MYSELF together for my caviar and champagne soiree, as Desi and Vito were going all out. They had ordered $1000 worth of caviar, $2000 in Louis Roederer Cristal, and $800 in truffles for Vito's special pasta. I could not let my insanity over a man get me off track.

I arrived at the party and could not have asked for more from Desi and Vito. Anyone I cared to see and say good-bye to was there, standing around the caviar bar. Desi, Vito, Bobby, Pia (who looked furious, as I guess someone informed her of my Italian escape), and Alexa, who just returned from a two-week cleansing from Miraval Spa in Arizona, thanks to Oprah's recommendation.

Alexa had lived in Manhattan for about eighteen years. She'd recently turned forty-four and every bit of her five-foot frame was a firecracker. She was an infamous real-estate broker to the elite and had just sold a 12.2-million-dollar brownstone to the new up-and-coming starlet, also known as the new CW (coke whore) in Tribeca. She dated all the twentysomething Wilhelmina models and had the red velvet ropes e-mail contacts for all the door lists. I read the *New York Post* "Page Six" daily to keep up on all the gossip, but also to see if Alexa had been up to any crazypants activity on her own. That's how we all kept up with her.

She typically made a story about every two months but as an "unidentified female." To this day, she has made some of the more memorable Manhattan moments to be covered by that page. Being single in New York and friends with Alexa guaranteed invitations to the best parties with the best eye candy—crucial therapy for a newly forced single life. Alexa's lifestyle was an exciting distraction to my own life, but hers not a life I desired. I wanted a co-pilot to fly through my journey. I wanted the partner that I was destined to be with. I refused to end up as a heartbroken, sentimental fool. I wanted my fairy tale.

"Desi, you really over did it. I'm just going to Italy for a week."

"Darling, that is true, but think of it as your funeral to this phase you are going through. We all have the highest hopes when you return. We will be celebrating your new self. I love you, sweetie." She gave me a tight squeeze.

I looked around the 3,000-square-foot Flatiron loft for Vito, to thank him as well. He was anxiously circling the room.

"Now, everyone, I just had the walls painted, so please be careful," he said, We were all aware of his obsession with white. I think he had his walls painted the whitest white once per month. We all repeated simultaneously, "Yes, Gestapo."

"Seriously, guys, be careful with your wine, leaning against the wall, or moving your chairs back to sit," he said as he walked behind Alexa, licking his finger and rubbing an invisible mark off the wall. "Last time we had guests, it was like someone took a stroll all over our wall. I mean how do footprints get on the walls?" he asked, looking at us intently, as if we had the exact answer that would settle his nerves and prevent such an occurrence from ever happening again.

All the furniture, vases, picture frames, and kitchen appliances were strategically placed, thanks to a feng shui expert they hired to help their karma. Desi was always doing crazy projects on a weekly basis, usually inspired by something she'd read in *New York* magazine. Of course, every new improvement was always "amazing." So, they hired a feng shui expert to look at all of those things in their apartment that they couldn't see but which existed.

The caviar bar was set up on the kitchen's island, and we all stood drinking champagne and finishing off the entire buffet. It was a carefully planned spread, and I could not remember the last time anyone I loved had made this kind of effort for me.

To the right of the island was a dining table that seated twelve. The table was set for Vito's pasta, which had achieved status among us, linguini with perfect slivers of black truffles, to be followed by an assortment of pistachio, chocolate, and strawberry hamburger-like French macaroons, a stunning apple tart, and Ciao Bella vanilla gelato.

"To having each other, as we will always be friends. We will always be here for each other, no matter the circumstance," Bobby said tearfully as we all placed a sufficient mouthful of pasta in our mouths and rolled our eyes to the back of our heads, as the truffles were orgasmic. "Can you rude pigs raise your glasses?" Something dramatic must have happened early in the day, as he was on his soapbox at the moment.

I raised my glass and said, "Thank you, guys, so much for all of this, and thank you for being here for me during my mess. To Desi and Vito, for being loving friends and always knowing how to create another unforgettable family meal."

"Yes, so lovely being acquaintances with them. Just for their truffle connection, it's worth it," Alexa mumbled, trying to push Desi's buttons. Alexa grinned at me, and I was dying to know why, as I wasn't getting involved with anyone's buttons this evening. "That's if Ms. Reynolds even returns. You know those Italians with blondes. You may just come back married and knocked up in nine days," she said.

"That's the pot calling the kettle black, Miss Alexa," Bobby quickly said, with an obnoxious giggle. Sometimes he was truly in his own movie, starring only himself.

"Alexa, darling, that's absurd," I insisted. "See, the thing with Italians is a whole mathematical code one must break in order to get close to them—a code that is more difficult than the damn Da Vinci Code itself. And then closeness only occurs if the man is not completely defective and can say the word commitment." I now realized that I sounded a bit bitter and could feel Pia shoot a look at me. However, I was on a roll. "One must assume, as a woman, that you are third on the totem pole," I continued, despite myself. "First is his mother. Second, himself, which includes his career. Third is you, if you are lucky. As a woman, if you can break the code, then one day he may actually put you near his mother in the list. In nine days, I will have crushes, dinner dates, and—I'm sure—a couple meaningless proposals, which of course were said only to get me into bed." Yes, I was bitter and had a disgusting flash of myself eating Jif with my cat.

Bobby quickly interrupted my rant. "Sweetie, you can be really nasty sometimes."

Vito cleared his throat extremely loud. "Bobby I think we get the pot is black and so is the kettle, if you follow me?"

We all started laughing hysterically and toasting our glasses, but he was not pleased.

"I was simply saying the idea of her going to Italy is perhaps not the best place to go and rediscover herself." Alexa made "air quotes" with her fingers as she said "rediscover."

"She might have mixed feelings about where she is going, and maybe she has not acknowledged those feelings yet," Bobby said, trying to save hypocrite-face from another verbal slap.

"You two are quite the duo sometimes, no?" Desi suggested and sent me a wink.

Pia quickly interjected, "I wholeheartedly, 200 percent agree with them. You know we are right, Miss Reynolds. That is why I am just finding out about this ridiculous hiatus now. I don't even have a chance to slap you with reality!" Pia looked around the table for backup, but Bobby knew better than to cross Desi. Desi was Bobby's access card to a summerhouse in the Hamptons and A-list parties. Pia cleared her throat, initiating a response, but Alexa only took an extra-long sip of her bubbly, and Bobby placed an insane bite of pasta in his mouth.

"Enough of trying to push my buttons!" I snapped.

"How rude," Bobby replied, flipping his head away from me.

"Honey, I don't know which one is more dramatic between these two," Vito said, while picking up our plates and preparing for dessert.

"Wow, Isabella, when is the last time you ate? It looks like you licked your plate clean," he said, laughing hysterically, although he received dagger eyes from the table.

"All right, scooper, the stage is yours. I will grab the sugar course. Start scooping," Vito said. Sugar wasn't his weakness, but sitting with all of our drama for too long was too much for him. We were a twenty-four-hour talk show, but he dealt with us, as he would do anything for Desi. He adored her, and it was hard to miss by the way he looked at her when he thought none of us was looking. That was the beauty of the depth of love—to need someone because you love him, and not love him because you need him in order to survive. That, and the way a man looks at a woman when others are not looking—that look of desire; Vito did just that, wholeheartedly.

I excused myself to wash my hands, as the aroma of the pasta was on my fingertips. I locked the door behind me and asked myself as I stood in front of the mirror if I felt like purging pasta—its heavy texture was most uncomfortable. Ice cream and pasta made me quite tense. I could already hear Pia telling me to hurry as the gelato was going to melt. Melted ice cream disgusted her and interfered with the other components of the dessert. I surprised myself that I was aware of her food neurosis. I took one last glance at myself and smiled, *Not tonight, Isabella.*

Everyone in the room changed the subject at the same time as I re-entered, a clear sign that I had been the topic of the table. I could never be sure if it was paranoia, but I wondered if they knew of what exactly took place in the bathroom every time I excused myself. Could they possibly imagine? Ignoring them, I started perfectly scooping and serving heaping spoonfuls of gelato for those at the table, who sat in extreme silence. This made the obvious even more obvious—I knew they knew.

It was now midnight and time for me to make an exit. I still had some last-minute packing to do and desperately needed a decent night's sleep, as my body was incapable of comprehending changes of time zones. My stubbornness had a mind of its own. My flight was departing JFK at 10:00 a.m., so I needed to get into bed immediately, if not sooner.

While I was standing on the corner, waiting for a cab, my cell rang. Before even looking at the screen, I knew it was the Italian. I knew he would want to talk or see me before I left. Life was funny that way. I second-guessed myself for two years, wondering if he wanted to spend his life with me, but I knew Santo the Saint would want to say good-bye for nine days.

"Hello."

"What are you doing, Isabella?"

"I'm heading home from my caviar and champagne party. I leave tomorrow for Italy."

"Come meet me at Cipriani's downtown for a drink. I want to see you before you leave. Please." He sounded like a little boy, his voice low and shy. The Italian did this when he was uncomfortable and fearful of rejection. He did not comprehend the concept of putting yourself out there.

As much as I knew not to go, I agreed. He did not deserve my time, my words, or my company, but I was incapable of listening to my head and let my heart continue to make all the wrong decisions. This is where my gut always failed me. Wasn't my gut supposed to "tug" me in the right direction? My crazy curiosity regarding the blog writer turned novelist and her suave Italian was eating me up inside, like ants on ice cream, and I needed to see his eyes when I confronted him.

Fifteen minutes later, my cab pulled up in front of the restaurant. The place was not crowded, as everyone was in the Hamptons, and the Bridge & Tunnel crowd had already made their way to the B&T clubs. The ones who could actually make it past the rope to the small lounge above Cipriani's were already up there, dancing the night away.

The Italian sat at a table with a glass of sauvignon blanc, waiting for me. At that moment, I regretted meeting him. I could feel the deep, hollow pain forming in my chest. Without saying hello, he stood up, and we exchanged cheek kisses and a squeeze hello. The shy, unconfident man who was on the phone less than twenty minutes ago was now a smiling and happy one. The actress inside me kicked into defense and the scene began.

"So are you already for your trip?" he asked.

"Yes, I can't wait. I have always wanted to do this, and finally, I am. I'm so excited to travel alone and see everything on my own." I reminded myself to slow down. I tended to overshoot when I wasn't telling the truth.

"Yeah, traveling alone is an amazing experience. Every time I do it, I learn so much about myself."

Yeah, sure, I thought, *that's why you are able to act your age and know who you are and what you want.* Did he already forget about the mist or fog and its lifting? "Well, I can't wait to go to all the fabulous restaurants, meet complete strangers, and just get lost in the landscape and history."

"Where are you staying?"

"I found a boutique hotel in Rome called the Fontanella Borghese that I will stay at for the first couple of days and then the Hotel Monaco right on the Grand Canal in Venice. Then I'm checking into the St. Regis for my last days in Rome. I wanted to end the trip with a bang, and for $860 per night, I think I will."

"Sounds nice."

During the second round of wine, things began to get a bit ugly. I guess I did not realize how drunk I had become with the ten previous glasses of champagne and now I was turning into the mean version of Isabella, as the Italian would refer to me when I was drinking a martini. Often, it was "Meanie the Martini," but he was lucky that there had only been one 'tini tonight.

"So, I thought it would be a great idea to pop into a bookstore, pick up the essentials and get a novel to read. I came across this interesting book—a collection of blog entries, *Don't Just Stir It Up—Mix It*. Have you ever heard of it?"

There it was: the grin with no eye contact. Despite the fact that he was such a great litigator, it was funny how I could read his face like the directions on a street sign. He did not deny it. "Isabella, you are not the first girl I ever dated."

Of course, this was *my* problem. He was the one who didn't have the decency and sense to at least lie and not hurt my feelings even though our relationship was over. But, being him, he was proud of that fact that he made a line in some book. The defective Italian just never got it. He would never understand that he had robbed me of our sweet beginning because some "tell-all" blogger had already written the story of how he had swept her off her feet.

Meanie the Martini officially had been released. Right in the middle of Cipriani's, I told him exactly how I felt, spurred on by the frustration and fear pent up inside me over the past two years. "Santo, you are no saint. I drank myself into another world to numb the misery that I felt when I was around you. I had been unhappy for much longer than you realized. I have given up trying to convince you to talk when you don't want to, to open up when you don't want to, to be loving when you want to be an asshole, to feel close to me when you want to be distant. I see now you just didn't want these things yourself."

"What are you talking about Isabella? What are you saying?"

"And here is a real kicker"—now it was my turn to grin—"I never baked those damn chocolate chip cookies. They were from City Bakery. That's right; I placed the purchased baked goods in waxed paper in a Tupperware container, you miserable little shit. The most hilarious part of baking was that you actually used to comment how I sometimes used too much butter or how the last round had been too chewy. They were from an f-ing bakery." It was then I realized that no matter what I did or how perfect I did it, nothing would ever make this little cannoli happy. It's like they forgot to fill this one up with the soft, creamy, sweet filling that made the delectable Italian staple so adored and comforting. He was defective, and I needed to comprehend that—there was no depth to him. It was what it was. He was an empty shell.

I looked over at his face and saw tears collecting in his sparkling blue eyes.

"Oh, my God Isabella. I …"

"The saying is very quite true," I said, giggling and taking the last sip of my drink.

"What saying is that?"

"It's not me. It definitely is you. Ciao."

I did not even let him respond. I stood up and walked out of the restaurant as fast as I could, not even caring that I got into someone's car service. I paid the driver $100 to just take me home. I turned off my cell and reminded myself that I would be on a plane in less than seven hours, and this would all just disappear.

13

THE CAR SERVICE TO THE airport arrived at 7:00 the next morning. The anticipation for my trip was overwhelming, and the intensity of my nerves was unexpected. I had always wanted to do a trip like this, and I respected myself at this very moment. Here was the perfect example of actions versus words. I was following through with my goal. The past year I had not been my old self: confident, ambitious, spontaneous. I had been an insecure, dependent, and emotional mess with the Italian. The bankruptcy of the company had made me become less of a risk-taker and even less of a dreamer.

Here I was, the first day of a new month, alone in a car, watching the New York City skyline disappear behind me. My eyes began to slowly fill with tears covered by my oversized Gucci glasses, but I did not feel the deep, hollow pain in my chest. At that very moment, just a couple of seconds in time, some of the pain I had been refusing to let go simply escaped from my heart. My soul got a taste of some fresh air, and I was terrified but excited at the same time. *Breathe, Isabella ... breathe.*

I checked in and went straight to my departure gate. Sitting by the window I stared at the plane, and suddenly felt afraid. Was I really going to another country where I knew no one and could barely converse? What would happen if I was kidnapped and some European convict held me for ransom or sold my organs to an underground medical mafia for money? What would happen if I forgot to exchange dollars for euros in the airport, and I couldn't pay the taxi or if I forgot to pick up an electrical adapter and I couldn't dry my hair? Being a blonde in Italy, of course, everyone would be looking at my hair. I took several deep breaths and clearly reminded myself that I had printed all my Expedia itineraries, confirmed my hotels, packed my travel books and maps, made some restaurant reservations, and practiced saying the address for the taxi to my first hotel in Rome: "Ottanto Quattro Hotel Fontanella Borghese."

A group of men and women that resembled an army of eight approached our departure gate. The men were dressed in neatly pressed gray suits, and the women in gray blazers, red skirts, and red stilettos. I felt like I was staring at soldiers going to war. Ironically, I was entering into a battleground—fighting myself to finally save my own life.

The plane began boarding. I got situated in my requested window seat, 33K, but then stressed out who would be occupying 33J. I took off my jacket and sandals, pulled my ponytail down, and wrapped my blanket and pillow around me. I was greeted by a plump, aged Greek woman with quite a thick accent. With her coal-black hair pulled tightly back, her weathered skin was clearly visible. She squeezed in next to me, and I assumed she looked much older than her age, probably from years of worrying, an unhealthy diet regimen and, of course, the sun. She looked at me and smiled. "Hello, dear."

I just replied with a smile, extending my hand to her and saying my name, "Isabella."

"What a beautiful name, my dear. A beautiful eight-letter name, *Eisai mia omorfi kopella* [for a woman who is beautiful]. Your number is eight, my dear, just wait and see."

In thirty seconds, the Greek stranger had intrigued me with the number eight, and I tried repeating "omorfi kopella" (beautiful) to myself a couple times. The word was so delicious and appealing for the lips.

"My dear, are you traveling alone?"

Hesitant to answer, as I hoped this would not result in a long lecture-like discussion, I simply nodded.

"Where is your husband? You must be married."

I could feel the disappoint on my face. "No, not yet, at least."

"What do your parents say?"

"Excuse me?" I asked, now a little perplexed by why she was even talking to me.

"Dear, as parents, we worry about our unmarried sons or daughters and the lack of suitors for them. How is it that a beautiful girl like you is not taken?"

"Well, I don't think my appearance has anything to do with it," I said, although I wondered myself.

"Isabella, beauty is a powerful thing."

I could tell by the solidness in her eyes that it was pure wisdom, and she was going to reveal insight that would result in epiphany for me. "Well, I moved to New York to—"

"My dear, what is your sign?"

"Okay, forget about New York. I'm an Aquarius."

"Oh, my, that is it," she said as she leaned back to take a better view of me.

"I'm not following. I'm sorry what is your—"

"You are a Valentine's Day baby, of course!"

"How on earth did you know that?" With all the things under the moon she could have said next, she guessed my birthday.

"Dear, oh my, you have been hit with the lead arrow. Cupid can be so mischievous sometimes, toying with our emotions and hearts."

"Cupid? As in the sort of chubby, nude baby with curly hair who carries a bow and arrow?" I reminded myself to relax—I needed all the help I could get.

"Two arrows," she said, like this was a crucial misunderstanding. "With him are two arrows, one gold and one lead. The gold arrow is for love, and the lead arrow is for hate." She shifted her body to her right side, now facing me as much as she could in her seat. "Dear, your heart has been pierced by the lead arrow."

As I looked down and touched my chest, my heart felt very much full of hate after everything that had been happening. "Well, thank you for the story. I apologize; what is your—"

"Dear girl, you must listen to this story of Cupid and Psyche if you ever are to embrace your soul and find your predestined soul mate."

She became involved in listening to the safety rules, so I pulled out the airline magazine to find out which movies were offered. I loved eating everything they served on planes, sipping wine and watching movies. I never felt the need to purge on a plane. It was something about being high in the sky, moving at a speed I couldn't feel, and being free. At that moment, I was above all my problems; soon, I would land firmly on my two feet to deal with everything and nothing at the same time. Watching a movie while in the sky was on my top-twenty list.

"Dear, please focus." She'd turned her attention back to me again.

"Sure. Please continue." The flight attendant walked past me, and I called out to her. "Excuse me, miss. I would like some red wine, please." She handed me the mini bottle of Chianti, and I quickly requested two while I had the chance. I knew I was about to participate in a deeper conversation than I was prepared for and with only an hour into my journey.

"In ancient Greece, Cupid was known as Aphrodite's young son, Eros. Aphrodite was the goddess of love, fertility, and beauty. In ancient Rome, he was Cupid and known as the young son of Venus, which is the Roman name for Aphrodite."

I nodded my head; I was becoming interested. How was it that I did not know anything about Cupid?

"Yes, dear, Cupid was a boy equipped with a bow and two piercing arrows, but at times he was very troublesome. Shooting his arrows to match couples, he was fond of watching them fall in love and seeing what would happen. You see, his arrows express emotions of desire and love. Cupid aims one of his arrows, gold or lead, at both gods and humans. This results in the deepest love of all among lovers whether they are divine soul mates or are mixed and matched.

"Well, my ex was definitely not my soul mate," I said. Flustered, I realized I had said that a bit too loudly, as the nosy gentlemen in front of me turned his head in my direction.

"The lead arrow, my dear."

"But why me? I was born on the day associated with love. I should have been shot with the golden arrow!"

"My dear, Valentine's Day babies are truly special and somewhat sensitized to love as a result of their birthday. However, there is not always an answer to our "whys" and "hows." It is very simple. Sometimes, life is such," she said with a stern nod. Then she smiled. "Ah, my dear, I have just given you the background but have not even told you the tale of Cupid and the beautiful Psyche." As her eyes grew wider, I felt myself shrink down into my seat.

"Cupid met his match one day by falling in love with a human. He fell under his own spell and became deeply in love with the beautiful Psyche. In my language, her name means "soul." Now, remember, his mother Venus was the goddess of love, fertility, and beauty. Here she was a goddess that possessed many supernatural powers, yet she was powerless in the presence of the stunning and angelic mortal Psyche. You see, dear, beauty is a power of its own. Venus was intimidated by Psyche's beauty, yet she resented and feared Psyche's beauty, and this was the reason for much of Psyche's pain. She wanted nothing more than for Psyche to go unnoticed and unloved by other men. Although people from everywhere would gather to see Psyche, she was never able to find a husband to love her. Her beauty was intimidating to more than Venus, as you can see. Her father and mother were very distraught that their daughter was unmarried. They sought answers and were eventually told by Apollo, the god of the sun and also truth, that Psyche was not meant to marry a mortal and that on top of the mountain she would find the husband that she was predestined to spend her life with. So, Psyche set off up the mountain to lie in a field of grass to wait. At this time, out of jealousy and envy, Venus sent Cupid to ruin Psyche by wishing her to fall in love with the most hideous, monster-like man on earth. When Cupid found her delicately lying in the grassy field, he slowly approached her to lean over her resting body and observe her beauty, which so threatened his mother. Unexpectedly, Psyche awakened and gazed directly at Cupid, startling him and causing him to wound himself with … what, dear?"

"The golden arrow?" I guessed, leaning on the edge of my seat as far as I could.

"That is right."

"Wait—why was Cupid startled just by her gaze? Was her beauty that seriously ridiculous?" I asked, feeling a bit silly by the way I'd posed the question to this very serious and wise woman.

She seemed dumbfounded by my question, almost as if she was wondering if she was wasting her breath by telling me this story. She responded slowly. "Cupid is immortal. Psyche is mortal; she is human. He was invisible to her, my dear, yet, she looked directly at him."

"Oh, right," I replied. "Yes, of course."

"So, he fell deeply in love with her. He surrounded her with the most magical life and overwhelmed her with riches. There was one condition, though. Psyche was never to look at him. Cupid only came to her in the night and would vanish before sunrise. She was never to see his face, as he did not want to be loved as the son of a goddess but for himself."

"Well, how would that work? How could he expect for her to love him?"

"Dear, although she could not see the color of his eyes, the softness of his hair, the charm in his smile, or the tone of his skin, his words and embraces were enough for beautiful Psyche to realize she had found her soul mate. By fate, she had found her complementary twin who held the qualities that summoned her hidden potentials and allowed her to achieve wholeness."

"That would be so lonely. Please understand that I hear what you are telling me about wholeness, but to know you have found your soul mate but to not live in both the spiritual and physical world together would just be ... I want my co-pilot by my side."

"Your co-pilot? What do you mean by this, dear?" she asked, confused, and I could see for a second that she wondered if we having the same conversation. "To continue, Psyche did begin to grow lonely. Listening to her doubts and not believing in her heart, she disobeyed Cupid's request one night while he lay sleeping. She snuck up on him, amazed by his beauty and realized that he was the son of Venus. But of course, the silly woman accidentally woke him. He asked Psyche why she needed to look at him, to see him. Was it that she doubted his love for her? Did she fear he was a monster? Did she not believe in them as a couple—two beings with one soul? All Cupid wanted was to be loved and adored as her equal, as her partner, not as a god. To punish her, he abandoned her."

"He abandoned his soul mate? How is that possible?" I started to feel the deep, hollow pain in my chest and the hot tears form in the inner corners of my eyes.

"Isabella, without trust, love cannot live. Hear me again, dear. Love cannot survive between two lovers under suspicion."

I could see her lips moving but could not hear her. I faded into my own head and could only think of how Santo and I had no trust between us.

"Dear, do not look so hopeless. There is a solution to all the worries and heartaches. Remember, hope dies last. If you can dream it, you can achieve it. With hope, all your dreams may come true," she whispered in a reassuring tone.

I repeated in my head: *Hope dies last.*

"Greek myths are real doozies at times, as it's not always easy to hear the honest truth about love. You must trust yourself, Isabella. Make that promise to yourself, for your soul. Psyche's journey is symbolic of the journey that every woman will travel."

"So, as a result of her mistake, she lost her soul mate? That was such an honest action. She didn't want to hurt him; she just needed to know. That is so tragic."

"No, dear. You see, Cupid realized that when you love someone, that comes with accepting the good with the bad. He came to life when he had found her, his other half. With her, he evolved. This divine predestined connection that draws two people together is a bond that remains, even after death."

"How do we recognize our other half?" I asked, yet I knew there was no clear answer.

"You will not see it; you will feel it. God has his tests. Your time will come."

Forty minutes later, I realized this Greek woman sitting beside me was a sign that this journey that I was heading on was right, and I was going to be okay. I realized that no matter what had happened in my past, it brought me to this very moment on this very flight, sitting by this very woman.

The woman sitting in 33J was also traveling alone, also running away, also scared. She had been visiting her son in Brooklyn for a month, as she had lost her job and her husband two months earlier. She was heading to her beach house in Palermo for a couple of months to be alone. 33J was a blessing and allowed me to realize as humans, we all go through the same obstacles even though we may have different stories.

"Dear, I should rest a bit."

"It's truly a pleasure to have met you," I responded. "Thank you for sharing this story. I hope you are right."

"The pleasure was all mine, my dear," she said, smiling as she leaned back to close her eyes.

I turned toward the window and stared at my reflection. If someone were out there looking in, what would that person see of my life? Could he see something I couldn't? Would I agree with him or even want to know? As I rested my head against the window, I could not help but question my life. For being born on a day of love, it was the one thing I never had without a price. This had always felt like the curse of Saint Valentine, as he always reminded me how unlucky I was.

These thoughts always made me miss Potato tremendously, as the love I shared with him was unconditional; he would never reject or hurt me. Always wanting to be loved had resulted in my putting huge expectations on myself, therefore setting the standard for everyone else to judge me. I realized that Dr. Goldstein was right. I had made the insane mistake of thinking that if I were the perfect daughter, student, entrepreneur, employee, friend, or girlfriend, I would be guaranteed love. How could my family not embrace me or my partner not want to marry me if I were perfect? The thing was, I wasn't perfect, and pretending to be was so very exhausting. I was eager to leave all of this behind me—for now, at least.

Ten hours later, I was landing in Rome. I never got the woman's name who sat in 33J, but as we went our separate ways with smiles, she said, "Your actions in life should match your dreams, my dear."

Everything felt a bit easier as I walked through the airport. I hoped that I wouldn't forget the sense of peace I acquired from my talk with 33J. I exchanged my money, and headed for the taxi line. The taxi drivers were so much hotter than the ones in New York. "*Excusi*, taxi?"

"*Si, signorina.*"

It was time for my well-rehearsed line that I had been practicing all week. "*Ottanto Quattro Fontanella Borghese, per favore.*" It was a moment for me, my first moment in Rome, and I was the only one to witness it. Lesson number one: stop underestimating my potential to do anything. I was capable of anything. I could travel alone any time in my life. Okay, I'd only spent ten minutes in this foreign land, so maybe I was getting a little ahead of myself. But that's what dramatic people do. *Dear God, I forgot to buy the adapter at the airport.*

Arriving at the hotel, I buzzed the gated entrance and immediately the door clicked. I entered into an atrium lobby with a serene fountain that was the home to a few koi fish.

"*Buon giorno*," the gentlemen behind the front desk greeted me. "Checking in?"

"*Si*, Isabella Reynolds."

He directed my attention to a huge bouquet of stargazer lilies behind him. "Madam, these arrived for you a couple of minutes ago. We will send them to your room shortly."

I mumbled "*grazie*," thanking him.

The Italian had already interrupted my journey, and I had not even been here for one hour. Now, my small hotel room would smell like the familiar, my past. With a sigh, I went to my room, quickly unpacked, and changed into a Theory denim skirt and fuchsia silk tank top. I slid on my silver metallic Jimmy Choo flat sandals and grabbed my matching oversized Prada shoulder bag that included all maps, euros, and necessities. I pulled my hair up into a ballerina bun, dabbed my lips with Rosebud salve, and covered my entire body with my must-have Skinceuticals SPF 30. I opened my hotel room door and put on my Chanel sunglasses, just as a bellman greeted me with flowers in hand.

"*Buon giorno*," he said while handing them over to me.

"*Grazie.*" I took the flowers, shut my door, eagerly headed out to explore and tossed another piece of the past into the trash, right where it belonged. "Completo finito!"

Walking around alone, I felt unexpectedly safe. I got a pistachio gelato in a cone and walked to the Fontana di Trevi to toss a coin and make a wish that I would find myself while I was here. I wondered if Bobby was right. Was Italy the best place for me to be? Here I was in Rome, the original home of my Italian, while he was in New York.

I headed to the monument Il Vittoriano to finish off the rest of my gelato. I remembered the monument from my Columbia University journey years prior—how I loved looking at it, as it resembles a wedding cake. I recalled standing there almost five years ago wondering about my own wedding. It was ironic that I ended up falling for a Roman. Now, I was standing in front of the same statue, wondering about my own wedding ... again. Staring at the gigantic wedding cake, I wondered if Bobby was right, and I subconsciously had another agenda without being aware of it.

After wandering around a bit, I walked back to the Fontanella Borghese, as I needed to make dinner arrangements for my first Roman meal alone. I was actually going to have dinner all alone. I was unsure how this would take place, but I was going to have a fabulous meal and eat whatever I wanted and guilt-free.

The restaurant the hotel recommended, Le Campagne, was five blocks away. I had imagined a darkly lit restaurant where I would fit right in and be somewhat invisible, so dining alone would not be so bad, but being a five-foot-seven blonde stands out, no matter the lighting and especially at Le Campagne, which I discovered to be a brightly lit restaurant. I walked back and forth before the entrance four times, then took a deep breath and headed in. I requested the table in the corner but noticed the majority of the people were men and all eyes were on me. Maybe my bright purple Alice & Olivia bubble dress was a bit too much. I requested a table for one. "*Buona sera. Un tavolo per uno.*"

The restaurant was not hip, nor did it have a trendy scene. Maybe when I asked for a restaurant recommendation with legendary appeal, the concierge at the hotel thought I meant senior appeal. This was going to be a very quiet dinner.

Le Campagne had a super antipasti bar and a display of whole fruits, vegetables, and fresh fish. Unlike my Chinese comfort food, nothing caused the "binge" signal to go off. Other than that, the décor was old and the atmosphere was a bit too stuffy for my taste. I just reminded myself that this trip was about discovery and since my choices recently had not proven to be the best ones for me anyway, I should keep an open mind.

When I ordered for myself, I was served with so many tastings, it was like eating for four people. The chef and staff were so eager to please me and introduce me to their talents in the kitchen, they were stuffing me slowly. I think I shocked my restaurant audience so much that they paid more attention to my finishing every bite than to the fact that I was eating alone. I dined on mozzarella y tomato, fried artichoke and zucchini, and pasta with grilled octopus in a spicy tomato sauce, while drinking several glasses of red wine. People continued to stare, probably wondering who I was, why I didn't have a companion, or how I ate so much food. I was aware that I was doing it, something I normally and comfortably would only do in the privacy of my own home—eat for four people. Being so thin and able to eat like that was shocking to people. They had no idea of my B&P cycle. I got a sense of control when I flaunted my abnormal behavior. However, I knew it was a lie as well. This skinny frame was fake perfect. I was not one of those people who could have her cake and eat it without purging. I had not figured out who I was going to be for the next week.

While taking a breather between my last bite of pasta and my first glance at the dessert menu, I wondered if I really could order anything else.

Dessert was a difficult one. I mean, who could decide between a fresh, creamy tiramisu and the sweet peach tart? The waiter seemed bothered by my dilemma so he cut a small slice of each for me to sample. I was amazed that he picked up on my pensiveness over the menu. An Italian responding to my emotion was unknown territory. However, the feeling of shame that I would be even be flattered by this was parallel to my low levels of expectations lately.

After dinner, I strolled back to the hotel, feeling free and lost at the same time—and a little bit like a fat girl. Having a quiet dinner with myself was crucial. No matter what, I was not going to purge while I was here. It was exciting to know that each day here alone was an opportunity to reinvent myself. I did not want to waste one moment and thought it would be a bright idea to request a wake up call for 8:30 a.m.

As I walked into the hotel, the same gentleman was working as when I arrived. "*Buona sera, Massimo,*" I greeted him. Can I get a wake up call for 8:30 tomorrow morning, please?"

"Of course, Miss Reynolds. Would you like a Roman or an American one?"

"I'm sorry ... what is the difference?"

"A Roman wake-up call requires me to personally come up to your room and wake you up," he responded with a sly wink.

I looked at his wedding band, staring for a good second to let him know his offer was not welcome. "An American one would be just fine. *Buona notta, Massimo.*" If an Italian fling was going to happen on my adventure, it was not going to be on my first night, with a married man, and especially not the night desk guy at my hotel. My standards were not that low during this Greek tragedy.

14

THE NEXT MORNING I WENT for a bite at Café Vitti, where I sat outside in the sun. It was only day two, and I had already adapted to eating alone. It was such an amazing experience that I could not believe I had never done this in New York.

I ordered a glass of champagne to celebrate myself—this was all that mattered.

Three glasses of champagne later, I headed to Vatican City for some spiritual inspiration. I hoped the Pope would not mind my buzz. As I made my way, I captured with my camera the quaint Roman streets, bridges, and the strangers surrounding me. I did not want to forget any of these moments of my vacation.

Once I reached the Vatican, I walked into the center of it all and sat down on the concrete ground. I looked up at the sky, which was so pure and blue it was as if the saints that surrounded the Vatican were watching over me. At least, I felt that way, and it had been a while since I had that sense of not feeling alone. This was ironic, considering I was far away from my life and very much alone. I wondered if the Vatican saints would do a better job than Saint Valentine, who seemed to have cursed my heart. Valentine had totally dropped the ball this past year. I was even comparing him to my previous Roman saint, Santo.

I decided to have lunch at Obika, the restaurant where Pia and I had our first dinner together. The restaurant was still the same—sleek and super-modern, with twelve small outdoor patio tables under a sunlit roof. As I walked in, there was no one. It was noon; was I the only one in Rome wanting to eat mozzarella? The small but quaint restaurant had two separate buffet bars, just like I remembered. One of the buffets was a dream for the cheese whore that I was: the freshest mozzarella in many varieties, burrata, and even ricotta. *Yummy!* Mr. Burrata was calling my name this afternoon. The other bar was filled with an assortment of pastas, cured meats, grilled vegetables, and an assortment of breads. I grabbed a clear square plate and assembled my Italian "for four" buffet. I loaded mozzarella, ricotta, salami, prosciutto, pesto pasta with squid, a vegetable orzo, a puffy pastry with ham, and an unknown white creamy cheese. I wanted to eat, eat everything and enjoy it, rather than using the food just to eat it and purge it.

I took a table on the patio to dine alfresco and watch the strangers stroll by. I had the entire place to myself, and I loved every minute. I could be the scene myself. Here I was, eating the freshest mozzarella and creamiest burrata my mouth had ever tasted, breathing in fresh air, and being in silence. No wonder the life expectancy was so extended here. I could not imagine anyone here using the expression, "I could just die." No one was judging or upsetting me. I was the American girl all alone in Rome.

"*Exusi?*"

Startled, I turned around and noticed a fortysomething, unshaven, average-looking man sitting behind me. There was something sexy about his seeming so average. I couldn't help but notice his overly tanned Mediterranean skin. "Yes?" I said, trying to smile through my shyness and not come off as uncomfortable.

"I have been admiring you enjoying the surroundings and burrata. I'm glad you approve."

"It is lovely," I confirmed and also wondered how much of a piggy he thought I was. I was exhausted with always being preoccupied by what others would notice with my relationship with food. "Approve?" I asked, attempting to save myself from myself.

"Where are you from?"

"New York."

"Ah-h ... New York. A very fast city but similar to Rome, no?"

"Similar?" I asked, unsure and wondering if I couldn't keep up because I was slipping into a dairy coma.

"Bella, it is not the pace of the city but the city itself. Just like New York, Rome, this restaurant, the weight of the sun on our skin, the sky, your burrata, this breeze, are all moments that hold the prettiest things. Can you feel it? Isn't it *fantastico* when you find the prettiest things in the tiniest moments and in the biggest cities? It is all very alive, no?"

God, this is why I loved Italy. These people were romantic about everything and found life in the tiniest details.

"Please finish your meal. I do not mean to disturb you. I saw you admiring everything, and I just had to speak to the blonde Audrey Hepburn," he said, with a very handsome and not-so-average smile.

"It was a nice meeting you," I said.

"Ciao, bella."

As I finished my meal, however, I was feeling like a fat girl, and it was a struggle not to think about B&P. I always reminded myself that normal, healthy people who did not struggle with food like this noticed the things I put into my head. To distract myself, I decided to walk to the most "touristy" place of all, the Spanish Steps. As I turned over the check that was strategically place on a sterling silver tray, I saw that it had been paid and was accompanied by a business card. The back of the card had a written note: "Bella, if you need a tour guide, it would be my pleasure." The front of the card displayed the contact information for a Mr. Mario, owner of Obika.

Smiling, I lingered through the streets that were filled with people chatting, laughing, reading, singing, licking their dripping gelato, and picking out fruits from the sidewalk stands. The sun warmed my skin, and the air was filled with the smell of bread baking. Everything was colorful, bright, and alive. Rome was filled with tiny bits and pieces of everything and nothing.

As I walked with no destination in mind, I was greeted with, *"Buon giorno,"* "Bella," "Excuse me, do you accept compliments?" "How about dinner?" and a lot of "Where are you from?" I simply kept walking and replied to everything with a smile. I thought about my great-aunt, as she always reminded me that the best compliment is remembering one's smile. A smile is the window into our souls, second after the eyes.

With the evening approaching, I walked to the Piazza del Popolo and sat on the steps as the sun set. I leaned back, closed my eyes and took in the cool evening atmosphere and music from the accordion in the background. I was excited for the morning as my 8:52 train to Venice would take me across Tuscany to another new adventure full of unknowns. Back at the Fontanella Borghese, I passed on the wake-up call and set my own alarm that night.

The alarm was pointless, as I could not sleep with the butterflies fluttering in my stomach from all the excitement. I was anxious that traveling by train in Italy was perhaps going to be a challenge. Or maybe I was just nervous, as I had never been to Venice. There was also the fact that I was going five hours away to a city that was literally floating on water. Meanwhile, I was the girl who did not go in the ocean past her lower thigh. I still blame my parents for allowing me to watch *Jaws* when I was seven. It took me years just to be able to swim in a pool by myself. Now, that's something Dr. Goldstein could have helped me with.

Though I had no idea how I was going to manage this next part of my journey, when I set out the next morning, I acted like traveling alone was typical for me. The taxi ride from the hotel to the train station felt like a dream. From my window, I saw Rome at its "Romest." All the tourists were still sleeping, and the locals were heading off to work or going on early morning runs; business owners were opening up their stores for a brand new day. It was a glimpse of real life and what it would be like to live here.

Leaning against the window, I let the fresh morning air blow through my hair. Closing my eyes, I thought about what my life here with Santo would have been like if things would have worked out between us. For the first time in years, I recognized my gut feeling telling me that a life with the Italian would have been the wrong choice for both of us. Moving to a new world with a man when I hadn't sorted out who I was would have been a crisis in itself. That morning on the way to the train station, I caught a glimpse of myself and it was more than my reflection in the window—not my fake self, but me.

Arriving at the train station, I took a deep breath and walked through the double doors. A cold gush of air hit me in the face, and I felt a tremor of anxiety at the chaos before me. It was the Italian version of Grand Central. People were breezing from all directions; voices shouted Italian over the public address system, and I'd forgotten to look up the Italian word for ticket. I had no clue where to go. It felt like someone had just slapped me in the face. I felt as terrified as I did the morning the car service picked me up to whisk me away from New York.

Taking several extra deep breaths, I pulled myself together and proceeded into the chaos. I asked myself, *What would a savvy traveler do?* For Christsake, I lived in Manhattan and had found myself in more crazypants situations than this. Following others, I then realized where to buy my ticket. I matched up the words on the departure board with the ones on my ticket and now knew where I needed to be in twenty minutes.

I headed toward a café for a cappuccino and a pastry filled with cream. There was no takeout in Italy. You were forced to stand at a bar and swallow your pastry and sip your coffee. In some ways it was more civilized because you weren't carrying around a paper cup, but in other ways, standing while eating and drinking at a small, crowded counter made me feel like a pig, fighting for its place in front of the trough.

When it was time to board my train, it was such a proud moment for me that my fear subsided. Once again, I found my own way; no one was holding my hand or hindering my learning process. This was more than a journey to Venice. Now I understood how a person's fear could paralyze her from doing the things she desired to do. Now, I understood what this journey was all about. Whether I was going after a new goal, moving to a new city, ending a relationship, or traveling to a foreign country alone, life was about moving forward and pushing myself out of my comfort t zone.

I sat in my assigned seat on the train and stared out the window, watching Rome pass, a feeling of satisfaction moving through me. I was eager to see Tuscany's countryside. Being on this train, allowed me to feel like I was getting farther away from my reality. It felt great, being temporarily free from my past, the pain, and the B&P. Being so perfect and accepted did not consume every moment of my day here.

Almost five hours later, I knew we were getting close to Venice. The countryside began to change and soon I saw more and more water. Sometimes, it felt as if the water would swallow our train, and we would just disappear into the unknown, and no one would ever find us. Finally, we were at the last stop, which was my stop. I walked out of the train station and found my way to Vaporetto 82, the boat that would take me to the Rialto Bridge. It was amazing; my first stop would be the famous bridge itself.

Ten minutes later, I was under the Rialto Bridge. I felt like I was in a dream. The quaint yet bustling alleys that were really streets felt like a maze. Still, I exited the vaporetto and went in search of my hotel along the narrow streets, which were lined by canals. It felt as if the water could rise and wash through these tiny streets, and that terrified me. This insecure feeling forced the weight of my presence and pushed me to stand up taller. I felt myself and was in no hurry to disappear. I had so much more to do in this world, so much more to live and give. Looking up, with only a glimpse of the sky visible above the narrow alleyways, I tried to feel reassured by the small rays of light falling upon me.

I reached Hotel Monaco, which was right on the Grand Canal and—I was thrilled to discover—right next to Harry's, the landmark restaurant that I had already reserved ahead of time for dinner that night. Harry's was the first of the Cipriani establishments, dating back to the 1930s. I quickly checked in, as I was eager to head out, not wanting to waste any time. I was already truly inspired just being here. The historic hotel was breathtaking, grandiose, and romantic. This was going to be extraordinary.

First stop was San Marco Piazza. I loathed birds but was dying for the dirty pigeons to surround me, as it was a tourist attraction to experience at least once. I walked through the piazza, trying not to shriek too loudly when the pigeons entered by comfort bubble. I spotted the ideal café to sit in the sun and sip bubbly. I ordered the most expensive bottle and watched the gondolas pass by. I felt my soul lighten while sitting there. The deep, hollow pain in my chest had consumed me for so long that I had forgotten what it was like to just feel tranquility. I embraced the day as I sat there, and was thankful for the time away from everything. The real challenge was just ahead, I realized—getting the pain to leave me for good.

I strolled back over to the Grand Canal Restaurant near my hotel. The restaurant terrace had splendid views of the surrounding islands, the Church of Santa Maria della Salute, and the floating gondolas with their shirtless taxi men astride them. Taking a table by the water, I took in all the views while enjoying every delicious bite of a plate of tomatoes and mozzarella. I sat there behind my big sunglasses and pretended to be someone important. This actually helped me with getting a table. Tall, blonde, American girl alone ... who could she be? It was a lazy afternoon, and it felt nice not to be in my reality, although this was part of my problem—my pretending.

My reality here, my life this very moment consisted of no work schedule, no saints (neither one of them), no apartment with Potato's smell, and no excuse to go somewhere private and cry for hours. *Perfecto.*

After lunch, I followed the lyrics of a Frank Sinatra song, around the corner to Caffé Florian on Piazza San Marco, where there was a small stage and a band of four Italian men dressed in neatly pressed tuxedos. For two hours, I sipped several glasses of Prosecco and finally, an espresso, while being serenaded by the orchestra. When I got the bill, I was amazed that they charged an extra eight dollars for entertainment. What whores those men were, in their little tuxedos.

I had three hours before my fabulous dinner at Harry's, so I decided to be a tourist. I took in the best views by going to the top of the Campanile Tower, then back to the Rialto Bridge for some photography. Dinner was going to be amazing, as Cipriani's was one of my favorite places in New York. Here I was in Venice, where it all began ... and dining without him. The thought crossed my mind that I had come here to mentally and emotionally torture myself with everything Italian—except my Italian.

Back at the hotel, I took a long shower, praying that the water wouldn't turn cold and that my hair would not become a complete mess. Airport security had confiscated my Bumble & Bumble deep conditioner, so I was screwed, not to mention the fact that I had no blow-dryer because I had never picked up an adapter. I tossed on a black Versace camisole, my dark high-waisted Seven jeans, and a cream Loro Piana pashmina and my black Manolos. My hair was working against me—I felt like Diana Ross—but I was blonde and in Italy, so they would all see me coming.

It was dark and breezy, and the sounds of the water and music in the air comforted me. And there I was, standing in front of Harry's bar. Suddenly, I felt paralyzed. I could not believe I was about to walk in and have dinner by myself at this restaurant. The past couple of days had been such a pleasant new experience; but this just felt too close to home. I would never do it at Cip's, but I held my breath, opened the door, and exhaled as soon as I was in.

"*Buona sera, signorina.* Would you like a table?"

"I have a reservation for one for Reynolds."

"*Un tavolo per* uno?"

"Yes, table for one."

"It would be my pleasure. Please follow me." He led me to a table in the front between two older couples. "My name is Alfredo. I will send your server right over."

"Grazie, Alfredo."

Seconds later, a twentysomething super-striking Italian (and tall!) was standing over me with a Bellini. Two more seconds later, another one came with a menu, and a third poured my sparkling water and squeezed my lime. Well, this dining alone didn't seem so bad. I liked it when people fussed over me, especially beautiful Italian men who were perfectly sculpted and appealing to the eye, similar to Michelangelo's David in Florence.

However, the question was, how would I eat in front of them? They would never see me again, and I was looking thin. Yes, they would definitely be thinking, "Wow, look how much she can eat and stay so beautiful." I decided I was just going to order and not worry about how little or how much I was eating. I decided there would be no purging again tonight. Of course, I started with the Cipriani invention, carpaccio, and followed that with the tuna tartare. Ordering the tuna tartare was a bit hilarious, as this was my notorious dish at Cip's every time when I was pretending to eat, with 'tini intoxication being my only desire. The tartare was followed by a half-order of orecchiette pasta with scampi in a spicy tomato sauce and then two desserts, which included a sliver of chocolate cake and one of the vanilla cream cake, another Cipriani classic. All the food was paired with the appropriate selection of wines and topped off with an "on the house, bella" Krug Vintage Grande Cuvee Jeroboam, my favorite champagne—a breathtaking symphony of flavors that put my taste buds in harmony; an instrumental experience with a steep price tag. I just kept telling myself, *When in Venice, do as they do*. I sipped my delicious treat and watched the hustle and bustle around me.

Francesco, another maitre d', approached to ask me to return the following day to sample some other Harry's lunch classics. My response was interrupted by the obnoxious couple beside me. A seventy-ish man in a gray pinstriped suit and binocular glasses was complaining about his martini. His drink was not served in a typical martini glass but in a three-ounce glass. As a result, he began to cause a scene and question if his drink was, in fact, a dirty martini. I wanted to say, "Sometimes things are not always what they seem, sir, but I would worry less about the shape of the glass and more about the age of your date." The woman was clearly in her mid-fifties, but she dressed and behaved like she was in her twenties. I wondered if she was capable of chewing her pasta with all the Restylane pumped into her lips and around her frown lines. *Maybe I should recommend the tuna tartare, which only requires swallowing.*

I observed their fake perfectness. A wave of shame passed through me, and I realized, *Who am I to judge?* I was fake perfect.

When I got the bill, I realized that there was a difference between the way a New York and Venice maitre d' took care of you. Of course, the whole restaurant fussed over me all night, smothered me with attention, and included a glass of champagne on the house, but the bill reflected every Bellini and glass of Prosecco I'd consumed and both slivers of dessert. A New York maitre d' would have thrown in dessert and the Bellinis. I thought the Bellinis were complimentary, a way to greet customers and served while reviewing the menu. None of it mattered, though—I had been paying the price my entire life.

After dinner, I walked back to San Marco piazza, wishing I'd worn a larger blouse because I would have given a million dollars to unbutton my skinny jeans. It was dangerous for me to dine alone and not have someone there to judge me and keep me from overeating. Now, I felt like a heifer and knew that I would have to refuse to see anyone for a week when I returned to New York. Here, I was as free as one of these Italian pigeons, eating every crumb someone gave me, pretending to be naturally thin when I was clearly in metabolic mayhem.

The music still filled the Venice night, so I sat down for a nightcap and took it all in. While sipping my Prosecco, I listened to classical music and watched the others around me. I was the only one sitting alone and this time, it felt nice.

Couples danced to the music, and I watched as they slowly moved back and forth, looking into each other's eyes and whispering or sometimes simply smiling at one another. For some, it seemed as if they never wanted the night to end.

I was thankful that I was alone and the Italian ex was not there to remind me of how much he had disappointed me. We had never danced like that in the years we were together. I was sure we shared moments, but the pain had somehow erased everything good now.

My thoughts were interrupted by my cell's ringing. I knew it was him. I hit ignore, even though I was dying to answer and tell him all about my dinner at Harry's. He did not deserve to hear my voice or learn of my new experiences, and I questioned why he still called to talk to me, even though he knew it was over. Why would I share any of these moments with him when he obviously did want to share anything with me? He lost me the day he exited our relationship without a fight. That was what I needed to remind myself: he gave me up without a fight.

As I headed back to my hotel, I promised myself that I would carry my phone on me only for safety reasons but leave it turned off. This trip was for me and if any Italian was going to influence me, aggravate me, or even speak to me, it would be one on this side of the pond.

15

MY SECOND DAY IN VENICE began with an early morning trip to the Rialto market; I woke to a sunny but chilly morning. The air was crisp, and it felt like a splash of cold water on my face. It was the perfect morning to explore the markets and perhaps become a bit more social. I wanted to become a part of the people and to interact. Even though I was not shopping for food, I liked to see how others lived and what made them happy.

It's hard to miss that Europeans take such pride in every detail—everything from the fresh whole fish to the vibrant colors of the vegetables and fruits presented in an organized pyramid manner, reflected their pride. I took pictures of the fiery red peppers that were stacked up like the Campanile Tower I had climbed at the beginning of my trip. The picture was to remind me about effort and to pay more attention to the small details in life; to put passion into everything.

As I walked around the market, I made eye contact with and smiled at everyone. *Baby steps.*

Heading back to Caffé Florian in San Marco Piazza, I wanted to sit and keep my mind on the music and stare at the lavender sky. The colors in everything took my breath away. All the drama going on inside me seemed to fade during those quiet moments. I wanted to have as many as I could and stuff these tiny moments in my pockets for safe-keeping.

I ordered a large bottle of Pellegrino to satisfy my thirst, a foamy cappuccino, and a flaky croissant. I was not even hungry, but the exquisite presentation of the coffee made me feel like a proper lady—it was served in a porcelain tea cup on a sterling silver tray, accompanied by a dainty silver stirring spoon. That feeling of being a lady soon faded as I took a bite into my crusty croissant and found, to my surprise, that it was filled with a tart strawberry jam, which oozed down my chin.

"*Sorpresa!*" said the waiter, who towered over me. "Ah ... how do you say in English ... oop-seh?"

"Very much a *sorpresa*—surprise—and that would be 'oopsie.'" I wiped off the sticky jam, trying to mask the redness of my face with the matching surprise that was smeared on it. This was not helping how I felt while eating the fatty crescent carb treat. *Perfect.* "Can you please bring me some additional napkins and a Prosecco?"

"Of course," he said, touching his chest like it was an honor.

"Grazie," I said, smiling. I needed something to calm my nerves and walk me away from the ledge. I put the damn thing down and buried it under my napkin.

Being alone felt nice, and more important, I was being able to hear my own thoughts rather than all the opinions and lectures of my friends in New York. As I walked through the maze-like streets, I had no destination. I just wanted to see where I would end up. My only agenda was to be lost.

An hour later, I approached a small café with twelve outdoor tables, Rosa Salva. It was quaint, quiet, and the perfect spot for more Prosecco and a view of the Campo Santi Giovanni e San Paolo. Considering I had known idea how I got here, I questioned if the Prosecco was such a brilliant idea. I was still feeling uneasy and completely anti-social now. I remembered how confident I was before my company went under, before I had failed to save Potato, and especially before Santo. I wondered where that Isabella Reynolds had gone. I needed to write in my journal, but my feeling now was mental exhausting, so I pushed the idea away.

It was time to head back to the hotel, as I had a reservation at Acqua Pazza for the best pizza in Venice, and I wanted to stop in the Basilica di San Marco to light a couple of candles for my loved ones. I walked in and took a seat to admire all the mosaics on the ceiling. I wanted to be closer to my spirituality or just to something bigger. While lighting candles for others, I lit one for myself. Slowly bringing the flame to my candle, I asked myself, *What about me? What about Isabella?* Closing my eyes, trying not to let the tears escape, I silently asked God to protect me.

Tonight at Acqua Pazza, I was going to have the best Venetian pizza, according to Frommer's Guide to Venice. I needed to blow off breakfast and not care about being so perfect here. I unfolded my map on the bed, to trace out the walk to the restaurant. There seemed to be only one clear way to the restaurant and the names of the streets were familiar.

I walked along Calle dei Fabbri, found San Luca, turned left, and continued on the straight path I had traced. After five minutes, I was at a dead end facing the Grand Canal. The map said nothing about swimming. The sky was dark; I was alone at a dead end and my fight-or-flight kicked in. Frantically searching the surrounding walls for an address, I saw that I was on Calle di Cavalli, and this was not the Cavalli with which I was so familiar. Backtracking by running to the last piazza I walked through, I had two other options, right or left. I went right, walked over a bridge, then under one and there I was, standing alone on an even darker and quieter street.

Suddenly, an image of an Italian newspaper headline filled my mind: "An American tourist disappears for a big pizza pie. Was Acqua Pazza worth the risk?" I told myself I should turn back; some Italian crazypants could have followed me, but was it possible that anyone was capable of being crazier than me at this point? My travel guide said this was the restaurant for pizza, so I decided it was worth the risk. I had already given up my reservation at Osteria da Fiore, a gathering spot for the famous and one that was awarded a Michelin star. Moving forward, following tiny street after street, turning left then right, I came to another dead end. *Reynolds! You should have taken that left!* Twenty minutes had passed for what was supposed to be a five-minute walk. I was feeling very insignificant on this tiny dead-end street, which was blocked by a wall. It began to feel like the walls were closing in on me, and I high-tailed it out of there again. Starving, I ran back to the piazza and took the left; it was the only option remaining. Lesson: sometimes we need a second chance. The street was crowded, full of people and music. I came to the end, and there was San Luca Piazza, but it was deserted. On the right was a large outdoor white awning, under which were twenty candlelit tables with navy blue tablecloths. It was perfect. It was romantic. It was Acqua Pazza, and I was ready to eat every damn pizza on the menu. At the entrance, a group of tall, dark, and handsome Italians were speaking among themselves. A suave one, wearing a cream tuxedo jacket and a black bow tie, looked at me with devilish grin. Oh, he had trouble written all over his perfectly chiseled face. "*Buona sera, signorina.*"

I flashed a smile. "*Buona sera. Tavolo per uno.*"

All of the men turned in a synchronized manner and looked at me. "*Tavolo per uno?*"

It was as embarrassing as being in a drugstore and purchasing a feminine hygiene product. *Aisle three needs a price check on regular Tampax.*

I confidently responded "*Sì*" and was seated at a table for two, where I ordered a glass of Prosecco to settle my nerves. The couple beside me had ordered and was sharing a large pizza. I took a deep breath, then said, "*Excusi*, I will have one of those with spicy salami, cherry tomatoes, and extra cheese."

"Ah, signorina, we only have that size."

"That will be fine," I confidently responded; tonight, I could feel Mr. Deep Hollow Pain was about to join me. Leaning forward and folding my arms on the table to reiterate my choice, I said, "Perfecto."

It was delicious, and I attempted to eat the whole thing, as the couple next to me stared. I felt like a fat girl at a Chuck E. Cheese birthday party. I didn't care, though. I was tasting it, using it, and fully aware of it.

The suave maitre d' walked over to the table directly in front of me to seat two dark-haired, overly tan, middle-aged, and chain-smoking Italian women. The women seemed very eager to see him, as he was as delicious-looking as the pizza I'd just devoured. Suddenly, the two women turned their attention to me. I soon realized that they were looking at me because *his* eyes were deadlocked on me.

"There is my future wife. Isn't she molto bella?"

"Sure. Um, yes, she is very bella," one said, as they buried their faces into their menus. I was flattered. He made me smile because an Italian had looked at me and said the word wife. *How cute.*

After finishing my pizza, I walked out of the square and back into the chaos of things. I noticed the crowd was moving left, so I decided to follow, and around the corner, there was my hotel! I could not believe my eyes, but this was typical of me. I had walked the entire city of Venice and somehow skipped a direct street that connected my hotel and San Luca Square.

I would leave this episode out of the storytelling when I returned home.

I went for a nightcap at Caffé Quadri and ordered a Prosecco. It was so romantic with the mini-orchestra playing and the bell tower ringing every thirty minutes, all under a full moon. I looked at the groups of people standing behind the café area. These people obviously did not want to pay for listening to the music. Couples of all ages stood there, holding each other, taking it all in. They were all so happy to be there, to be with each other, even when the ridiculous *Titanic* theme song filled the air.

I felt the tears begin to swell in my eyes. The Italian and I never had that. If he was sitting here right now, he would be smoking away on one of his short, fat cigars, drinking a glass of Pinot Grigio and laughing at these people who were simply enjoying their lives. He would not be holding my hand or saying I was beautiful or that he loved and adored me. He would not be looking at me as if I were really even present. Lesson learned: there is a significant difference between being in love with someone and loving someone. I was clearly beginning to see the difference and that I loved him as a person, even when he was not the best person he was capable of being.

It began thundering and pouring rain, so I moved at the fastest pace I could to get back to the hotel. The thunder was constant and outrageous, and the lightning bolts lit up my room throughout the night. Pulling the covers over my head, I prayed that it would not rain too much—I feared being washed away.

The next morning I decided it was time for me to educate myself with art and culture. I would be heading to the Biennale Art exhibit. According to my artsy friends, it was so amazing that I would just happen to be in Venice during the exhibit, and it was a must-see. In the elevator, heading to the lobby, I looked in the mirror and smiled back at myself. Being alone was becoming so amazing. I woke up when I wanted. I dressed how I wanted, even though my clothes were getting tight. I ate how much I wanted. I didn't even feel alone. Lesson: I am really enough; anyone else would just be an extra something special.

In the lobby, there was complete pandemonium. It seemed that Venice had become flooded overnight and at one point had been on the verge of evacuation. My "remain calm" pep talk turned to shit quickly and flew right out the window. I was officially in alarm mode.

I went back upstairs, grabbed my cell, and sat in the middle of the bed. Who do I call? What do I do? Of course, my luggage did not have any of the essentials for an Italian monsoon. I rolled up my jeans to my knees, put on a pair of Havaianas flip-flops that felt like butter between my toes, a blazer, and my pashmina around my neck. I overloaded the Fendi spy bag with all the necessary essentials: map, cell, camera, passport, lip gloss, novel, and an umbrella.

I headed down Calle dei Fabbri. This was not so bad. I was freezing my ass off, but I was hoping any sign of hypothermia would not set in until I reached the Biennale exhibit. But the museum wasn't close, so this walk was going to be a bit of a hike. A couple minutes later and already wet, I came to San Marco Plaza, which was crowded with people, making it difficult for me to cross. There it was—my worst nightmare. We were flooded, trapped, and forced to walk along makeshift walkways. Metal stands were set up and topped with plywood for us to walk on above the inches of grimy water.

I followed the other tourists, hopping up on the walkways and crossing the flooded piazza. This was not fabulous, and I felt so far from glamorous. I was wearing a hideous outfit that was only suitable to keep me warm—and not doing a very good job of that—and here I was on my first runway and feeling so far from being a model. At the end of the runway, the only thing to do was walk through two inches of water. Everyone was wearing rain boots and yellow ponchos, which were absolutely hideous, and I refused to take part in such a fashion disaster. "Fashion before warmth" was always my motto. As I walked along the edge of the Grand Canal and up and down a series of bridges, the largest gush of wind and rain blew me down. It seemed to happen in slow motion. I felt my right flip-flop fly off, my left arm going into the air. My right arm held the umbrella, which hit me on the head, eventually breaking my fall. I lay there, face down on the steps, in a twisted, awkward position. Five Australian men came to my rescue. They all wanted to help, each grabbing an arm, leg, my flip-flop, which caused an even greater scene.

I jumped up, said thank you to all of them for their efforts, and limped over to the side, away from the traffic. I was now covered with dirty water speckles. My forehead was scratched from the umbrella, as it had gotten caught in the bobby pin holding my bangs back. My large toenail was missing a piece of Lincoln Park After Dark polish, and my 24-carat diamond-encrusted bangle bracelets were bent into my arm. "*Just breath*," I said a little too loudly while pulling myself quickly together. There was nothing glamorous about this. The art mission was aborted.

Back at the hotel, I put the artsy culture lesson behind me and took a long hot shower, washing the day off of me, literally. However, there was nothing I could do about the paint chip missing from my toenail. It was poking fun at the perfectionist in me. Needing to glam my world back up, I headed to Café Gran. All the cafés were comparable yet exquisite for a late-afternoon lunch fit for a princess.

Sitting my exhausted and bruised body at a quaint corner table by the window, I watched all the poncho-wearing tourists outside in the misery. I ordered the most expensive lunch I could, with a bottle of Prosecco. I deserved it. I could not get enough of the juicy tomatoes and creamy mozzarella here. I topped it off with a double espresso and bite-sized rich chocolate truffles.

After another fabulous food experience, I ran back to the hotel to safety and warmth and to hide under the covers. The thunder was the only thing that starting up again. The deep, hollow pain was not present.

16

THE INTENSE BRIGHTNESS FROM THE sunlight woke me up early on my last day of Venice. Even though my trusty map and I did not have the best track record, I had several destinations to hit before tomorrow's departure, including C. dietro La Chiesa, Teatro La Fenice, and Vino Vino bar for their wine selection and their risotto di pesce, which I had read about in a travel magazine. My last stop would be Le Café for a sweet surprise before heading back to the hotel to get ready for this 999 Club that was a must-see and be-seen-at recommendation.

Later that day, as I sat outside at a café enjoying the sun and the ever so slightly chilly breeze, I smiled that my strategically planned day worked to perfection and I checked off everything on my must-experience list. Closing my eyes, I wondered what my life would be like if I stopped planning, worrying, and living in my head so much. I had the rest of the afternoon to relax before hitting the infamous and private 999 Club. Tonight, I was going to live it up, Isabella Reynolds style.

Post-breakup, I had still remained cordial with Santo's Italian social circle from the years we were together. I had not seen them, but somehow there was an understanding. His friends were under the impression that Santo and I split ways amicably. Nothing was ever demonstrated or verbalized otherwise. Luca, a tall, blond, crystal blue-eyed Italian from Naples, was a multi-millionaire and heir to an Italian fabric company. We had met one night during a private event at the Soho House. Of course, the Italian interrupted that, as he could not fathom being stuck in his office while I was poolside in my Missioni string bikini, sipping champagne and making lots of new "boy" friends. Looking back, I think his part-time job was ruining my life. I giggled at the idea.

I had called Luca before I left New York to let him know my travel plans, and Luca informed Christian, the owner of the exclusive 999 Club in Venice, to put me on the list and expect my arrival. The club opened at eight o'clock, so I planned on arriving early to have the perfect place at the bar to sip my champagne. I slipped into a Versace black pleated mini-skirt, paired with a black silk camisole and black velvet blazer. Thank God, the weather had lifted, as it was four-inch Manolo night, and I would not have exposed my two-week-old pair to unforgivable weather. These babies were such an investment, it was a shame that my renter's insurance could not somehow extend to cover any water damage on them. My New York apartment was home to my investments—my shoes. If I didn't polish myself up, I would indeed be the old, single, Jif-eating woman who lived in her shoes.

Reaching yet another square that was full of tiny cafés and restaurants, I could not find 999. I asked all the locals who crossed my path, but no one knew of the place. I guess exclusive here really meant exclusive.

Suddenly, I saw a tall (yes, another one), dark, and very handsome Italian boy; he must have been in his early twenties. He was pushing an outdoor table from a pizza joint out of the way to expose a large solid metal door. The door had 999 written across the center. I began to question Luca's sense and wondered if I was about to end up in an *Eyes Wide Shut* moment. Venice did have all those eerie but delicate papier-mâché masks everywhere.

"*Excusi*, is this the entrance to 999 Club?"

"*Buona sera, signorina*. You must be Miss Reynolds. We are expecting you."

Impressive.

"Luca said to keep our eyes opened for a conspicuous blonde. Isabella, *sei bellissima*," he said as he took my hand to place a kiss on it. "My name is Massimo. Please, this way." He touched my arm and led me up a long flight of steps.

I questioned if this was really safe to be alone at a mysterious place. I stopped letting all the Prosecco go to my head and continued up the steps.

We reached a narrow stairway lined with a red velvet carpet and dimly lit crystal chandeliers. At the top of the steps, he pushed through a beaded drape, and there I was—in the middle of this secret place. It reminded me of an Ian Schrager hotel bar, similar to the Rose Bar at the Gramercy Park Hotel. He announced my arrival, and another tall, gorgeous man, whom I assumed was the maitre d', said, "*Buona sera, signorina.* I am Francesco. Drinks or dinner this evening?"

"Just a drink tonight," I said. I wasn't comfortable here, even though everyone knew Luca. What would they think of me? An American girl walking into a private, dark, unknown place in another country, all alone?

"Perfecto, madam. Please follow me to our private upstairs bar."

I tiptoed up a glass staircase and could see the small bar to my left. It was very dark, as only candles and a tiny chandelier above the bar lighted the room. It was quite seductive, yet somehow romantic.

Massimo was already at the bar, talking to a woman with auburn hair and a blunt bang cut. She was loud and had round cheeks. Uncomfortable already, I took a seat at the opposite end of the bar. As I looked up from the drink menu to order a glass of champagne, Massimo was standing over me. In Italian, he asked if I wanted a drink.

Now that we were on a first-name basis, I guess he was trying to seduce me with his language, which was working.

I thanked Santo for teaching me the basics. "A glass of champagne, please," I responded.

"Of course, bella. I want you to meet Story. She is American, too."

Story was a thirty-three-year-old celebrity hairstylist from Beverly Hills who had just broken up with her boyfriend and was on a three-week journey through Italy to find herself. I guess this is where all the lost souls drifted. She resembled Punky Brewster, all grown up, with chubby cheeks and a thunderous personality. She talked so loudly that I was sure the surrounding patrons wished she would tone it down a bit. Still, it was nice finally meeting a girl, even though it was my final night in Venice.

Three rounds later, the three of us were all sitting next to each other at the bar ordering another bottle of champagne. The long stem flutes sparkled in the dim light from the tiny chandelier that hung above us. As the conversation continued along with the name-dropping of who we knew and what we did, a heavy-set gentleman in a well-tailored suit interrupted us. He had diagonal sideburns that accentuated his overweight face but showed off his winning smile. I wondered what Story, the hair expert, thought of this and if she would dare say anything to him.

"Ciao. I am Christian, the owner. It is great to finally meet you, Isabella." He placed a gentle kiss on the back of my hand.

"Well, Ms. Reynolds, it seems like you do know everyone," Story said as she studied me again.

Christian grinned. "Shall we drink something?"

I giggled. "I wouldn't have it any other way."

"It is our great pleasure to have you with us tonight. Luca is a very dear friend of mine and said you would be gracing us with your presence. You must stay with us throughout the night and celebrate your visit to our home. We won't take no for an answer. We are supposed to show you the best time while you are in our city," he said, giving me the deepest grin I had ever seen.

I had sipped down so much champagne that I excused myself and headed downstairs to the ladies room to regroup. I wanted to toss my hair a bit, retuck my silk camisole, and swipe blush to my cheeks.

As I got to the last step, I noticed it was pitch black and there was no one else in the place, with the exception of the drinking companions I had left upstairs. The restaurant was closed. Facing the mirror, I dabbed on a touch of my favorite Christian Dior pink gloss around my lips, stared deep into the mirror, and reminded myself, "This is your time. Live. Have a blast."

Tiptoeing back up the steps to the bar, I discovered the music had grown so loud that the glass walls were vibrating along the staircase. "Ah-h-h, Isabella! Welcome to the after-hours party. This is for you, our special guest," said Christian. I noticed that they had kicked out everyone except for Story and me—my own private event at an exclusive, unknown club. I deserved to be adored by all these non-defective Italians who actually liked to have fun. A fresh flute of champagne was passed to me and I delicately placed it in my right hand, along with a skinny yet sexy-looking cigarette in my left. I didn't smoke, but I thought, *When in Venice, do as they do.* After a couple of puffs, I grabbed the tuxedo hat off of Christian's head and twirled around the room.

Massimo kept popping in and out of my conversation with Story, occasionally kissing my exposed freckled shoulders or gently running his hand along the back of my head and twirling the ends of my hair. "Isabella, doing anything for the next hundred years?" he asked as he squeezed my hand. It was obvious that he had a crush on me, but what was I going to do with a twenty-four-year-old Italian boy in Venice?

At that moment, I recalled what 33J had said about the power of beauty. In the past, what would make me feel strong and reassured, I now realized, had merely caused a temporary and meaningless thing between the Italian boy and me. However, I was on a journey, so what could a little bit of flirting hurt, right?

I knew I seemed shy to everyone, which I was, but shy girls can be trouble and slightly dangerous when least expected. I pulled out my cell and walked to the dark area of the room on the other side of the staircase. I knew he would follow. He swiftly snuck up behind me, silently wrapping his arms around my waist, and whispered in my right ear, "Oh, my God, I just want to softly kiss your lips, Isabella. I want to make love to you." Slowly turning around, still tucked in his arms, I leaned forward, closer to his lips, and whispered, "No." He continued on and on, just like a little boy would beg. Then again, he was only twenty-four. Most Italian men did not even leave home and their mother's or nanny's side until they were in their late twenties or early thirties.

For some shock value and, of course, to drive him crazy, I broke free, ran my tongue slowly across his lips while looking him in the eyes, and then quickly walked back into the other room to join the party. Of course, he followed. He was too eager and impulsive for my taste, and I was completely distracted at times with his outfit. Five minutes at Bergdorf's with him, and I could totally change his life. He had on a cream sports coat with a black satin shirt, paired with blue pinstriped black pants. It was so bad that I was simultaneously analyzing his outfit and kissing him. Still, he was charming, with a boyish grin and an accent that was melting me.

We played cat and mouse throughout the night, unaware of everyone around us. By the time I headed back to my hotel, it was six o'clock in the morning—I had to catch a train in a few hours! The idea of missing my train and losing my room at the St. Regis made me crazy.

We all walked outside, and there it was—a private, breathtaking view of Venice, with all the residents and tourists still asleep. Who knew that a night of champagne, funny cigarettes, and misbehaving with an impressionable Italian boy would result in something I was so thankful for at that very moment.

"Miss Reynolds, would you do us the honor of joining us for breakfast? There is a stand that serves the best *pan du chocolate*." Christian looked at me so endearingly, and his hands were clasped as if in prayer. I could not pass on a chocolate croissant, and it would improve my condition by soaking up the twelve glasses of champagne I'd devoured.

We walked through the maze-like streets, each of us with a pastry in hand. As I bit into the crunchy crust, I found the chocolate was warm and oozing. I could not think of anything sweeter at that moment. My mind was clear; my world at this very moment was blameless. I closed my eyes and inhaled Venice at its finest.

"Bella. Isabella." Massimo said. "Please take my last bite. It would make me so very happy to feed you." His mouth opened, watching my lips. Saying no didn't cross my mind, nor did the fact I was eating this fat girl food in front of a delicious Italian stranger. "Grazie, Isabella." I slowly leaned in and took the last bite out of his fingertips as he watched every chew, smiling like he'd just witnessed the most precious thing.

"I really must get back, but it was so nice meeting all of you," I said, staring in Massimo's direction. I did not want the night to end, but he was not worth the St. Regis.

I also knew the two men would fight to not let me out of sight just yet, and the attention was flattering. Christian practically leaped in my direction. "I will walk you to your hotel, bella!"

"But you live near Story's hotel," said Massimo. "It is easier for me to walk Isabella home, and I would be honored."

I said, "Well, I don't want to be a burden, and I'm very flattered by both your efforts, but it only seems right that you walk Story home, Christian."

"You both are completely pathetic!" Story fumed. "I mean, what is it with Italian men and blondes? I will walk myself home!"

"No, no, it will be my pleasure" Christian said, rolling his eyes and shooting Massimo a dirty look.

"Perfecto! Isabella, this way, bella," Massimo said, smiling.

After Christian and Story were out of sight, Massimo placed his hand on the small of my back, and we began our stroll through the deserted streets of Venice. Things had dramatically shifted between us. Neither one of us knew what to say, but I could sense we both did not want to reach my hotel as fast as we did. Crossing the last bridge, Massimo pulled me into him and stared intently into my eyes. "Can I come up?"

"What will they think, you idiot?" I was concerned the hotel staff would see him.

"What floor are you on? Maybe I can come through the window."

I could not help but laugh in his face. Here was this young and very eager young man, willing to climb up the side of the hotel to spend time with me. Just then, it crossed my mind that Santo would not even leave a pair of clothes over at my apartment. "Massimo! You are not climbing up the side of my hotel like Spiderman."

"Well, I refuse to let you out of my sight. I will show you more of Venice. You will join me, yes?"

"Of course," I said, doubting my choice.

We headed through the quiet and empty San Marco Square. There was not a pigeon in sight. It was absolutely breathtaking having the entire square to ourselves. As we walked, he stopped about every two minutes and pulled me in to kiss my lips softly and tightly squeeze me. Even though we were the only souls around on this early morning, I still could not let go 100 percent. I was worried about the public displays of affection, even though there was not even a pigeon that could see me. With each kiss, I let myself get lost in the moment. I let go, freely.

As we continued our walk along the Canale di San Marco, I noticed signs that indicated we were heading toward the Giardini Pubblici Biennale art exhibit. And then it began to sprinkle, and I suddenly became panic-stricken that my new Manolos would get wet, and I recalled my dramatic wipe-out incident on one of these bridges. "We have to get out of the rain. My shoes!"

"Your shoes?" Massimo asked incredulously. "Isabella, I live one block away. We could go back to my flat." It was either fifteen minutes back to my hotel, or one block to his flat. I made the not-so-ladylike decision, but it was for the sake of the shoes. "Let's go!"

Running to his place, I reminded myself to behave and do the right thing. *Isabella, do not get caught up in the moment. Do not!*

I stumbled into his apartment; it was the smallest living space I had ever seen. *He will not understand the Manolo story. Do not even attempt it.*

Drenched from the rain, we stood in his small space, looking at each other. The light from the bathroom allowed us to see each other's profile. What seemed like forever was in actuality about thirty seconds before we started ripping each other's clothes off. I was finally getting rid of his hideous cream jacket; it had been troubling me all night.

We looked directly at each other without moving our eyes away for a second. "Isabella, I'm in a fairy tale," he whispered in Italian, while picking me up. After taking a couple of seconds to translate his words, I—for once—said what I wanted. "*Ho voglia di te, Massimo*," or "I want you, Massimo."

Between all the kissing and removing of clothes, I had decided, what the hell? No one was around to judge me and even if there had been, I was the only boss and judge of me.

One hour later, he was sleeping, and I was trying to find all my clothes. I did not want to risk leaving anything behind that could identify me with him. I stood over the bed, watching him sleep. The attention was entertaining, but I was searching for something so much deeper than desire, something that he could never give me. He was so peaceful and, at that moment, I realized I was thankful to have met such a free spirit. Grabbing my damp Manolos, I took one last look at my Italian fling and then tiptoed outside. It was now 8:30 a.m., and I had approximately an hour and twenty minutes to get back to the hotel, change, pack, and boat it back to the train station. *The St. Regis Rome, here I come.*

17

WITH NOT A MINUTE OF sleep and after suffering what seemed like eternal hell in the Venice train station, I was finally on the train to Rome for my last night, although I'd been able to squeeze in a three-minute shower before stuffing all my belongings in my bag. Wrapping my pashmina around me, I pulled on my oversized shades and prayed I could sleep the entire four-hour trip. I could not believe my adventure was coming to an end. I was so ready to check in to the St. Regis Grand Hotel for some princess time. I preferred this over the up-all-night, "anything goes" party girl I had pulled off for the past fourteen hours.

Once I arrived in Rome, I walked directly to the taxi line and was off to the hotel. The goal was to check my sleepless body into my room and order the entire room service menu, then have a bubble bath with some bubbly somewhere in between.

Seven minutes later, the taxi dropped me off right in front of my castle. From the outside, I could have never imagined what I was about to walk into. If heaven was not the inside of the Rome St. Regis hotel, then hell was just perfect for me. As I walked in through the revolving door, I could see the large crystal chandelier centered in the lobby ceiling, glimpses of the recently polished marble floors, and red velvet pillows strategically placed amid the opulent decor. The scent from the over-the-top flowers throughout the lobby was causing a phenomenal, transporting experience. The atmosphere was pricey—just how I liked it.

Turning right, I walked directly to check-in. "*Buon giorno.* I'm checking in," I said confidently.

"*Buon giorno.* Welcome. Your last name?"

"Reynolds. Isabella Reynolds."

"Yes, Miss Reynolds, I have your reservation for only one night."

The desk clerk's words made me realize that my trip was coming to an end. I would be back in New York tomorrow evening. For the first time in eight years, I was not looking forward to returning to my city. "Yes, only for tonight."

Well, even if it is my last night, at least I'm doing it in style, I thought as I made my way to my room. I loved being overwhelmed with the sense of elegance and glamour that surrounded me. The plush carpet and halls all reflected Empire Regency and Louis XV styles. I placed the key into the door of room 708, and my mouth—and almost my Louis Vuitton luggage—dropped to the floor. The cloud-like bed was calling my sleep-deprived body. I threw my luggage in the closet and fell back into the center of the bed, while staring at the crystal chandelier. I whispered, "Perfecto."

I was sleep-deprived, but also, my body ached in more than just the usual places. Stretching out, I noticed a handwritten note placed on the nightstand. "It is our pleasure, Ms. Reynolds, that you are joining us." Next to the note was a Venchi Italian pure milk chocolate block and mini-bottle of Pellegrino.

"Hello, my little freebie friends. You look yummy." I placed a piece of the chocolate block in my mouth, and the creamy treat melted on my tongue immediately. It was the richest thing I had ever tasted—well, today, at least.

Being the chocolate whore that I am, I completely forgot about the most important part of being in this hotel. I still had to inspect the bathroom. As much as I did not want to leave the bed, I only had one night to make the most of this entire room.

As I opened what I assumed to be the bathroom door, the oversized white cotton robe caught my attention first. I stripped off my clothes and slid into it.

I immediately turned on the hot water to run a bath and began smelling the Italian soaps and spa products on the vanity. *Hm-m ...vanilla lavender bubble bath sounds just delicious.* I poured the entire bottle into the steamy water.

Next, I went to the mini-bar for a bottle of champagne and the room service menu to review while soaking. I turned on the "do not disturb" light so there was no risk of interruption.

I gently eased down into my steamy bubbles with a flute of bubbly. I was Julia Roberts, and this was my *Pretty Woman* moment. Reynolds at the Regis was worth every inch of a new pair of four-inch Manolos.

After an hour of soaking and elegance that I never wanted to end, a not-so-pretty sound came from my stomach. Taking a deep breath, I slid under the layer of bubbles and took in the silence for as long as I could. Coming up for air, I rinsed off and then slipped back into the plush robe and wrapped my hair in a towel on top my head. Hopping on the bed, I ordered Italian for four. I guess some habits follow you wherever you go, but this wasn't about purging and control. This was indeed about comfort, and I recognized this was part of the vicious cycle as well.

The room service menu was quite extensive. "I would like to order the tomato and mozzarella, the St. Regis burger with fries, the potato and cheese ravioli with tomato and mint fondue, the loin of lamb encrusted with a mustard herb sauce, accompanied with thyme-seasoned artichokes, a large bottle of Pellegrino, and of course more champagne. Oh, and an assortment of breads, with butter at room temperature ... please."

"Of course, signorina, and I see it is just you joining us for one night. Will this be for just one, signorina?"

The "for four" secret was out of the bag. My choice was either to confess to this stranger that, yes, everything I had just ordered was for one, or do something completely absurd and say, "Of course not! This will be for two." I could either look like a fat pig or like a whore who was having a guest in her room, even though she had checked in alone for one night.

"Signorina?"

"I apologize for the delay. Yes, this will be for one. Grazie." I decided I would rather look like a pig than a whore. I also decided to see how it felt to own my shame. Maybe a taste of it would force a change.

While waiting for the food, I opened the armoire doors in front of the bed and discovered a large flat-screen TV. Perfecto! Movie time. This would be a satisfying distraction for the Humiliation 101 I'd just experienced. A tasting menu would have been a bit more convenient for my needs, but finding a solution to my issues would be even more convenient. There would be no elegant or gracious way of me to accept a room service cart with four entrees, a basket of bread, and a bottle of champagne for one person in the hotel bathrobe. Mr. Room Service was just going to have to accept my less formal way of doing things.

When I heard a knock at my door, I quickly pressed Audrey Hepburn's *Roman Holiday* for the night's feature film. I contemplated turning on the shower and closing the bathroom door to give the impression that I did have a guest for dinner. I forced myself to consider bingeing bulimics existed here as well.

It turned out that my room service waiter didn't even bat an eye as he rolled in my dinner cart. So that night, in the plush robe, with a buffet of gourmet food, I shared my Regis room with Audrey Hepburn. I was excited as I settled into the cloud-like bed with my spread on the bed before me, but something was wrong; I was uneasy. I felt sick before even tasting a morsel of anything. I sat there and looked at all the food, enough to feed a small group of children. This felt bizarre. I purged to be in control, but this was quite out of control. I had found comfort in the routine and in the quantity of over-ordering. I had found comfort in the anticipation, tension, and release of all of this, rather than in myself. I took the lamb dish and the bottle of Pellegrino and champagne and wheeled the rest of it outside my room. I enjoyed my dinner "for one" and Ms. Hepburn.

Falling asleep, it seemed that every cell in my body was smiling. Escaping the streets of New York was one of the best decisions I ever made. It also allowed me to escape from my dream company frustrations, the pain of being without Potato, and this so-called heartbreak. I was beginning to realize it was the rejection that hurt, not living without Santo for the rest of my life. My whole perfect life I'd fought to have and keep was being peeled away like layers of an onion, only to expose my very fake core.

What began as a dreamy night sleep turned into a restless night of bad dreams. In my luscious room, within my temporarily perfect world, my peace was interrupted by the nightmare of the large roaches crawling everywhere. The shortness of breath startled me awake. *Not again!* There had to be a way to get rid of these mental insects.

It was already 6:13 a.m. and I was leaving the hotel at 9:00 for the airport, so I decided to get up, grab my bag out of the closet and whatever outfit was closest to the top, and head downstairs. I would end the morning with a foamy cappuccino and some sweet little treats while doing what I did best—observing others, as I'd had enough self-observation for the week.

I knew I had to make sure to take my newfound insights back to Manhattan. All the loss over the past couple of months was beginning to make sense to me. These recent events had somewhat slapped me in the face, forcing me to wake up and drink a dose of reality. I was fighting to get my life back; I needed to learn, to accept, and to acknowledge, as unfair as it all seemed to me. It was actually quite shocking that I had succeeded for this long as the "fake perfect" me.

Journal entry—July 11

As I sit here at the airport, I see the day approaching, as the baby blue sky filled with pink cotton-candy clouds are beginning to fill with planes. We are all returning to our "homes." I sit here calmly, no chaos or decisions to make or avoid at this very moment. I hear my voice whispering to me softly, the little voice that is my sense of reason when my heart and head are pulling me in different directions and I even avoid those "gut feelings," as what I want is not always what I need. My unselfish and unbiased inner voice represents the child within me. It is telling me to not be scared, to not worry, to just believe, and just be. What is the quote? "If you can believe it, you can do it." I watch the planes take off with what seems like turtle speed, and I remind myself how incredibly fast they are moving. I do hope time slows down a bit and becomes my friend, although this Italy trip has shown me that it is the quality of my life, not the quantity of how long I live that matters. Quality is the word that keeps repeating inside me right now. Quality ...

I. R.

18

I LOATHED VOICEMAIL. IF I wanted to hear what someone had to say, I would have picked up the phone in the first place. Because I was out of the country, however, I had no choice. Anything could have happened while I was in my own little world. Julian and Clay had called to schedule a date, as did Alan, with his annoying and slightly desperate attempts. I knew Pia had to be the last message: "Isabella, it's Pia ... you know, your best friend who you have not had a real conversation with in forever. What's going on? I want to hear about Italy, and I want to hear what happened with Dr. Goldstein. Meet me tonight for dinner at Jewel Bako, 7:30 p.m. in the East Village."

I had arrived back in the city less than six hours before and already someone was trying to make me accountable for my actions. Now that I felt better than ever and had a plan of action for how to not be a crazypants, I was prepared to face Pia for some Cuban czar time.

We had not spent any real time together since my silent yet hysterical Nobu breakdown, and she has been trying to reach me for the Q&A on why I had broken up with Dr. Goldstein already. I had avoided her at my going-away dinner, but now that some time had passed, I could show her that things were looking up, and my going to Italy was not a sneaky secret to still being connected to Santo.

Our dinner convo would be about my Italy insight. Also, Pia could catch me up on the past *Us Weekly* headliners that I missed during my new tomato and mozzarella addiction, Prosecco episodes, and Venice monsoon. I knew Pia was concerned and that I needed to answer her questions, but at times, she could be a bit too analytical and protective.

Jewel Bako was going to be a new experience for both of us. When it came to our dinners and ordering, Pia tensed up over unfamiliar menus. With any new restaurant, the omakase was always my first choice, as it offered a taste of everything that the chef recommended. Pia was allergic to the omakase theory, as she was a control freak and had to make substitutions for everything. She even controlled the timing and order of what we ate, demanding that they go light on the rice with the rolls, as well as extra sides of chives, spicy mayo, and ponzu. In reality, it probably would have been smarter for us to sit at the sushi bar. That way she could just instruct them directly on how to prepare her food so she didn't have to redo everything once it was placed in front of her.

As I walked into the small and surprisingly quiet sushi spot, I saw Pia immediately—her face was glued to the menu.

"So how does the menu look? Do you approve?" I asked, flashing a smile and giggling.

"Actually, I'm so excited; this is going to be a long dinner," she replied, leaning in to greet me with a kiss. "Well, I guess this is a stable sign that the great-aunt is not in our presence tonight."

"Well, I can see that you are going to be on your best behavior this evening," I pointed out while rolling my eyes.

"I have already ordered a cucumber sakitini and your champagne. Now we can review our options."

"Well, thank you. Maybe the czar did bring her manners." I giggled while she took her turn to exercise her eyes.

"Sir, excuse me! We would like to order a couple of things while we look over the menu," Pia eagerly yelled at the waiter, even though he was already approaching us. During the first hour, we consumed a variety of rolls, sashimi, and tartars with Pia's buffet of extra sides. We were appalled by the toxic soy sauce they brought to the table. Water retention and designer labels do not mix; it's like oil and water, or even worse, Roberto Cavalli and Coach. Pia was sure to point it out, and I nodded to firmly agree. That was the beauty in bulimia and carrying many sides to myself.

A slightly chilled bottle of Pinot Noir was placed on the table and I knew the Q&A was about to begin.

"So, Italy ... let's talk about that choice, Isabella.

Already getting defensive, I could not hold back. "Okay, take a pill, please. I prefer to have dinner with Pia, not Dr. Goldstein's sidekick. Everything is wonderfully wonderful. I'm doing fantastic."

"Are you for serious?" Pia had the same look on her face that she had the day I asked her if we should walk into an H&M and see what all the chatter was about. "Isabella, you've been back in reality for less than twenty-four hours. Why did you cancel Dr. Goldstein? Why did you choose Italy, of all places? Have you talked to Santo? And by the way, how is work going? I'm just so worried you are not dealing with any of this. You can't run away or conveniently deny you have problems."

"Pia, I'm good."

"Good? What happened to wonderfully wonderful?"

"Italy was an eye-opening experience. I dined at the best restaurants. I took long walks, even though I often ended up lost, at a dead end, or in fight-or-flight mode. I walked around and said *buon giorno* and *ciao* more times than you can even imagine and when I wasn't doing that, I drank Prosecco. Then there was that fling in Venice." Anticipating the czar's response now, I just held my breath.

"But, what did you learn? Why did you choose Italy?"

"Why do you keep asking me, why Italy? What's the big f-ing deal?" I ground my teeth. I was dying to take an extremely large sip of my wine, but I hesitated. Pia would see it as a defensive move. "I love Italy—the people, the language, the food, all the prettiest moments in the tiniest details."

"Isabella, you think this has nothing to do with holding on to him?"

"I know how much you disapproved of my Roman saint, but is this about your validating yourself, or my well-being?"

"What the hell are you talking about?" Pia said furiously, her eyes set in a deadly squint.

"I seriously think all those mental sessions, Pia, have turned you actually mental." I sat there as numbness slowly rolled up my body.

"By the way, Miss Reynolds, you don't have flings," she said, squinting at me so much now that her eyes were almost closed.

"Well, wake up, buttercup, because I did!" I shouted a bit too loudly. I looked around and saw that I now had an audience.

Pia waited for the other patrons to direct their attention back to their food or their own company. "Or maybe you got caught up in numbing yourself with partying and feeling all the enjoyment, while desperately trying to suffocate this pain. You can do that all you want, but as soon as you let up a bit, it will still all be very much alive. Your actions need to destroy the damn monster."

"Dr. Goldstein has ripped out your heart and replaced it with another brain. You can only think with your head. Take off that big hideous rational hat and be a supportive friend.

I'm moving forward. Everything happened for a reason, Pia, and I'm realizing this now, for reasons that you can't simply understand, as this goes back even before our friendship."

She looked unconvinced. "What is your next step, Reynolds?"

"First step, I'm giving a four-week notice for my job at the end of the month. Life is too short. I'm crawling out of the big black rabbit hole."

"And financially speaking, what is your goal?" she asked, with a quick glance to my chest where the Krugerrand would have rested.

"Well, my crazy Cuban czar, I'm selling a couple of my skin care formulas. They are just sitting there, and another company could do some genius beauty work."

"Nine days. Nine days in Italy, Isabella, and now you tell me you have come to terms with Potato, the defective Italian, and your next career move? Are you serious, Isabella?"

"Well, I guess Prosecco and promiscuity can cure a lot, Pia."

She shook her head, but then, distracted by the sight of dessert being delivered to the table next to ours, she said, "We need a seasonal finale to this meal. Dessert?" She was grinning now.

"I'm up for it. But let's head out of here to Max Brenner's chocolate factory. I passed it on the way here."

"A chocolate factory?" Pia whispered.

"Request the check while I head to the ladies room, and then we can head to the chocolate place," I said.

"Why are you going to the ladies room?"

"To pee. Isn't that what it's for?" I turned quickly and walked away. I could feel the almost "deer caught in headlights" expression sting my face. A trip to the new version of Willy Wonka-land would be worth purging $400 worth of sushi and sashimi.

As I looked in the mirror, I reassured myself that Pia's question was a coincidence. I hadn't been lying at dinner when I said I had changed. This would require baby steps, not cold turkey. I never wanted anyone to know—that was part of my ditching Dr. Goldstein. While my reflection stared back at me, I was reminded how good I'd felt in Italy without purging. I was not going to do this to myself anymore, but how could I say no to the "treat for two" that I'd read about on the menu when I'd walked by—two types of chocolate and a warm toffee caramel fondue, served with chunks of banana bread, banana slices, strawberries, and a personal grill to roast marshmallows. I needed my chocolate fix after that dramatic tango with words over dinner. I could feel myself painfully anxious, almost frustrated, almost nauseated, and I pulled myself out of the ladies room and back to safety.

Journal entry—July 12

I'm twenty-nine years old and feel like I'm learning to tie my shoes all over again. I am fighting for myself and with myself at the same time.

There is no guarantee here, and I have a lot of hard work and difficult choices ahead of me, but God, those are the ones I just know have the biggest rewards. I'm blessed for having this chance to realize my mistakes, learn lessons, and have these little but gigantic things called choices. I refuse to be on the road to nowhere or some somewhere. I want to be on the road to everywhere.

I am excited to begin my new life with my brand new post-Italy self, and I have quite a hectic schedule to keep my mind busy. I just need to focus and remind myself that my heart is my light. My heart is my guide. Here is my chance to create a new story for my new soul. Going to the chocolate factory tonight brought me back to childhood, when I used to sit in front of the TV in my Minnie Mouse pajamas and watch Willy Wonka and the Chocolate Factory. *At that moment when Mr. Wonka pushed open the doors and all the kids walked in, mouths dropped and eyes were wide open as he went into his "Pure Imagination" song. "Hold your breath. Make a wish. Count to three. Come with me. And you'll be in a world of pure imagination."*

I'm wishing ...

I. R.

On Tuesday I had my matchmaker date with Clay, the multi-millionaire, at Bette, 8:00 p.m., then to Beatrice Inn, where we danced on the upstairs sofas (as it seemed to be the thing to do—everyone else was doing it) until 3:30 a.m. The Ivy League graduate, a self-made billionaire, brownstone-living sort of handsome man was way too petite for my taste. He was the kind of guy that I would always feel fat around no matter how skinny I was or could become; the kind of guy with whom you would not feel confident walking down a dark street. That was the good news. The deal-breaker was the conversation over my red snapper sashimi and his quail. It seemed that Clay has commitment issues, but thought Sylvie and her team would be the most effective approach to meeting a quantity of women with quality.

On Wednesday morning I left a message for Sylvie—"Thanks, but no thanks"—wanting to avoid the Q&A. I asked her for the next option. That evening I had drinks with Alexa at Waverly Inn, 6:30 p.m., then off to the *America's Next Top Model* after-party at Socialista, 9:00 p.m., with Bobby. After six 'tinis plus three glasses of bubbly, I made it home at 4:15 a.m. From the mascara stains covering my pillowcases, I know that I cried myself to sleep ... again. Talking about change was much easier than acting on it.

Thursday night was dinner with Brady at Perry Street, 8:00 p.m. I was eager to see him and had been anticipating this date since our lovely afternoon before my Italy departure. The time with him was unexpected and everything I could possibly imagine. Dinner, two bottles of wine, and a glass of champagne. Home by midnight and thought about Potato. Cried myself to sleep around 1:30 a.m. Tomorrow would be a brand new day for change and quality of life to start.

On Friday, I had a picnic dinner with Julian and Bugsy along the Hudson River, 7:00 p.m. We stopped by Flatiron Lounge for drinks, then back to his apartment for a three-hour makeout session. We definitely had chemistry for making out, but that was the extent of it. The chef was obsessed with food, which was an obsession that hit too close to home for me. Even during the coming-up-for-air breaks while on the couch, he would speak again of Marseille, the history of the royal family, his favorite rose petal macaroons, and Marie Antoinette. However, the real deal-breaker was when my hand moved up his head and I came across a clean patch—a rather significant bald spot.

I guess that fact that he was six foot three had prevented me from noticing this at first, but it was something that upset me. It was as if he had been keeping it a secret. I guess he couldn't help that he towered over me. Maybe I was making an excuse or being too picky, but I felt betrayed.

My "new self" was failing miserably. I could feel myself walking forward but stepping backward. Even acknowledging it felt draining, and I did the only thing I knew to do. I crawled under the covers. Tomorrow would be another new day with better intentions.

19

THE ITALIAN WAS HEAVY ON my mind during this sun-drenched Saturday morning, and all I could think of was Bobby, Jesus, and watermelon therapy. On impulse, I quickly called Bobby. "Hey, you. Wanna meet at church?"

Bobby always read my mind. "See you in twenty, darling!"

We knew we should not really drink before 11:00 a.m., but if we were having "brunch," then a mimosa, Bloody Mary, or a watermelon martini was acceptable. What was not acceptable was staying at the bar from 11:00 a.m. until 6:00 p.m. When most people kicked off their shoes and leaped out into the New York City sun, the breeze and the brightness made our position at the bar even more delightful as it prolonged our bad behavior.

The bottom line was that as entertaining as my week had been, the deep, hollow pain had kept me up almost every night, and Potato and the defective Italian had been weighing heavily on my mind, shoulders, and what was left of my heart. Watermelon martinis, Kettle 'tinis, and flutes of champagne were my pain relievers of choice. My life had more holes in it now than a screen door. This therapy, my therapy, numbed the pain and the time passed by faster than any other technique I was willing to accept at the moment.

"Bobby, findyourperson.com is not helping me find my person."

"Well, I would say at least you are getting—"

"Bobby!" I quickly interrupted and contemplated if I should be confiding in a guy about this, as he would look at it as an opportunity to checkmate with a new woman every night, rather than find his soul mate.

"All right, Miss Prude with so many rules I have stopped counting," he said while turning the bar stool around toward me to demonstrate that I had his undivided attention, with all jokes aside. "Reynolds, talk to me."

"I'm not finding my person. It is like I have hopped on this carousel of men, and it is going around and around, week after week. I want to get off this ride.

"Sugar—"

I interrupted him accidentally with a giggle, as his Southern accent was coming out, and that was my blood-alcohol test as to what drinking level we were at.

"Maybe you will find your soul mate on findyourperson. com, but maybe you won't. The point is that you are out and meeting people and living rather than the alternative."

"The alternative?" I asked with a smirk, then took a sip of my martini.

"Isabella, you need to live your life. This is it. Make it happen. All of these moments are your life. You keep waiting to wake up one day as if everything will be fixed and this deep pain you always refer to will just be gone. Poof! Just like that. Honey, each date, each laugh, Italy, and so on is part of your healing process. It is your life. Life is not an "until then." Life is happening right now, at this very moment. It is not all going to be perfect, but it is balancing out the pain with some happiness until happiness is the end result. Slowly but surely, eventually, you will find your balance."

He was right. I wanted my plan of action to rid the deep, hollow pain and to be perfect. Here I was again, expecting everything to be perfect, like none of the past would have mattered because it was so imperfect.

"Reynolds, I know you know this. I just know right now that you have lost yourself, so you just need reminding. Findyourperson.com was doing nothing but filling up your address book with men you clearly were not ready to date. All the men looked good on screen, but it is impossible to experience any of them, as your heart is broken and unavailable as a result of everything that had been stripped away from you. They were merely distractions and allowed you to ease back into the swing of things."

After almost five hours of liquid therapy and feeling nauseated, I found myself in the ladies room holding my ringing Pinkberry. Pia was calling, of course. I knew not to answer. I knew my voice and the weightlessness of my words would be heard. I pressed "ignore." Focusing on my reflection, I decided I didn't look so bad after all. I wet my fingertips and slicked back the stray hairs to clean up my ballerina bun. I swiped my cheeks with some blush and applied a touch of gloss to my lips.

Making my way back to the bar, I noticed Bobby on the phone, grinning from ear to ear. "What's going on now?" I asked.

"We're leaving," he said in a surprisingly macho-man tone.

"I'm not going anywhere."

"Isabella, we are going to go meet the Frenchies." Bobby was pushing me to go and meet all of his friends that he had met while living in Paris. I was not dressed appropriately to meet up with civilized people—people who were not aware that I was just going through a dark phase and was not always this much of a mess. This was just me for the past couple of months. Just a phase.

"Hey! You are coming with. It's just a casual tiny bistro on the Upper East Side, Bilboquet. You are not ditching me just to go home, cry in your pillow, and look through your boxes."

"First, do not insult me. Second, I know the place on 63rd off Madison, but—"

"Oh, no, don't even try to get out of it, you stupid little woman. There is a perk. The VP of a major skin care brand from Paris will be there. This is the perrr-fect networking opportunity, now that you are about to escape that rabbit hole you are always bitching about. Although that salad place you eat at every day sounds fabulous. What is that Japanese miso—"

"Bobby. Focus, please," I said, now actually tempted to go. "Let's go. Move it. Move it." I quickly turned around, looking over my right shoulder. "Bye, Jesus."

Jesus winked at me, "Come back soon, beautiful."

A short cab ride later, we walked into the earsplitting and boisterous bistro, where there were four loud-mouths taking up a booth. It was French chaos. Bobby and I wedged in. After we got situated as best as possible, a glass of champagne was placed before me. "Cheers" occurred before the introductions, which was fine by me. To the point, and no wasting time. Thank God they had their priorities straight. This was my type of crowd. The champagne was delicious, too.

These four were definitely all Frenchies. There was the VP, his boyfriend, what I assumed was their drunken woman friend (the French version of me) and Twin 1. Bobby referred to his two of his friends, who are brothers and identical twins, as "the twins," and I had never met them before but apparently I would be tonight.

"So, where is Twin 2?" I asked, wondering if addressing his friend in that manner was completely inappropriate.

"He's on his way," Twin 1 responded. "My name is Jean Luc, and Bobby never shuts up about you."

"Isabella used to run her own skin care company. She created creams, formulas, and um … Sugar, what are those thingies called that are liquid with the dropper?"

"Bobby, it's called a serum."

He was totally being obvious and calling me out in front of Mr. VP. "Oh, yes perhaps that's what it is. You know so much about the skin care business."

So I said, "I just returned from Venice recently," as I kicked him under the table to shut him the hell up.

"Ouch!" yelled Mr. VP as he looked around the table.

Shit, Isabella.

Bobby broke out in his obnoxious laugh, accented with his drunk Southern accent.

"Oh, here comes his inner Southern belle," Twin 1 said, distracting everyone and saving me from having to apologize and admit that I was playing rough footsie under the table. Twin 2 had now joined us and squeezed in, pushing us all closer and closer together. In this frame of mind, I had a hard enough time keeping people straight. Sprinkling identical twins into the mix just seemed cruel.

"Sorry I'm late. Champagne, please, and now," he said, as he removed his jacket.

"You have to be f-ing joking," I muttered. I never thought it was possible to cause another scene within two minutes of my first one. But what could I do? Twin 2 was wearing the same shirt as Mr. Florida, Mr. No. 8 from the bookstore before I left for my Italy trip.

"Excuse me?" Twin 2 said, hesitating to remove his second arm from his jacket.

"Isabella, what is wrong with you?" Bobby was now yelling at me, his Southern charm no longer present. "Sorry, William. I really can't take her in public these days. I told her to just go home and sleep off all those martinis. Anyway, William, Isabella, Isabella, this is William."

"I'm so sorry; I lost my head for a moment," I mumbled, staring at him, wondering still if this was a joke.

He sat directly across from me, wearing an orange and gray version of the mysterious man earlier today in Three Lives & Company with the Florida T-shirt.

Why was the universe playing such a cruel joke on me? "Excuse me, I need to go to the ladies room." I could not stop thinking about Mr. No. 8, Mr. Florida from the Three Lives & Company bookstore, and Mr. Konstantino before my Italy adventure. Was William walking in with the identical No. 8 T-shirt a sign? 33J alleged my number was eight.

Walking into the powder room, I noticed that both stalls were vacant. I put down the seat and sat there, closing my eyes and taking a couple of deep breaths. Before I got a minute to myself, the door to the ladies room opened. The stranger on the other side did not go into the vacant stall adjacent to mine. I could see her heels directly outside my door. She was practically leaning up against my door.

What could this possibly be about? All I needed was another scene. Act III in this tiny Upper East Side bistro. I could picture "Page Six" in the *New York Post* tomorrow. "Three strikes and the crazypants was out and escorted from upscale bistro Bilboquet. Banned from the Upper East Side." Included would be a photo of my drunken self.

I slowly opened the door and suddenly the woman came pushing through, pinning me up against the wall. It was the Frenchies' drunk woman friend, whose name I had forgotten. And she had me up against the wall, her arm pressed against my chest as she attempted to put her tongue down my throat. With my free hand, I began beating her with my Fendi spy bag.

"What the hell are you doing? Help! Help! Someone help me!"

She stopped her assault, her expression absolutely puzzled. "What is wrong? I thought you wanted this?"

"I'm not into girls. I didn't want this. I don't want you. I don't want to be drunk. I don't want this deep, hollow pain. I don't want to cry anymore. I don't want my dog to be dead. I don't want to eat another salad in my rabbit hole. I don't want to be a serial dater. I don't want this curse anymore from Saint Valentine. I don't want …" I stopped, realizing she had run for her own life and out of the ladies room. Was it possible that I'd scared her? Was I actually scarier than an aggressive delusional French crazypants?

Bobby ran in. "Sweetie, what's wrong?"

"Please just take me home. Please, Bobby. Please," I pleaded, crying. "I was just manhandled by the most petite woman in the world."

He was amused and giggling. "Well, shall I contact Guinness Book of World Records?"

"Please, Bobby."

"Okay, Sugar. Okay."

As he walked me home, I wondered if this actually had been a lesbian experience. A girl kissed me.

"So, I don't think I will be receiving a call from Mr. VP any time soon ... or in my lifetime. Maybe it's a sign that skin care is not for me anymore."

"Sugar, I think you are right about that one."

I looked up at the sky and rolled my eyes. "Christ, that was completely and purely French chaos."

On Monday, August 1, I went into the horribly unglamorous rabbit hole and gave my one-month notice. My original plan was to do it first thing in the morning, but my nerves numbed me and every two hours I would approach Mr. Maxwell's office, pass his door, and continue to walk toward the kitchen. It was like breaking up with a boyfriend. Sometimes the hardest things in life are the most rewarding; that is why fear is always a factor. The guilt of letting someone down or telling him it was over would paralyze me. My first-year review mark was approaching so I needed to drop the ball before the big sit-down with the partners.

I decided to send an e-mail first and was surprisingly anxious as I sat before my computer to compose it.

Mr. Maxwell, please let me know a convenient time to speak with you regarding my upcoming annual year review. I would like to discuss some things. Isabella.

I quickly sent the e-mail and waited for a reply.

Isabella, please stop in my office now.

Now? It was the middle of the day. The majority of the creative team and partners were still taking lunch. I was expecting that I would do it at the end of the day and then run out the door. I was not ready for a Q&A right now!

I walked into his office and sat down across from him. It was such a Hollywood moment, as the actress in me came alive and took over. "Mr. Maxwell, I have been struggling with this decision for some time now. I really have enjoyed this past year here at Cosmetique Labs and especially working with this team. However, I am not able to give 150 percent to you at this point, as I am distracted with personal issues at the moment."

The truth was that I was not sure what I wanted to do. But I knew this position was not for me. I wanted something more true to myself and worth living for, as I wanted to kill myself every morning I walked into this office. After Italy, I told myself I would no longer settle—settle for any man, job, or excuse for not being simply happy. Some drastic and unbelievable changes were about to occur in my life. The revolving door had been going around and around, and I decided to step in and enter happiness, leaving misery and chaos behind me.

"Well, Isabella, I am shocked and did not see this coming. Can we talk about a salary adjustment? Make a counter offer? Are you leaving us for another firm?"

I immediately thought of others in my life at that very moment. If only he had noticed the asset I was to him, as Mr. Maxwell did.

Surprisingly, fifteen minutes later, he was supportive, and I was relieved. It was over. I had ended my relationship with Cosmetique Labs. I just had to ride out the storm for one month—they were happy for the extension from a standard two-week notice.

Post-Italy, I was a different Isabella. No one was going to make me feel guilty about anything, not even my Krugerrand. No one, not even myself, was going to sabotage me.

20

Journal entry—September 5

AFTER ALL THE SUMMER MONTHS *of drinking and dating and drinking some more, I am happy the summer is over, along with my job. I never approved of wishing days away. It was wishing life away, but I am desperate for a change. Maybe change will come with this new fall season. Change in colors, a change in me. I pray that it is at least a possibility. I am reminding myself that my actions must match my dreams. They just must.*

I. R.

I woke and had six new voicemails.

First message: Alexa. "Isabella, please call me. I have to tell you about Mr. Gorgeous who is about to buy my penthouse listing on Central Park South. Anyway, the real reason I'm calling is to tell you I went to see Dorthea again [her infamous psychic] yesterday, and I have so much insight for you. We taped our session, and she saw your love life and your soul mate!"

I did not believe in these readings but, of course, Alexa didn't care. She lived her life always waiting and wondering if Dorthea's insights would come true.

"So, his name is Jeremy. Jeremy H-something. He is your soul mate, Isabella. You will have three children in the order of girl ... boy ... girl. You both are from Manhattan but will actually meet on vacation somewhere. He will love you for your vulnerability and your laugh and you will love him for the security that he gives you."

I wondered if Alexa remembered Dorthea's reading about the blue-eyed lawyer who was a sharp dresser. I would meet him surrounded by a body of water. She thought the Italian was my soul mate two years ago. Dorthea had failed to notice that he was a wolf in sheep's clothing. She had failed to mention that this same woman had seen not one but two soul mates for me in a two-year time frame. The soul mate theory was something bigger than a psychic's insight or a pretty word that makes a story perfect. This mystical connotation, finding a profound natural affinity for your other half, was not something you find with a psychic. That was purely a convenience theory and I knew better to follow it as a lead. It would only lead me down another wrong path.

Here is what I know. The word "soul" is part of the word, as your soul does the finding. Not a friend, matchmaker, or website, and especially not a site that uses the word in the URL. You find your own person by listening and being connected to your very own self. A big job that only I, myself can do. Love makes you vulnerable and to find the real deal, you have to face both the known and unknown. You have to face yourself.

Second message: Sylvie. "Hi, Ms. Reynolds, darrrling. So, it is raining men right now, and I must and will introduce you to one of my other potentials. I think he could be your soul mate, and he looks great on paper, and you would look great on his arm!"

I pushed the delete button. She was fired as far as I was concerned. Dorthea and Sylvie both knew my soul mate? Maybe I should set up a conference call and they could compare notes.

Third message: Italian. "Hi, it's me. Just wondering what you are doing. Maybe we would could grab a salad and take a stroll together. Call me. I would like to talk. Call me. Call me, please." As much as I knew not to call him, after everything that had happened, I considered it.

Fourth message: Brady. "Hello there. Good afternoon, beautiful. From your failed efforts to return any of my calls since our last dinner, I guess you are not interested in pursuing this. That's a shame. I hope you enjoyed the rest of your summer. I'm sorry I took up any of your time. Take care, Isabella." The truth was, I enjoyed our last dinner when I returned from Italy. I just was not emotionally available to anyone until I figured myself out.

Fifth message: Chelsea Animal Hospital. "Good afternoon, Miss Reynolds, this is just a reminder that Potato's upcoming vaccinations are due next week. Please call to schedule his appointment."

The blood rushed to my head and the deep, hollow pain in my chest swallowed my heart. I could feel my lip begin to shake and the tears burst from my eyes and slide down my face. "When will everything stop? Just stop!"

Sixth: Italian. "Hi, it's me again. I did not hear from you, and now it has become a bit late. Are your still up for a late lunch and stroll? I really need to see you." I needed to cling to something old. This was the one time that he would really be my Saint Santo, as he loved Potato as well. Wiping my tears, I pulled myself from my bed and peeked through the blinds, hoping that it was raining outside my window. It was the one thing that might keep me from an afternoon walk with the Italian.

No such luck. I went back to the bed and lay flat on my back, closing my eyes. I just wanted to forget about the world that was spinning outside my door. Lying there, I could sense the vulnerable little girl buried deep inside me. I had pushed her so deep that she was scared of me, of this woman I was becoming. She was losing her innocence and her giggle. With each passing day, I wondered if she would ever resurface. I wondered if I would glimpse that innocence and peace in my life again. In my heart, I imagined what it would feel like to live life in a childlike manner. I imagined what it would be like to live fearlessly, instead of worrying about the consequences of my every action.

Completely surrendering to the deep, hollow pain, I called him. We decided to meet in one hour at Magnolia Bakery to do our bench routine. Two pink and two chocolate buttercream icing yellow cupcakes with sprinkles.

As we devoured the sugary treats and poked fun at each other, I felt so much lighter. I looked at him, with icing in his teeth, and me with icing on my lips and fingertips, and felt something about to go down. Would I finally get the apologies, the answers I had desperately wanted to hear from him?

"Isabella, I have something I want to tell you."

Tears began to fill his light blue eyes, which were now sparkling, making me a bit soft.

"Santo, you can tell me anything," I said as I squeezed him and smiled.

"Isabella, I have decided to move back to Italy and not be a lawyer anymore."

"Wow." It was the first thing that came to my mind and rolled off my tongue. Was he serious? I was letting him do it again to me, but this time it was covered in sticky sugar. "Why are you crying? This sounds like a great idea."

"Yes, I know ... I know ... I'm just ... I don't know, Isabella."

Again, he did not f-ing know. For someone who was exceptionally intelligent, he was the most brainless, most oblivious man that I'd ever met.

I could feel the deep, hollow pain in my chest beginning to deepen, making my entire insides feel raw. Everything began to seem colorless, odorless, and tasteless with the exception of the sugary substance that I felt coming back up and stuck in my throat. "Santo, I'm sure if this is something you believe you want to do, then it is the right decision. Follow your gut instincts. I'm sure you'll do just fine." I could not believe what I heard myself say. Sitting there, he just grinned like he wanted to say more but did not want to break down in front of me. After about a minute of both of us staring at the ground, we went our separate ways.

While walking home, I could no longer hold the tears back. They were becoming so heavy that all I could do was let them fall from behind my oversized glasses, making sure to wipe them away as soon as they hit the top of my cheek. I immediately called Desi, which was not the smartest idea because as soon as she answered, I suddenly found it difficult to speak.

"Hola!"

"Desi …"

"Isabella, what is wrong. Are you okay? Where are you?" She could hear me crying. "Just come to my house, now."

"Okay" was all I could whisper.

When I arrived at her apartment the front door was wide open, and she was waiting in her bedroom for me. "Hey, it's me," I called to her. "I will be right there; just going to the bathroom." I went into the guest bathroom and finally released the sugary substance I was dying to purge since I had left the bench. Since I had left him. Here I was, purging again, even though I had promised myself in Italy that this part of me was over. I was so used to the deep, hollow pain in my chest and the emptiness that had taken over that I could not stand to even have two cupcakes with sprinkles in me.

"Isabella, are you okay? What's wrong? Are you sick?"

Great, she had been standing on the other side of the door. "Yes, I'm fine. I will be right out."

I opened the bathroom door slowly as I knew when she got a glimpse of my swollen, splotchy pink face that she would see my condition. Anyone's diagnosis would be "definitely a disaster."

"Sweetie, what has happened? Tell me."

I pulled out a barstool and took a seat at the island in her kitchen while she opened a bottle of wine. Months ago we were celebrating my so-called funeral and my friends were sending me off to Italy. I was right back here and in an even bigger mess.

"Which do you prefer, Gavi or sauvignon blanc?"

"Vodka on ice with two limes is what I need and want."

"Well, you know I have no problem with that, but I'm out of vodka." She picked up the phone, dialed the nearest liquor store, and ordered a bottle of Kettle One. "The vodka will be here in fifteen minutes. Let's have a glass while we wait, okay?" she suggested.

"That will work." I watched the wine fill my glass. I was so embarrassed, praying she would not recall how I was supposed to be in much better shape at this time.

"Tell me, Isabella, what is wrong now?"

The word "now" stung like a bee.

"He is moving back to Italy. He is really leaving."

"Wow," she said.

"Desi. Can you believe this?" I swallowed down my glass of wine, placing it down for her to refill.

"Well, there is your answer, Isabella. Stop believing in someone who doesn't exist. Stop waiting for him to be your friend. I mean, if you need another friend, let me know and I will call the deli back and order that as well." I started giggling as she tucked my hair behind my ear and gave me a huge hug.

When the doorbell rang, I had already gulped down a second glass of wine. I could feel the carefree attitude the alcohol brought begin to take over. Mr. Kettle One had arrived. She pulled two glasses from cabinet, filled them with ice, poured vodka, and topped them by squeezing two freshly cut limes.

"Perrr-fect," I mumbled.

"Cheers, my love," she said, kissing my cheek.

"I know why this is all happening."

"And you know it has nothing to do with Santo, right?" she said, now holding her breath, waiting for the correct response from me.

"Yes. All of this has to do with one person: me."

Three vodka on the rocks later, Vito walked in from work. "Hello, ladies. Already started, I see. It's only five-thirty, girls."

"Sweetie, Isabella had a hard day. We were just having a drink to calm her nerves." The mention of "a" drink caused us to both look at him and not at each other for fear of giving ourselves away.

"Are you hungry? Call Bobby, and let's meet at Aspen for dinner. Tell him to meet us there in fifteen."

As we walked to West 22nd between Fifth and Sixth, I almost started laughing at myself for meeting him, knowing nothing good would come from it. I was more upset with myself and that I lost control at the bathroom when I got to Desi's. Fifteen minutes later, we were in Aspen …well, not really, but I felt free and far away from Magnolia Bakery, that park bench, and especially Italy. Every detail in this restaurant transported the patrons into feeling as if they were dining in a ski lodge. The four of us walked past the long, dark, wooden bar, all admiring the same Lucite deer head above. The music grew louder and louder as we headed toward the back and comfortably squeezed into a white leather banquette booth. The music was loud, causing them to sway to every beat and causing me to smile, as sound somehow smothered the pain. They ordered what seemed like the complete menu. The small plates kept coming. We devoured the polenta fries with gorgonzola sauce, fresh tuna tartare with homemade hand-cut chips, a variety of bison sliders, tacos stuffed with fried brook trout, wild boar sausage, and the grilled corn on the cob that was covered with Mexican cheese and a lime-chile sauce.

This time I skipped the tuna tartare. I killed the polenta fries, double-dipping each bite into the melted cheese sauce and almost refusing to share the corn on the cob. That was not the smartest, as it was not the easiest thing to eat with a mouth full of perfectly white porcelain veneers. Having the perfect smile could be such a hassle sometimes.

As I made my way to the ladies room to remove any kernels from my smile, my cell began to ring. It was Santo. What did he possibly want now? It was almost 9:00 p.m., and he never called this late. I pushed my way through the line in the ladies room and locked myself in a bathroom. "Yes?"

"Isabella, it's me." I rarely heard this serious tone in his voice. I felt numb. I was scared to speak as I was not sure if I wanted the conversation to move forward.

"I'm in a restaurant bathroom and will be home in a couple hours. Can I call you back then?"

"It will be too late then, Isabella."

"Too late?"

I could hear the tears in his voice, a routine I was sick of, but his words interrupted and stumbled from his lips. "I tried telling you earlier. I tried but just could not do it. I'm at the airport. I'm leaving New York tonight for Rome."

"Is something wrong? Is your family okay?

"Isabella, I'm moving tonight. I'm leaving tonight. I'm

calling to say good-bye." Falling against the wall inside the bathroom, I fell forward to my knees and just looked at my phone, not knowing if I even wanted to speak. I couldn't even take a deep breath.

"Santo, you are calling me from an airport to say good-bye to me after everything, like this? This is *me*." I felt like our so-called invisible anything and everything slapped me across the face and then disappeared into thin air.

"I'm glad you're out of my city. I want you out of my life. I want you to just disappear!"

Immediately, I hung up the phone, turning it off as my heart could not bear any more pain. After everything, where was the respect or courtesy of calling me from the airport to say a final good-bye? At that moment, I wished Potato were still alive. I knew things would not be so bad with Santo if Potato were still here. It was the combination of everything and the weight of it. The deep, hollow pain now felt like an endless void. I could no longer hear the voice in my heart, the voice inside of me to tell me what to do.

Kneeling in the bathroom floor, I closed my eyes and tried to collect myself. I had no idea how long I had been in the bathroom at this point. I thought of a picture he had taken of me on the beach one summer in East Hampton. I was walking on the sand along the edge where the ocean comes up to touch the shore. I was walking alone, each footprint stamped into the wet, silky sand. He had taken a picture from behind, without my noticing. I remember seeing the picture and wondering why on such a beautiful day, I was looking down at the earth and walking away from everyone. Why had I looked so lost? I knew that Santo was not the beginning of my forever. I somehow always knew.

Suddenly, I felt disgusting with the fried, greasy, fatty food in my throat and could not help but purge. I never wanted to go to Aspen again. The deep, hollow pain did not go well with a full stomach. I was getting used to feeling empty. Not just my stomach but my mind, heart, and soul.

I collected myself. I gathered my bag and a couple of items that fell out of it when I was on the floor. Tossing the bag on the sink, I stared at my reflection in the mirror.

Dear God, Isabella, how can you have an honest relationship with anyone when you can't even have one with yourself? Where did perfect get you?

I attempted to fix my makeup, but no concealer would hide this mess. Not even if it was rated the best by *Allure* magazine. I moved my bag out of the way, washed my hands, and rinsed out my mouth a couple of times before heading back to the table.

As I passed the bar, I stopped to order vodka on the rocks. I was worried that after getting sick, I would lose some of the numbness the previous efforts had given me. It was never about the food or the alcohol, just the purge and the numbing. It kept me company, as I was already now too alone.

In one sip, it was gone. Staring at the empty glass of ice, I realized I forgot to squeeze my two limes. I realized I could not accept a membership to this path I was heading down. As I stumbled back to the table, I felt weak, and my bag felt extremely heavy .

I could also feel the loneliness in the midst of the restaurant crowd. I could not hear anything, but since I could see everyone at the table dancing and having a wonderful time, I slid back into the banquette, smiling and moving to the music.

I hid my pain. I hid it all. Staring in the mirror that hung on the wall in front of me, I stared into my sad eyes. I thought, *I have failed me.* I was surprised no one noticed because tears made my blue eyes wet and sparkling. Thankfully, no one was in their right state of mind to notice anything.

Two hours later and five more vodka on the rocks later, the party moved back to Desi and Vito's loft apartment. Walking back, I staggered behind. My entire body was numb, and I had no idea how I was even walking. "Isabella, get your ass moving. Come on!"

"Okay, Bobby." I started running on tiptoe to protect the heels of my Manolos from my drunken stagger.

Then, it happened. I don't know how but suddenly I was lying on my back—flat on my back with my designer clothes and pea coat covered in God knows what. All I knew was that I felt sopping and my head throbbed as it hit the ground. I lay there staring at the sky. I was everything that I feared. I was not perfect. It did not matter how perfect my outfit was, my hair, my body, or my smile. My inner self was showing at this very moment, and it was nothing short of disgustingly ugly.

"Isabella! What are you doing down there?" Bobby, Desi, and Vito each had grabbed a part of me and were pulling me to my feet.

"You hit your head so hard. Thankfully, you are so wasted that it could not have possibly hurt too much. Thank God," Bobby said. He seemed so happy for that, but if he only knew how much everything else hurt ... "Isabella!" Bobby screamed so loud and horrified, we all stood still. "Why are you wet? Where did all this water come from? Oh my God, did you pee your pants, you crazypants?"

"Wait a minute," Desi said, grabbing my spy bag. "Sweetheart, why is your bag full of water?"

Everyone was just staring at me and I really wasn't sure what was going on or why my Fendi was full of anything.

Bobby was horrified again. "Were you carrying a bottle of vodka in there, you insane little person? Oh, be careful, Desi, her bag is probably full of glass, too!"

"It must be from the sink!" I cried.

Trying to take control of this odd and frightening situation, Vito said, "Desi, let's get her back to our house."

"Hold on!" Desi interrupted. "Isabella, why is your $2500 bag full of water or vodka or whatever it is?"

My eyes were blurry, hurting, and hardly open. "He's gone. He called from the airport. The saint is gone."

"Free at last, free at last!" Bobby screamed. "The cord is cut."

Desi shook her head at me, confused. "The bag, Isabella, the bag?"

"The faucet must have had a motion detector. I didn't know it was filling my bag up."

"Wait just a minute," Vito interrupted. "You are telling me you carried your bag entirely full of water from the restroom, back to the table, and sat there for another hour?"

Desi started to giggle. "Come. We are almost to my home. It's nothing all your friends can't cure."

"And the Fendi?" Bobby asked, concerned.

"It's just Fendi. Isabella is a bit more important, Bobby." Desi shot him the evil eye.

Inside their apartment, I sipped an Earl Grey tea without even taking off my coat and asked Bobby to put me into a cab.

Finally home, I stumbled off the elevator and turned the corner to my apartment. There it was, sitting in front of my door—an arrangement of twenty stargazer lilies blocking the entrance to my apartment.

I brought them in and placed them on the coffee table while settling onto the couch. I grabbed the card but hesitated, not knowing if I should even read his words.

Isabella, I could not leave without sending you these. I never left without doing so. I will miss you terribly. Sending you a squeeze and big kiss.

Here I sat, alone. Potato was gone, but his smell wasn't. The Italian was gone, but the smell of his flowers wasn't. All I had was myself, but even I felt no longer here. I felt as if I was losing everything all over again.

I stood up, grabbed the lilies and card and took it all outside to the trash chute. "Ciao," I whispered.

21

THE PHONE RANG AT 7:30 A.M., and of course it was Pia. No one else had the nerve to call that early, but she had her personal training appointment at 5:30 a.m. three days a week. However, I had not slept. I was still sitting on the couch, staring out at the moon and now the sun.

"Finally! Where have you been? I have been so worried, Isabella."

I took a deep breath and focused, as I did not want to slur my words. I had just stopped drinking five hours earlier and was still a little intoxicated. "I went over to Desi's for dinner."

"Why don't you ever answer your phone?"

"I did not want to be rude and be on my phone while I was a guest at their house." "Isabella, are you okay? You sound funny."

"What are you talking about? What are you saying? I'm just tired. I'm just so tired of everything. I can't take any of this anymore. I need to go. I need to finish getting ready for work." I really just needed to hurry up and make the sick call as there was no way I was making it in today.

"Listen to me, Isabella. Listen good. I think you need help. Please consider going back to Dr. Goldstein."

"Are you out of your mind? I already know what I need to do."

"Isabella, you are not perfect. No one is perfect. Why do you put this perfection label on yourself? Why do you feel that you have to live that way?"

For a split second, I actually considered another mental session with Dr. G. and thought she could help me get started with the "get up and dust yourself off" routine I needed to start immediately, if not sooner.

I was trying to think about the past couple of months, measuring my alcohol intake. Yes, I was going out a lot. Yes, I drank when I was out. Didn't most people do that? I mean this is what I needed to be doing. Was I supposed to just sit at home and cry in my pillow? (Well, it's not like I didn't end up doing that anyway.)

"Isabella, are you listening to me?"

"Yes, silly, I hear you, but you have no idea what you are talking about. There is no problem. I'm just in a bad place and a bit of a beautiful mess. I know I can handle this. It is me, for Christsake. This is life; it can't get in the way. Life can't destroy life; only I can and I won't let that happen.

"Isabella, life is full of lessons, and loss is one of them."

"I am experiencing a couple of difficulties at the moment, but I will get through this. Now, I'm getting off the phone as I have a lot to do today. I need to say good-bye."

"Okay. I just pray you know what you are doing."

"Thank you darling. Let's do a dinner soon. Love you."

"Love you, too, Reynolds."

I hung up the phone and tossed it on the couch. This was definitely a gym and steam day. As soon as I flipped on the light, I saw what appeared to be a disaster staring back at me. Another night of Isabella. Another night of not washing my face. I thought of the reflection I'd seen the night before in the mirror at Aspen. There was no way I could leave my apartment today.

I picked up my phone again and called in sick. It was best to stay in and relax and enjoy the chilly day, as today was my last official day of the rabbit hole anyway. My good-byes had been said, along with the cake at lunch to say farewell. I put on my Columbia University sweatshirt, and ordered Chinese for three (I was trying to make some changes in my life).

Journal entry—October 16

It has been over a month since my last journal entry. I'm wondering if it would be easier to just write backwards.

I'm sitting in Union Square Park, sipping an extra-hot soy latte on my favorite park bench across from the playground. I'm sipping while trying not to burn my tongue or the entire inside of my chest, as it is a bit chilly today.

I'm watching this little blonde girl swinging. She has an adorable blunt bang short haircut. I can't stop admiring how it suits her and her age. She must be around six or seven years old. She is swinging alone, staring at her feet while she's kicking her little feet forward, then swinging them behind her with all her force to get higher and higher. She probably thinks she can almost touch the sky. I watch her little feet and then look at mine and contemplate that she has greater strength and weight in hers.

For some reason, I can't get past "go" and collect my life back. This mess is following me everywhere I go. I am beginning to feel closer to it, then myself. I want to try and reach the sky. I sit here in disbelief. I cannot believe that I'm still here in this mess. How could my own heart fail me so badly?

I love this bench. It suits me more than the rabbit hole I was sitting in. I'm going to head to 79th and Madison to Le Maison du Chocolate for a cup of hot cocoa and get lost in the MET museum. They are hosting the "Art of Love in Renaissance Italy" exhibit. I'm going to go remind myself of Cupid and 33J. I'm going to go and find inspiration this afternoon. I will find my voice again. I will swing high and attempt to reach the sky, again.

I. R.

Journal entry—November 22

It is 5:30 a.m., and I'm lying on the couch. I dread the flight that is scheduled to take me home for Thanksgiving for an extended holiday vacation.

As much as everyone complains about the effort of traveling to spend quality time with each other, at least I can say I have somewhere to go for the holidays. With all of the loss, I often question the definition of "home" and what it really means.

My flight is scheduled to leave at 7:30 a.m. from LaGuardia airport. As I write this, I'm watching the time pass by, minute after minute. I considered being a no-show this year. Maybe I am enough for this year. Besides, my skin and my energy is a clear mirror into what I am feeling like on the inside. And then there is the turkey and pecan pie pounds I will gain while home. Having to sit with my perfect pearly white smile at a table with my entire family asking "How is New York, Isabella?" would only make the food I was trying to eat feel like razor-sharp fingernails sliding down my throat. I am so very tired. I am mentally, physically, and emotional exhausted. I do not want to get on that plane. Am I a terrible person?

I. R.

Glancing over at the clock again, I saw it was 6:49 a.m. I continued to lie there and just watch each minute pass. It seemed to go fast. At 7:31 a.m., one minute after my flight departed from New York, I called my family to say I would not being joining them this year. I was sick in bed with the flu.

I called Bobby and Alexa and asked if I could join them this year for dinner. For the first time in my life, I was abandoning my family. I was not going to be there for them. I needed to begin this mourning that Dr. Goldstein referred to. I was ready to march forward.

22

AFTER THE THANKSGIVING BOYCOTT, I became even more anti-social, disappearing from every scene. Just like Thanksgiving, I did not go home for Christmas or make any fabulous plans for New Year's Eve. I was trying to slow down and deal with myself. By being around everyone and the Q&A, it would have just refreshed the pain that I was trying to live through. It would have just kept bringing it back when I had not entirely gotten it out the door yet. I wanted to see if I could hear the voice that used to be with me before "perfect" took over. I desperately wanted that little girl inside me to feel safe and to come out again. I wanted that purity, that honesty. I needed to find a way to change. I was beginning to see the vicious cycle of my fake perfect world. The fake perfect me. The idea of perfection had consumed me. I had no idea where my lies ended and my truth began. My truth was lies, and even my lies were lies. I had no idea if I had any truth left.

I spent Christmas with my New York family—Bobby and Alexa. We went to Alexa's apartment in the East Village; I brought the wine, cheese, and dessert from my favorite French bakery, while they spent hours in and out of the kitchen. Setting up dinner on the coffee table, we sat together on the floor by the fire. We ate. We laughed. We were thankful for us. However, we were not thankful for such full bellies as, at one point, we all had to unbutton our designer skinny jeans, but most important … I didn't purge.

It was that night that the opportunity presented itself. It was that night that if I had not been listening, if I had not been a bit aware, the moment would have passed me by. I would have missed it—the opportunity to wake up and take control of my life. To stop the spinning out of control and fight my way back. To fight for everything I wanted for myself and in my life.

After dinner we just lay around on the floor, surrounding the fire. We were full. We were silent. The room was consumed with warmth and the sounds of crackling wood.

Alexa began to speak, waking us a bit from our fullness. "We should do something. Right now. Together."

Bobby sat up, which seemed to require so much effort. "Honey, we just ate like fat kids. I would call that something. We should promise never to tell anyone about this tonight. Look at us!"

"Like what?" I asked, ignoring Bobby. I could not help myself, as I sensed something in the room that evening. I felt a part of me that I had not felt in a long time. A part of me that was ready for something new. A change. For the first time in a while, I felt clearer. I had silence within me. I was listening.

"Well, since we are here together this evening," Alexa continued, "and a New Year is approaching us, we should make a list of goals for the New Year. We should write them down and give them to each other. We can support and help each other out."

I sat up and tried to hold back the tears that were beginning to form in my eyes. "I think that is a fabulous idea. This is exactly what I need. I need this. I need change. I need to make some promises to myself."

We each took some paper and a pen and went to different areas of Alexa's apartment for privacy. I stared at the blank page before me and didn't need much time to think on what needed to be written. I put pen to paper and effortlessly wrote what came to mind.

New Year Resolutions for the new "me"
- *Take better care of myself.*
- *Learn to love me.*
- *See my family more.*
- *Be imperfect.*
- *Attend church (the real one) and become more spiritual.*
- *Read a novel each month.*
- *Find a charity to become involved with and give back.*
- *Laugh out loud.*

- *Take responsibility. My actions must match my dreams.*
- *Learn to say no.*
- *Celebrate both my accomplishments and non-accomplishments.*
- *No more Chinese for "four." Depend on me and not B&P.*
- *Believe in me. If I can dream it, I can do it.*
- *Stop searching and start living.*
- *Write more in journal. Acknowledge my feelings.*
- *Declutter by cleaning out the closet.*
- *Always forgive. I will not be my own prisoner.*
- *Love wholeheartedly.*

In a month and two weeks, I would be entering my thirties, and I was determined to break the doom-and-gloom cycle, curse or not. I was not only determined, but I would carry my Krugerrand as a positive reminder.

Journal entry—January 1
I woke up early this morning. I feel an unexplained excitement. This is a new year for my new soul.
I. R.

As I walked to the gym, I took in deep breaths and enjoyed the chill in the air and the strength of the breeze. While waiting to cross the street, I stood next to a girl holding a yoga mat. *I should add that to my list*, I thought. I'm always hearing about the benefits of yoga. It was hard to believe that I'd lived in this city for so long and never attended a class.

That was probably equivalent to never going to a Barney's sample sale, visiting the Museum of Modern Art, or sipping a Bellini at Cipriani's downtown.

I entered Equinox but headed straight to the café. I needed a double espresso. While waiting, I stared at the menu. I had been a member for over a year, stood in this very line a million times, and I had never noticed the extensive organic menu that my gym offered, with a wide variety of juices such as Red Gulp. Ingredients included beets, parsley, watermelon, strawberries, and ginger for "cleansing, detoxing, and rejuvenating," the sign proclaimed. Those three words—*cleansing, detoxing, and rejuvenating*—made the Red Gulp call my name, just like the ham and cheese sin at Le Bergamot once did. All my years of nutritional studies never touched upon the holistic aspects of the field. Universities focused more on the clinical aspect of the science. Of course, I understood fasting, but Columbia didn't include Red Gulps in its curriculum.

"I'll take a Red Gulp."

I watched as a rather petite man behind the counter grabbed solid chunks of raw ingredients and forced them through the loud contraption that I assumed would extract the very liquid I was to suck down. It was a bright red, thick concoction, not as pretty as my watermelon martini, I must admit, and I was guessing it would not be served with a perfectly placed fruit wedge.

I slowly took a sip, watching the juice come up through the straw toward my lips. Yep, it was warm and completely disgusting. I did not taste any watermelon or strawberries; I tasted beets, with a bit of an earthy grassy after-taste. It caused me to gag a bit, and I made an embarrassing choking sound. Of course, this caught the attention of everyone in the café. Even drinking a Red Gulp was dramatic for me, but I didn't care if others were looking at me or not.

One … two … three … I sucked it down. I just kept repeating those three words to myself: cleansing, detoxing, rejuvenating. *If anything, think of your skin, Isabella. Beets are loaded with nutrients and betaine for cleansing.* The taste was definitely an appetite suppressant. This drink alone would help me attain resolution number twelve: no Chinese for four.

As a result of my newfound nausea, I digested a bit, and then used one of the computers available for members to browse the Internet for information on juicing and my new little friend Mr. Red Gulp, as he would be replacing everything Kettle or 'tini. The results displayed "juicing recipes," "juice fasting," "holistic retreats." *Retreats?*

At the top of the listing was a juice-fasting retreat in Long Island, New York. I did not even need to click on it before knowing that I would be going there. As I read through the website, it called out to me. "Five-day fasting retreat." "Juice only." "Detox." "Rejuvenation." "Cleansing." "Daily yoga." "Life-changing." Was this a sign or coincidence?

Scrambling for my Pinkberry, I dialed the contact number for Lotus Holistic & Healing Yoga Retreat. "Good afternoon, I'm calling to inquire about the retreat and your availability."

"Of course. The next juice fasting retreat with daily yoga is January 11th through the 16th. Check in would be the evening of the 11th with a prefasting meal. The cost is $2400 and includes room, juicing, yoga, and workshops."

"Workshops?"

"Daily discussions on various holistic topics and meditation." Something clicked, locked, and I could hear myself reading my credit card digits over the phone. Five minutes later, my Pinkberry buzzed as the confirmation e-mail for my holistic retreat trip was booked.

I had to call Alexa and tell her what I'd done; to tell her how much I appreciated her resolution idea. "Well, hello, Ms. Reynolds. How are you today? Starting your resolutions, I hope!"

"Alexa! You are not going to believe what I did!"

"What, Isabella? Where are you? Did you hop on another plane? Are you in the United States? We just made our lists less than twenty-four hours ago."

"Wow, you guys really think I'm insanely insane. I'm on U.S. ground, darling. I woke up this morning, saw a girl with a yoga mat, had a Red Gulp and ... I am leaving in ten days for a holistic juice fasting and yoga retreat somewhere in Long Island. I think the area is considered the 'other Hamptons' and is somewhere near our Hamptons."

"Wait just a second. Slow down and take a deep breath. I need a minute to connect all the dots. Isabella, have you ever done yoga? Not eaten for five days? Do you like juice?"

"Well, no, no, and no, but sometimes the best things for us in life are not always the easiest, right?"

"I think it is great that you are aggressively pursuing change and beginning your resolutions. But let's not forget that you are an unbearable monster when you don't eat. The martinis suppress it, but I don't think they will be serving them between yoga and self-reflection hour. You know that, right?"

"Yes, Alexa. I have a week to wean myself off of MSG, kill the Kettle, and drink some juice. What do I have to lose?"

"Well, you have already lost your mind. I guess nothing, really."

"Did I mention no cell phones are allowed? I even asked if that included BlackBerries. The girl who took my reservation was not amused."

"Isabella, that Pinkberry is like a sixth finger on your right hand. You are going to go mental there."

We both started laughing as it was clear I was a crazypants; neither one of us had to say it. Fasting. Purging. Martinis. Juicing. Happy. Just wanting to die. I was all over the place.

The day before I was to depart, I called Desi to tell her about my five-day fast and how she would not be able to reach me. Sometimes Desi was not the best person to go to. Twenty minutes later, we ended up at Pastis for bleu-cheese burgers, fries, and champagne. She said I needed a last supper. I hesitantly agreed but could feel the anxiety for being away for this period of time and not being about to B&P. I knew this was not a terrible thing, as I was going here to let this controlling routine go. I was superior to this cycle. I was stronger then, it as I gave it life and I could also take it away.

Then it was Sunday, the day I had anticipated. The car service would be there at 2:00 p.m. to pick me up and take me out and away. Maybe the Pastis cow I devoured yesterday had not been a clever idea.

Besides getting away for an entire week, I was looking forward to comfy clothes, no makeup, reading novels, and no food (especially Chinese) or alcohol. Most important, I was standing by for the inner peace and silence to surround me.

I grabbed my Louis and tossed in a bunch of cotton pants, tanks, socks, cashmere hoodies, and my must-have products, which did not include any makeup. This was going to be the cleanest week of my life. I hoped my own body would not reject itself.

The car arrived right on time, front and center outside of my building. I tossed in my bag, slid in, and put on my Gucci shades.

"Ms. Reynolds, are you ready?" the driver asked. "We should arrive at your destination in one hour and forty-five minutes. Will there be any additional stops before we leave the city, madam? "

"Actually, yes. Can you please stop at the first corner here on the right? I need to make a tiny stop."

I quickly went in to my French café to order my ham and cheese sin with a large, freshly squeezed orange juice. I smiled at the girl behind the counter and as always, she flashed me her smile of recognition. And then it clicked. I didn't want people to recognize me, especially not like this. The secret binger, the anxious food addict, the woman with a hole in her chest, on the other side of the counter, hiding behind big shades.

"Bonjour," she said.

"Hello. Sorry, I have had a change of heart." I walked out sin-free and paused for a moment in the sunlight. The warmth reminded me how nice it felt to not walk in shadows but toward the light, and so I headed back into my rescue ride.

This "other Hamptons" was not going to include yachts, lobster rolls, Mr. Cristal, Mr. Cavalli, or Mercedes chauffeuring people to their must-get-to scenes to show off. I placed my iPod ear buds in my ears to avoid any conversation with the driver and any questions regarding where I was headed.

I had been in the car for twelve minutes. Just another hour and thirty-three minutes to go. *Now what, Isabella?* I could not make any phone calls; my plan was to just disappear. I turned around to see the Manhattan skyline fading behind me. As I turned back around, I told myself that this would be different from Italy. I was running away then. Now, I knew I was going to go and fight for the new me. I wouldn't return this time until I got it right. I started freaking out within minutes and craving a something from Starbucks or even a Diet Coke. I had only been in the car now for twenty minutes, and I could feel the onset of a panic attack. I was actually surprised I didn't pack a handful of Zone bars or some mini bottles of Kettle in the secret inside compartment of my toiletry bag. *Focus, Isabella.* I took my mini-panic attack for exactly what it was and acknowledged the test that would occur on this trip. I would have to fight discomfort, pain, loneliness, and all the above, with me and only me. It was necessary to create a new relationship with food.

I rolled down the window, pulled back my shades, and turned up the next song, "Fix You" by Coldplay. This was a bit too relevant so I forwarded to the next song, "The Story," by Brandie Carlile. I stared out the window and watched the trees blur by. This was what my life had become over all these months. Just one big blur. I was floating from one day to the next, drinking, purging, crying, dancing, falling, and crying some more. *Where had I been and what and who had I missed?*

I had lost more than three parts of my life, but eight months of my life. Gone. Just like that it had passed me by, and I let it happen. Brandie was exactly right, I needed to create a new story, not of where I had been but where I was going.

I took a journal with me, as I was never one to freely express my feelings. It was always much easier to put a pen to paper and not be forced to own things 100 percent.

Journal entry—January 11
The night before: the prefasting meal

I'm here alone with strangers and, surprisingly, not uncomfortable. I have checked in and settled into my room. Nancy, a sixty-ish woman and the director of the retreat, has just given me a tour of her home. She is so in love and connected to her mission with yoga and juicing for all of us. She has created beautiful paintings throughout her home. They are as much alive as the people within these walls. To witness the beauty of her relationship with her mission, beliefs, efforts, and passions is a confirmation that I have not been in a true relationship with myself. Her artwork captures a world of emotions, as it's so lifelike. I stand close to her paintings, trying to see where the stroke begins and ends, but I can't find it. I stare into her ocean waves, the sparkling eyes of a little boy, the color of the sun, the shapes of the strawberries. Her work inspires me to want to examine life closer. To see the details. The retreat is at her home. Not just any type of home, but an odd, rectangular-like shape, similar to a barn. The couch, drapes, carpet, bedding are all organically made. The water throughout the house is filtered and pure. I have never seen anything like this. All the rooms are separated with white linen, sheer drapes, and no doors. Her life is transparent, open, with nothing to hide behind. Everything is open and connected in its own way. Her most important place, her home, that houses everything meaningful to her is clear and clean. Every detail of her house, her diet, has been thought through. The rectangular windows that line the walls shape the sunlight that enters the room. The room is heated by the large fireplace, which fills the air with the woodiest smoky aroma. This is where we will have our morning yoga and meditation daily at 9:30 a.m.

At 5:00 p.m., I joined the other three guests for our last meal. Our prefasting meal. We gathered around the table and introduced ourselves, as Marisol, the juice chef, placed the prefasting foods before us.

All of us are similar in age but come from very different backgrounds. The thing that is connecting us is the reason we are here. We are all looking for change within us ... our lives. All of our problems are different, but our purpose is the same.

Abbey has recently lost her father to a heart attack. Heart disease runs in her family. Her father was only fifty and had the attack while shopping for dinner at their neighborhood market. For not only herself, but for her father and her widowed mother, she is here to have a healthier life.

Jasmine is here to learn how to eat better on a more consistent basis. However, I can see through her, as I see a bit of me in her. By the way she looks at lack of food on the table, I know she is here to not only lose weight. She is here because she is tired of purging, or because she not does have the control to starve herself at the moment. This is the ideal world for her, this place, where someone will enforce the fast, the restriction. I think she definitely is "packing," and by that I mean coping methods of choice.

Laurel has admitted to us that she has been using cocaine for the past two years to numb herself from recent events she would not share. What began as an indulgence has now become her addiction. It has now become her life. She is not willing to go to rehab. She feels like she can do this on her own.

All three of these women remind me of myself: the death and loss of a loved one by a disease, the eating disorder which forbids you to ever accept yourself, and self-medicating with a negative means of coping, as my 'tinis had become toxic. I am all three of these women. All three of these women are me.

We broke up the heavy table talk and started making jokes about the food. Our last meal consisted of a couple leaves of organic romaine surrounded by a shaved cucumber peel and topped with a teaspoon of pumpkin seed and Udo oil. What looked like pasta was actually zucchini strands with a blend of a tomato puree and topped with basil. A sauerkraut mixture was served on the side, which I completely passed on. Forget about a nice glass of wine; we were not even served water with our meal. Drinking did not occur while eating to protect the digestion and absorption of these nutrients.

After dinner, which took about five minutes to eat, we scattered around the house for some privacy and quiet time. I sat by the fireplace in the floor and sipped some peach detox yogini tea.

I still can't believe I am here ... I do not feel alone. I have never felt so connected to my pain. Almost as if it and I were here together, working together, as we now wanted the same thing—to move forward.

As I was returning to my room for the night, I passed a sculpture. It was made up of multicolored glass balls in various sizes, all natural colors, all stacked on top of each other. It resembled a spine, perhaps a person's core. That is what I'm going to focus on while I'm here, my core. While walking away from it toward my room, I felt myself stand up a bit stronger.

Until then ...

23

IT WAS THE FIRST MORNING of the fast, and it was 8:10. I had slept for twelve hours and had dreams all night about the upcoming days and nights. It was less than a month from my thirtieth birthday. Here was my first step to taking better care of myself. I laughed at myself and checked two resolutions off my list.

After starting my morning off right with a multiple-head turbo shower, I put on what I considered yoga-like clothes by Vince: a pair of cotton black pants, a tank top with a black cashmere hoodie, and black cashmere socks. No four-inch heels for a week. The house was freezing, like the Arctic Circle. Nancy kept it like this, as it enhanced the detoxing process. I wrapped my hair in a ballerina bun, and for the final touch, smoothed on my Jurlique moisturizer and a dab of shea butter across my lips. I was looking forward to the end of the week and flaunting healthy features again.

As I walked out of my room, I could hear the sounds of Regina Spektor's "Better" playing and smelled the woodsy aroma from the fireplace. Everything was cozy. The girls were sitting around on various oversized chairs, covered with blankets, reading and occasionally sipping from small clear glass bowls.

"Good morning, Isabella. Please come and get your potassium broth."

"Thank you. What exactly is this for?"

Everyone looked up from their novels at Nancy, waiting for a response. I guess no one thought to ask.

"As soon as you are situated, I will go over everything, including the retreat rules," Nancy responded. "I am very excited about the next five days for all of you. This is the beginning of your new beginning. A new way of thinking, feeling, eating. A new way of living. A new way of being. Let's get down to business. The retreat rules are simple and must be followed."

She then read from a paper, which we all got copies of.

Retreat Rules

- The "F" word is prohibited. (By the way, this took me a second, but she was referring to "food").
- There is no eating for the entire five days during fast.
- Two juices per day will be served, one at noon and one at 3:00 p.m.

- Potassium broth is offered to keep your electrolytes up and so no one faints during yoga. This will be served at 9:00 a.m. and again at 5:30 p.m..
- The day is yours to spend how you like. I recommend taking this time to reflect, to feel. You can use any area of the house or even take nature walks. (I laughed. Take a walk? Leave this house? I knew better. I would find a Starbucks, a Zone bar, or perhaps a tree twig if I was hungry enough. I put myself in lockdown.)
- Promptly at 8:00 p.m., movie night begins. We will meet in the gathering area.

"Does anyone have any questions?" she asked, surprisingly serious, as yesterday she's been all sweetness.

We all looked at each other. No one asked Nancy anything. Across all of our faces were signs that we clearly just hoped for the best.

"Okay, ladies, let's get ready for yoga. Please grab a mat, remove your socks, and take a spot in front of the fire. Our first session will focus on breathing and meditation."

We all got situated; I made sure to be in the back. I had no idea what I was about to do or if I could even do it, for that matter. We all sat on the mats with our legs crossed at the ankles, and our palms resting upward on our knees.

"Let's close our eyes and begin to breathe. As you exhale, repeat ohm …"

Well, she lost me at close your eyes. I was already uncomfortable at this point. I closed my eyes, slightly separating my lashes to catch a glimpse of what everyone else was doing. I moved my mouth in the "umm" sound, but nothing came out. I felt completely out of my element. Also, after a couple of minutes I realized it was not "umm" but "ohm," which sounded a bit like "home."

About fifteen minutes into what seemed voodoo-like, I got the hang of it. I was letting go. I was letting go of the fear of doing something that seemed so extreme and unusual. I raised my voice a bit louder with each "ohm ..." and at some point even forgot to peek at everyone else. I was saying my "homes" and keeping my eyes closed.

As always, I spoke too soon. Nancy said, "Now take a deep breath in, pull your head upward to the sky and your sexual organs down to the earth. Straighten your core." *My sexual organs?* I could feel myself blushing and felt ridiculous at being almost thirty and embarrassed because an adult said "sexual" out loud.

After several poses with names like tree, triangle, cobra, and downward-facing dog, we came to a prayer pose, and my first session came to an end.

"Please lie on your backs and extend your legs out. Lie still and remain with your eyes closed."

I could hear her standing up now and moving around, but I was scared she would see me if I opened my eyes to peek. All of a sudden, she placed a blanket on me and a pillow on my stomach, like she was weighing me down. "Please relax. Remember to breathe. Stop thinking. Take this to fill up with peace, with silence. Start your process of change now."

I was trying not to think. I was trying to be silent inside, but I could not stop wondering how long I was suppose to remain on the floor with a pillow on top of me. Now whispering, she said, "When you are ready, please move back to the table for your first juice." We all removed our pillows and blankets and gathered around the table. While waiting to be served our first cocktail, I noticed that table was covered with markers and paper. I was hoping that we were not going to be asked to draw our sexual organs.

Marisol placed a glass filled with green juice in front of each of us. Wait. What was this? I had practiced on red juices; this was green.

"Your first juice is made of spinach, cucumber, celery, parsley, and green apple. We refer to it as the Greenhouse Effect. Now, before you take your first sip, smell the juice. Become one with the juice. Now take a sip and hold it in your mouth. Feel these living things in you. Taste the life inside you."

Jasmine politely interrupted the silence, "Nancy, how did you find such balance? How did you figure it all out to get your life like this? If you don't mind sharing."

I glanced at Laurel and Abbey and realized they were wondering as well. It was comforting to know that I wanted to know the formula to personal success.

"Dear, think of the colors black and white. They are both extreme and at opposite ends of the scale. Black is being not focused and life passing you by. White is being your 'things to do' list for each day, month, year of your life. The list that robs you of actually living. Although these two colors are both extreme and opposite, they are actually one and the same. Neither has balance. So ask yourselves, ladies, what about the gray?"

We all sat there in our comfy clothes, legs crossed and sipping pensively.

"Albert Einstein once said, 'Life is like riding a bicycle. To keep your balance you must keep moving.' Think about this, girls," she said as she walked back into the kitchen.

After our first insightful liquid gathering, I returned to my room to rest. Being anti-social was not a concern here. Quiet time and reflecting were very much promoted here, as the goal was self-awareness. I was surprisingly sleepy just after breathing and sipping. The chaotic carousel of my life stopped and for the first time in a while, I felt the effects from beating up my body and spirit so much.

Drifting off, I imagined standing in my apartment bedroom before my framed pictures of my loved ones. All of a sudden, I found myself standing in my childhood home in the small town in South Carolina. I was alone, tiptoeing down the long hallways. It was silent and the house was empty of people and furniture. Where were my family, the dogs, our friends, and even the nanny? I walked to the front door, stepped outside, and headed down the driveway. I looked around the land; there was no one, not even our dogs. I was all alone. What was I doing here? Why was I in South Carolina?

The town consisted of about 20,000 people. It was one of those towns where everyone knew each other's name, and people often called each other by their first and middle name. The town had one stoplight, one movie theater, and a one-stop shopping center, Sam's Club. The town was saturated with every fast-food chain imaginable.It was ironic in a way. I was living a life in Manhattan that did not resemble anything that I came from. Growing up, my only hope was to just blend in and not seek any extra attention, and now my fake perfect world was consumed with being unique, standing out, and being the best. The fog of the delusion was clearing a bit and the two sides to the story in my life were revealed: the real one and the fake perfect one.

The sound of whispering woke me. I saw Jasmine standing behind the sheer curtain that hung in the entranceway of my room. "Isabella. Sorry to wake you, but it's time for the 3:00 p.m. juice."

"Oh, my God, I slept the whole afternoon. Thanks, I just need a couple minutes."

I realized that is wasn't the loss of my company, Potato, or the Italian that caused me to fall apart. It was me. It was the way I had been living and seeing myself in the world. I was not being true to or honest with myself. All these years, cracks had formed, and then the three-strike curse shattered me. The curse was not from a Saint Valentine.

I took my place at the table as Marisol placed another concoction in front of me.

"Thank you."

"Of course, Isabella."

I smelled the dark, reddish-brown juice.

"Ladies, this juice is what we refer to as Bleeding Hearts. Begin inhaling scents of tomato, beets, lemon, carrot and celery."

"Too funny—Bleeding Hearts. You said a mouthful there, sister," I said, as I looked around and realized everyone was giggling. I took a slow sip and held the nutrients in the back of my mouth for a couple of seconds before swallowing. I wanted to appreciate it all. I wanted to sip it slowly to make it last, as this was my last meal of the day. I simply wanted to slow everything in my life down, as I was beginning to figure some of this out.

I excused myself from the table, grabbed a blanket, and lay down beside the fireplace in front of a large window, directly in the sunlight. We all seemed to be enjoying the self-reflect mannerisms and keeping to ourselves, so I didn't feel terribly rude. I sat there and sipped, occasionally opening and closing my eyes. The sunlight was intense; it felt as if it was penetrating deep into me, warming my insides. I had missed this feeling. The pain had hardened me, along with the excessive martini therapy, numbing me from feeling much of anything these past six months. Finishing the last of my juice, I lay on my back, pulled the blanket to the top of my chest, and finally closed my eyes, just wanting to fall asleep again.

Potato and I were walking down 20th Street toward home. It was fall, and the seminary bells were ringing. The block was full of nuns, and the sidewalk was lined with golden leaves that had fallen from the trees that lined the streets. Potato kept barking at the nuns covered in black from head to toe. He tried to eat the leaves. He was behaving like a mad, wild dog. One of the nuns looked up at me while passing and smiled. I was immobile under her gaze. What seemed minutes could have only been a second. As I directed my attention back down to Potato, he was gone. Fear shot through my entire body as I helplessly looked around. He was nowhere. I raised my hands and noticed I was no longer holding his leash. As I turned to find the nun to ask her if she had seen my dog, she was gone. Everyone was gone, and I found myself alone, standing on the street, surrounded by fallen golden leaves.

I was a having a Dorothy from *The Wizard of Oz* moment. I was standing on this yellow brick road, wanting to click my heels to go home. To go home and find Potato sleeping on the couch. I now knew that I was in a dream. I knew this as I knew, without a doubt, that he would not be there waiting for me.

The chill in the air woke me, and I was shivering. The sunlight was gone, and it was close to dark. It was 6:00 p.m., and I was due for a mug of potassium broth.

Marisol was setting up the area near the flat screen in the living room. It was two hours until movie time. I was actually looking forward to getting comfy and watching a movie, as this was a new adventure in its own way, similar to my airport escapes.

I took my mug of electrolytes back to my room and prepared a hot bath with Epsom salts to assist in the entire detoxification and purification process. While the water filled the tub, I tied my hair into a ballerina bun and strategically applied a fruit enzyme mask. My reflection in the mirror this time seemed slightly familiar. I was staring at a girl who acknowledged that she had problems and was on her way to correcting them. For a second, I felt the little girl inside. I think she smiled back at me.

Slowly sinking into the steamy bath, I exhaled, taking in every second. Everything was silent. This allowed me to clearly view this path of self-destruction out of this game we call life. My thing was that I did not want to be that girl anymore. That girl had cracked up over the years, becoming unglued, and there was really nothing else to do but shatter into bits and pieces. I did not want to continue being a crazypants. I did not want to be a woman who lived in a fake perfect world, never mourning disappointment or acknowledging loss in her life, never exposing the actress. I was eager to be a woman who would grow from all of this. All of the lies, bad choices, pain, abandonment, and loss. I was ready to become a woman who would say, *Whatever it is, it's okay. I am strong; I will be fine.*

That night, I tried to watch a movie, but I became irritated every time an eating scene or food shot was in the picture. My stomach did not growl, but it was yelling for attention. Obviously, my only choice was to sleep it off.

24

Journal entry—January 13 (day two)

WHY DO I PRETEND TO expect so much but live with so few real things in my life? Why am I still so desperate to find this unexplainable love? I continue to hurt only myself. I continue to inconvenience only myself. Does any of this truly exist? If so, can it honestly last forever? Will I have found that crazy insane love for another? Each time I lose at anything, another part of my heart feels broken. I'm weak. My body and my soul need a break. I simply cannot handle another painful event right now. Do we just experience these circumstances throughout life to reveal portions of who we are? Is there an alternative? Does one exist? What comes with "I love you"? What comes with "I love it"? A promise? A bond? A self-sacrifice? With all of these unknowns, how can I not live in fear?

Today is not so bad, but without any distractions or numbers, I feel beat up. The same routine, but with the Eye-Opener (apple, celery, lemon, and carrot) and the Virgin Mary (lemon, celery, tomato, spinach, and beets). I can't believe it myself, but I am not hungry. My skin is glowing and I feel alive, especially because I'm feeling, yet no tears here ... yet.

Until then ...

It was the morning of the third day, and it seemed I couldn't sleep past 7:15 a.m. I felt productive before I even left my bed. As I lay there staring out the sheer oatmeal curtains at the sun, I could not ignore that my stomach was definitely screaming at me. Placing my hands down on my lower abdominal area to shut it up, I was startled. *Oh, my God! Hip bones!* No purging. No 'tini therapy. Waking up before noon with my porcelain skin and my hip bones jutting, I almost fell out of bed. I could see that I got addicted to things quickly. Juicing was becoming my new best friend.

Following my morning shower routine, ballerina bun, black sweat suit, and a nice morning massage, I headed for yoga. I was getting used to the cult-like language, including references to my sexual organs. This surprised me, as I was always shy when it came to conversations regarding private matters like this, even around my best friends. Just as I was getting comfortable, Nancy announced that we would be working with a partner today. *A partner?*

I was paired with Abbey, the five-foot Asian girl. I felt absurd, at five foot seven, towering over her noticeably smaller frame. Even though I was thin, I could see the fear in my partner's eyes as she looked across my chest at my swimmer's shoulders. As Nancy demonstrated the spine stretch, I watched in horror. My partner sat behind me with her legs spread open; I sat between her legs with my back toward her and legs tucked in. Next, she was supposed to wrap her arms around my legs and roll me back on top of her. The problem was that her short arms could not reach around my legs, as my wider shoulders and 32 C chest was causing a bit of an issue.

Eventually, Abbey was able to lock her hands around me and roll me back, making me dreadfully uncomfortable—it wasn't good for my "Am I fat?" complex. This complete stranger was embracing me, and I was lying in between her legs. I sat there with my eyes tightly closed, praying this moment would end. The French chaos flashbacks were coming into play.

"Abbey, so sorry, but I need to run to the ladies room. Must be all the potassium broth." I whispered so Nancy would not hear me. I paced myself until I got to the corner and then ran down the hallway, only to hide in my room behind the curtain-like door. This exercise was way out of my comfort zone. So, I did what I do best. I hid in my room until I assumed the exercise was over and prayed that I would not wake up with a "stress bump" tomorrow morning. I felt guilty for abandoning Abbey without a partner, but I was sure Nancy would step in to take my place.

My friends had a theory about me and my comfort zone around women. I was secure in my sexuality but suffered from what they referred to as the "Sister Theory." As a result of not growing up with sisters, I was uncomfortable doing things around girls. Things like undressing in front of them, using the bathroom with the door open, or demonstrating affection, such as hugging for more than five seconds. The locker room at my gym was torturous.

While I had some free time, I decided to sit there and simply collect my thoughts by writing.

Journal entry—January 14 (day 3)

I have been thinking about power lately. About keeping it and not let anyone or anything rob me of it. It is frightening to think how people can and will take your power, causing you to doubt yourself. This is your own personal test. This is where your strength is challenged. This is where your "self" must prevail. Each time you give in to fear and doubt, a small piece of "self" is lost. If you're not careful, you could be left with nothing. You will have lost yourself and that is everything. Nothing to be. Nothing to offer. I'm hiding in my room and abandoned another person because of my own fears. I have robbed her of the experience Nancy was trying to teach us. Look at me. I have removed myself as a result of fear. I have been so wrong. Giving up some power, having doubt, experiencing fear does not take a piece of my "self" away. Letting go is frightening, but experiencing the challenge is how I would prevail. I am not losing my "self" each time. I am creating a new one with each uncomfortable obstacle. I feel so ashamed; I just failed myself and Abbey.

My entire life, I have tried to "fix" everything and everyone—everyone but me. Being here makes me realize that letting go each day is allowing me to see my worth.

I. R.

I could hear Marisol's voice and now knew the morning juice was being served. As I went to rejoin everyone, Nancy popped around the corner. "Isabella, what happened to you?"

"I'm so sorry. I was just feeling a bit light-headed and had to take a break to splash some cold water on my face. I'm much better now."

"Please join the others for your juice," she said, staring at me pensively.

Today was a nice surprise. Day three's concoction was the Berry Patch, with strawberry, blueberry, apple, and lemon.

Marisol gave me my juice with the warmest smile and said, "It is my pleasure."

Sitting around the table, smelling the juice, and watching each other sip slowly had become our normal routine. It was funny how none of us would admit that we were hungry as we watched to see who among us was the fastest sipper. That was the dead giveaway. None of us wanted to seem like the pig at the table, which was quite entertaining as we had not eaten in three days.

The days felt long and short at the same time. Today had passed quickly and soon enough, we had made it past our second juice (another Bleeding Hearts), two cups of the "so you don't pass out" broth, and then it was movie time. I decided to skip movie night again and head to my room to spend the evening alone.

This was the end of day three, and I felt myself getting

anxious and irritated. My teeth were hurting a bit, which I assumed, was because they had not chewed on anything in days. I was tempted to slip Marisol a fifty for just one almond, but knew nothing would come of it. I could see myself waking up the next morning and seeing the bill taped to the refrigerator and Nancy humorously using me as an example of bad behavior. A simple thought of biting and chewing that almond could last for minutes. I found myself now constantly thinking about food, but not B&P. Being here and not having access to food allowed me to keep an eye on my emotions and triggers that cause these unhealthy coping ways.

My eyes grew heavy; I could no longer fight the weight and let myself gently fall into a deep sleep.

Journal entry—January 15 (day four)
I had a lovely dream last night.

It was spring in Manhattan. People were out and about. My quiet, tree-lined street was so refreshing. Walking down the street to Le Bergamot, I admired the magnolia trees and the chirping of the birds. They were singing so intensely. It was a perfect Saturday. I walked into my favorite French café, only to find it empty, waiting just for me. I took my corner table at the window and ordered a double espresso and, of course, the ham and cheese croissant. It was so peaceful, so familiar. I stared out the window, watching the sunny day begin to turn a bit cloudy. A storm was setting in, and I looked forward to being trapped inside the café to sip coffee and stare out the window.

It was then that a man, who seemed in his late twenties, slowly passed by. He turned, looked at me, and stopped abruptly. We both looked into each other's eyes. His eyes were emerald; they froze me like kryptonite, and I became stuck in the moment. Suddenly, it started pouring rain, forcing him to look up, away from me. He never looked back and unexpectedly ran around the corner. I had never seen him before but felt like I had known him my entire life. He looked at me with such recognition.

When I woke, I could not get him out of my mind—his masculine chiseled face with the small dimple in his chin, his head of black hair, and those eyes. How could it have been a dream? I sat up in bed, wondering if I would ever see him again. The feeling was so intense; he felt familiar and real, so much that even though I was asleep, this was so much more than a dream. Was this a premonition or perhaps a past life catching up to my future one? When I came to a state of completely awake, I remembered. It was him. It was Mr. No. 8. It was Konstantino.

Starvation must have been kicking in. I was left with only hunger pains this morning and, of course, a stress bump centered perfectly on my right cheek for all to see. Obviously, my secret weapon to immediately rid this visitor from my face was my whipped egg yolk applied with a Q-tip every thirty minutes. But I had no access to yolk. I couldn't even pay someone fifty dollars for an egg to smear on my face.

Tomorrow is the last day. Carlos, my driver, will be picking me up at noon. I'm looking forward to returning to reality and creating a new map. I am really looking forward to having a life again.

P.S. Nancy has promised she has saved the best for last. Tomorrow morning we will be sipping Pick Me Up (peach, pineapple, and orange) and then another Greenhouse Effect for dinner. Yummy … yummy … as there is literally nothing in my tummy.

Until tomorrow …

As my bags were placed neatly in the trunk, I turned around one final time and looked at this place that had transformed me. That had forced me to re-examine myself. I had been spiraling out of control and reliving each day with the deep, hollow pain. In these past five days, I realized that was okay to let go of that pain and that there was no reason to feel guilty for doing so. It did not mean I was forgetting and letting go of the memories.

I knew I had a lot of obstacles ahead when I returned to the concrete jungle and Manhattan mania. I needed to make a "Things I Must Change" list.

I sunk behind the driver's seat and caught a glimpse of myself in the rearview mirror. I looked fabulous, and I was not even blown out, manicured, pedicured, or dressed from head to toe in any of my favorite men. My skin was glowing, with no discoloration or even surface capillaries staring back at me. There was nothing like not having dark circles under the eyes or not having to hide late-night imperfections with dabs of foundation. I was looking at my classic, clean face and couldn't agree more that less is best.

My hair was pulled tightly back into a ballerina bun, and I was cozy and comfy in my black cotton sweat suit. I felt pure and, I must admit, super skinny, as I had shed seven pounds from the liquefied spinach, beet, and God-only-knows concoctions, as well as the intense yoga therapy. I never would have guessed that standing around making warrior poses and pushing your sexual to the earth while stretching your head to the sky could cause such a transformation.

"Miss Reynolds, please fasten your seatbelt," Carlos reminded me. He flashed me a boyish smile in the rearview mirror when he caught me checking myself out.

"Thank you," I said, and thought, *Yes I have one hell of a ride ahead of me.*

To start off my Manhattan maintenance plan, I scheduled an appointment for a superficial exfoliation, a microdermabrasion. I just loved how the tiny aluminum oxide crystals flowed over my skin. Increasing skin cell turnover never felt so good.

I pulled out my journal; I wanted to document everything. I never wanted to forget this very moment. I turned on my iPod and started writing all my emotions as they flipped through my heart like a deck of cards.

My chest was full of an intense energetic feeling, like it was going to explode. I could feel my soul smiling and the spirit of that little girl who once lived inside me. I had never felt stronger in my life.

Journal entry—January 17 (Manhattan-bound) -
I'm listening to "January Rain" by David Gray. The song is calm, clear, and gentle. Gentle enough to write and feel to. To unleash the mind

and heart and let it wander. I sit here, both secure and insecure at the same time. It is a nice balance. A balance in response to Einstein that I won't forget to keep moving, but will always remember I control the speed.

This past week, I learned that truth and only truth is my identity. This is what gave me this newfound power, and I didn't want to lose it. I knew better, though. As human beings, we get so caught up in life; in our own wants, rather than our needs. Our fears rather than our own confidence. My living such a dishonest lifestyle led to more deviant behaviors. Without truth, I'm not doing myself justice or any of the people in my life. Perfect doesn't exist. That is why it was always impossible to live under the "P" theme. I lived for it, rather than for me.

I feel prepared to do anything to protect it, to keep it. I realize what living really means to me and the journey is our life, not the final destination. Every moment, day, month, year is what counts. Living for myself, loving myself, is the foundation of who I am, who I need to be and where I will end up. I had a self-revelation, or should I say, my self revealed itself.

My truth is, I am a human being and my imperfections are just as special and unique as my perfections. They are equally beautiful. I am blessed that I had the strength to lift my head out of this black hole. Something in these past five days clicked. I am not sure if I can ever truly explain it or perfectly define it. The retreat changed my life.

We only have one life. Anything can happen from one second to the next. If we don't live it, if people don't try to fight for something, then what's the point? Life sometimes seems cruel, but it's just the way to clear our path (or help us clean out our closets) so we can see the choices we need to make and all our opportunities ahead. Everything is an opportunity. Everything is a possibility. It is simply up to me. That is my power. That is my truth. No one and no circumstance like fear can rob me of this, except for me. In fact, the next time fear comes knocking at my door, I will say, "Thanks for stopping by, but my house is already full with hope, passion, dreams, and heart. I have no room for you!"

The most important thing I needed to do is love me. Love is different for everyone. There is no one-size-fits-all in love. I not only need to learn to live with my feelings, but I learn to embrace them, positive or negative, and learn from them. I admit that they are not problems just with my emotions but also with several relationships in my life, including food. I admit it. I own it.

I am ready to live my best.
I. R.

"Miss ... madam. We are entering the city."

"Already?"

"Yes, you have been quite busy back there. Would you like to stop before your final destination?"

As I watched the car move through the crowded city streets, I felt slightly nervous. "Stop, Carlos! Please pull over, right there. I will return shortly." I slowly exited the car, and I stumbled a bit, as I could not believe what I was doing. I opened the door to the small store. I stood there and looked around the menu and all my options. The room was full of symbols and signs.

"Excuse me. I'm ready. I want Chinese, the symbol for

"truth."

"Please read over the consent form and sign at the bottom."

I grabbed the paper and quickly scribbled my signature.

"Where would you like it, sweetheart?" The process came so naturally, the decision so easily. I sat down and placed my left arm on the table and flipped my wrist over, facing up. "Right here, centered on the inside."

"You have a birthday coming up, I see, sweetheart. Wow, Valentine's Day. Your man must have a tough job," he said with a wink. "How about a sweet pink for a sweetheart?"

I was a Valentine's Day baby, and I needed a little color in my life. "Sweet pink would be lovely."

The intimidating twentysomething man with black latex gloves and more piercings than I had time to count secured my wrist. He began wiping my wrist with rubbing alcohol, and the aroma was so overwhelming that my nose burned and my eyes teared. He filled the needle-like instrument with my sweet pink request and put the wand to my wrist.

"You ready, sweetheart?" He looked up at me with anticipation.

"Go for it," I said, leaning back. The noise was nail-bitingly loud and not so soothing. There was no pain. There were no second thoughts. I don't think anything could top the deep, hollow pain that I had been living with, certainly not a pink needle. Two minutes later, there it was—my "truth" symbol.

I admired my freshly done "tat." I laughed as I thought of the next time this Southern belle returned home—Miss Reynolds and her pink tattoo.

25

AFTER WALKING INTO MY APARTMENT, I dropped my bag and fell onto the couch to check all the missed voicemails over the past five days. "Please enter your password, then press pound. ... You have seventeen new messages." I began erasing messages until I got to the very last few, which would have been the most recent. "Hey, there, Isabella, it's Alan. I haven't heard from you in months and wanted to see if you would like to join me for dinner tonight at Cru, say 8:00 p.m.? I hope you are wonderful. Big kiss"

I wasn't sure what to do. This was my first evening back, and I was tempted to see my perspective now with a findyourperson.com failed potential and in Cru, as they had the best martinis in Manhattan. I wasn't ready to call up any of my friends, as I didn't feel like talking about what it was like not eating for five days and my desperate thoughts of paying the housekeeper fifty bucks for one almond. I felt fabulous and looked great.

I scrolled through my phonebook and pressed send. It went straight to his voicemail. "Hi, Alan, it's Isabella. Dinner sounds great; I will see you there at 8:00 p.m. Looking forward to it." It would be a nice relaxing dinner; he did make me laugh, even though he eventually got on my nerves. For some reason, the evening would always start off fun but then quickly turn into "I love you, Isabella. What would make you happy? How about a brownstone with a bulldog? Do you love me, Isabella?"

The thing was, Alan had good intentions; he was just a mess from his crazy divorce, ex-wife, and his super-high maintenance four kids. I mean, would there really be any energy left over for all of my high maintenance? I never questioned that I was a complete handful. Wasn't I supposed to be the one who traveled with so much baggage? Plus, I assumed Alan, being in his mid-forties would soon be going through his midlife crisis—he was already in love with a twenty-nine-year-old and always talked about his abs. Now that my head was a bit clearer, I thought that maybe I'd been too hard on him. Everyone deserves a second chance, right? Well, after my episodes, I was a firm believer in perhaps two or three chances, unless the issue was cheating. If cheating was the case, then I was a firm believer in running away.

I had not eaten in five days, and there were strict rules for breaking the fast. Over the next couple of days, I was to drink only water and tea and consume fruits, vegetables, and clear soups. Being able to order off the menu and then not get sick and spend the evening in the ladies room was my challenge.

After a nice long shower, I was in my closet contemplating what one should wear after a week-long retreat and being cleansed to the bone. As I began trying things on, I was overwhelmed with choices, as everything looked fabulous on me. I glanced down at the tat to remind myself again of the past week at the retreat. No partying, no bingeing, no purging, and look at me … I felt amazing and happy.

I decided on a pair of skinny J Brand jeans with a navy V-neck Donna Karan blouse, tucked in. I grabbed my Chanel clutch and slipped on my four-inch black Manolos. I felt a tingle in my toes after a week of wearing socks. I couldn't swallow putting on a lot of makeup on my newborn nourished skin and didn't need it. I lightly brushed on some powder with a swipe of blush and some mascara. As I stood there in the bathroom my reflection staring back at me, I could not help noticing how I was smiling. Not my fake pearly white smile, but my smile.

Walking into the restaurant, I noticed Alan was already sitting at the bar.

"Well, hello there, beautiful," he said. "Dear God, you look breathtaking!"

"Thanks, I hope you've not been waiting long."

"No worries. I thought I would have a drink at the bar. I really wasn't sure if you would show," he said, his grin confirming his mistakes on our last date.

We sat at a snug corner table. "What kind of wine do you feel like having?" he asked.

"You decide; I will be pleased with your choice." I knew if I said I wasn't drinking it would spark up the conversation of "How?" and "Why?" The fact was, Alan was fully aware of how much I drank, and I was fully aware that we could order a bottle of wine and I could fake-sip on the same glass throughout the entire dinner, and he would finish it.

The menu was perfect for breaking my fast. I ordered the roasted shallot broth and the salad of baby greens, substituting the dressing for olive oil and lemon juice. Alan never questioned anything and or realized I wasn't drinking. He was always too consumed with his ex-wife's drama and his needy kids.

"I mean, can you believe she wants more? She has the house, the cars, our friends, and a direct link to my wallet each month." He finished with his hands in the air, waiting to see if I could think of anything else.

"Darling, you have your pride, a fresh start, and the responsibility of a role model to your kids," I responded with a firm nod.

"Seriously, she wants me to be miserable. She is ruining my life. I have nothing left."

"Alan, you have wonderful kids. Did you ever think what she wants is what you are doing right now?"

"What is that, Isabella?" he asked, leaning back into his chair and folding his arms like I couldn't possibly understand. Obviously, he didn't get any of it either.

Trying not to be distracted by the cufflinks, I said, "For her taking up every minute of your life with misery." He began to speak again and I zoned out. I sat there nodding as he complained. Then, it hit me. Was this what I was missing by being numb this whole time? I looked at him across the table, observing and occasionally agreeing, but all I heard was "Blah. Blah. Blah." This older man sat across from me. This man, only after a handful of months of knowing me, was in love with me and wanted to buy me a brownstone and a dog. This man wanted to take care of me. I was being desperate with this him. Sitting there confidently, I knew what I wanted not from but with a man. Alan was not it. I wanted an equal, a partner, someone to stand beside me, not in front of me. I wanted to share my life with someone. Someone who could learn from his mistakes instead of reliving his history and all of his regrets. I now saw that he had not even learned from his mistakes, as he was so bitter. He had not mourned the loss of his "things" and had not realized that what was important was the respect from his kids. I knew this would be our last encounter. As soon as I left Cru, I knew that he would never be a part of my crew, as he was sinking his own ship.

Journal entry—February 8

It has been two weeks since I returned to the city. I am feeling great as a result of continuing the yoga, sucking down a daily juice, and no Jesus and watermelon therapy. When I awoke this morning, I focused on deep breathing to clear my mind. As I lie here and write this morning, I realize something is not here. The deep, hollow pain. I inhale and exhale, feeling the lightness of my soul. I know what I have to do today. I know that it is long overdue.

I. R.

I threw back the blankets and brought my legs around to the floor with only my toes touching. I pressed into the wooden floor, testing my stability. I felt strong, secure, and surprisingly ready.

I went into the bathroom, pulled my hair into a ballerina bun, and splashed some cold water several times on my face. It was time to clean out the hall closet, removing all the mental cobwebs and the closet of pain.

I could hear my phone beeping; I had a text message.

Good morning. I'm in New York for the week, arrived last night. Are you free for lunch this afternoon? Santo.

Talk about timing. I needed an honest good-bye with him. I needed to say good-bye to the Roman saint as well as cleaning out the closet. Now that I had found my truth, I wanted to see Santo.

I replied to his text. *Meet me at Ernie's, 1:30 p.m.*

That would be the perfect place—my church, my house of pain, in which I wasted months of my life on watermelon therapy and tears on this man. I was ready to stare my past in the face. This time, there was no fear, no need to show my teeth and scream. None of that would be necessary, I realized.

I arrived first and took a seat at the end of the bar. Jesus was in position as usual. "Hey, beautiful. I haven't seen you in quite a bit. Watermelon 'tini or Kettle on the rocks with two limes?"

"Hey, I will have an Earl Grey tea and a bottle of a Pellegrino, please."

"Is everything all right, Isabella?"

"Better than ever. Thanks for asking, Jesus."

Santo was running late. I passed the time by sipping my soothing tea and taking in the restaurant. I didn't like it at all and couldn't believe I spent so much time there. I wondered what else I hadn't realized for months.

"Ah, Isabella. I'm sorry."

"Hi, Santo."

"Sorry I'm late; it was a rather late late late night."

He'd had a late night? This was the guy who thought staying up past 1:00 a.m. on a Saturday night was crazy.

"I didn't get home until close to 5:30 this morning."

"Excuse me?"

"We ended up at 1 Oak," he said.

Damn it. I had forgotten to send him my restaurant list—that was my place. "You went to a club, Santo?" It was then I started analyzing him a bit closer. He was a mess. He looked weathered, exhausted, and now, I realized, smelled like the night before.

"Would you like to just sit at the bar for lunch or get a table?"

"Oh, I can't eat, Isabella. Excuse me. Let me have a glass of sauvignon blanc," he said to Jesus, who hesitated for a second, curious to know who my friend was. It seemed that even Jesus did not approve of the saint.

"Santo, you are drinking more on an empty stomach?"

He didn't respond.

"Jesus, I will have another tea and the yogurt and granola. We will be eating at the bar. Sorry, I will be eating at the bar."

Santo's head jerked back toward me. "Ms. Reynolds is not drinking?" He looked confused, waiting for my response.

"No, I'm not drinking. I guess you could say some things have changed for me." How the tables had turned, and I was thankful to be sitting on the less messy side. For the next hour, he complained about his life, never once asking me anything beyond how I was doing. Wait—my mistake. He did ask if my granola was good.

Sitting beside me today, he resembled the mess I once was, and I resembled my better half. As much as I wanted to be there for him, to listen, I reminded myself that I was not his "PG"—his perfect girlfriend—anymore. I reminded myself that I didn't need to be a perfect person. It was unfortunate that this man next to me never really knew me. It was not completely his fault. I hadn't even known myself until a couple of weeks ago, but he was not capable of even seeing that.

We walked out of the restaurant and briefly hugged a final good-bye. I put him in a cab, as I wanted to take a stroll. I watched the cab head south down Seventh Avenue. He turned around and waved a couple of times. As I watched him ride away, only one thought passed through my heart: *How did I ever think he was the one, my person?* Santo was just like my other saint, Saint Valentine. At one time, it was thought that two Saint Valentines actually existed. Santo, although one person, had two completely different sides, and it didn't help that I only saw the one I wanted. However, the same rang true about me. Nothing was his fault. I don't believe the saying that love is blind. It's more like love is blinding. Love makes you blind. Completely and ridiculously stupid.

We rarely made each other laugh. We didn't have our "own" language or favorite place or song. He never knew when something was on my mind or even recognized my different voices, even my "disappointed" one. We would often go to bed angry. He would be passed out fast asleep, while I lay next to him, concentrating on the hurt and loneliness inside of me. All I had were my silent victories. My little secrets. Well, not the homemade chocolate chip cookies anymore, now that I had confessed to that one.

I simply smiled and realized it had stopped being about us a long time ago. I had been in competition with myself for his "favorite woman in the world" title. There was my honest good-bye. Good-bye to him. Good-bye to us.

After lunch, I was ready. It was time. It was necessary.

Once I got home, I went to the closet. With both hands, I pulled the doors open at the same time and slid them back. Face-to-face with all the boxes, I struggled with where to start.

Did I start with the least painful, or did I get the crying over with immediately and just start with Potato's belongings?

My goal was to spend the next couple of hours removing and promising never to fill the closet with pain again. I started with the company boxes first. I pulled box after box down, cursing myself for never sending anyone skin care products for Christmas. After the sale of the formulas, I meant to get rid of this stuff. Actually, I really shouldn't have been so hard on myself, considering I was pretty incoherent during the holidays. I decided to toss out half of the products and place the remaining products, for my personal use, back in the closet. All company files, headshots, press releases were carried out (several trips) to the garbage chute at the end of the hall wall and tossed. Wow, what an improvement already!

Next up was Italy. Everything to the garbage chute and tossed. *Ciao! Arrivederci!* Just to prove to myself that I was no longer angry, I did keep the $5000 vase and all the designer handbags I had received as gifts. I did experience a breakup, and I felt that I did suffer enough, so it would only be right to keep these items and use them on occasion, when necessary. I placed them on the couch to be reintroduced to my own closet.

It was now down to the final box that sat in the back of the closet. This called for me to step inside the closet and slide it forward to the front. I sat down on the floor, took a deep breath, and opened each side one at a time. There it was:

Potato's abundance of toys, feeding bowls and, of course, all of his designer collars, sweaters, and winter coats.

I touched each item, smelling and embracing every one of them. As the tears poured down my face, I finally mourned my Potato. The difference was that I did not feel the pain that always accompanied the thought of him. I actually found myself smiling as I cried. There was no doubt that I missed him dearly. The difference was that I was consumed by all of the things that we did, not that tragic day. I neatly placed everything back in the box, taped it together, and slid it back into the closet. I would never get rid of his belongings. I closed the closet doors, took a deep breath, and walked away.

26

I COULD HEAR THE PHONE vibrating against the wooden floor. Slowly opening my eyes, I noticed it was still dark. "I'm trying to get my beauty sleep, people!" It was officially Valentine's Day; the clock read midnight. I was thirty years young and even though I was dying to sleep, I would have been devastated if my family and friends did not call at the strike of twelve to say happy birthday. Every year, it was a contest to see who got through first at exactly twelve and not a minute earlier. I fell back to sleep after all the warm birthday wishes, leaving Bobby's rendition of the Happy Birthday song on my voicemail.

I woke up the next morning, excited to start my best new year. Walking into the living room, I pulled the blinds open to take a look at my day. There it was—the sweetest surprise: morning blizzard in Manhattan. A snow-covered New York City was one of my favorite things in the world.

Oversized snowflakes came from all directions, resulting in a mass of white outside my window. I sat on the sill, taking it all in. I began imagining myself inside a snow globe, looking at the outside from within, at my world being completely shaken up, with everything flying around me. I knew that life would eventually settle back and still continue, even if everything did not fall back into its original place. It's how we live our lives and carry on that makes all the difference in the world.

After quickly throwing on a Juicy velvet sweat suit, a Northface hooded down coat, and a pair of Uggs, I grabbed my keys and headed to the lobby. The snow was such a surprise that my smile caused my face to hurt. It was also smart to check my mailbox as I expected an abundance of birthday cards with money. The elevator doors opened and to my surprise, I was greeted by a very stressed-out Miguel.

"Happy birthday, Ms. Reynolds."

"Happy Valentine's—wait, how did you know it was my birthday?"

He gestured behind him, and as I looked over his shoulder, my mouth widened and my jaw dropped. The lobby had turned into a florist shop full of an assortment of fresh flowers, which included Santo's damn stargazer lilies, dozen after dozen of red roses, along with happy birthday balloons. The rest, I would have to figure out when I returned from my walk.

"Where did all these come from?"

"Miss Reynolds, we have received deliveries nonstop

this morning. I didn't want to wake you, as I thought you would sleep in on your birthday. Are you heading out?"

"Yes, just for a short walk. Can you please have all of this brought up to my apartment while I'm out?"

"Of course, not a problem," he said, finally taking a deep breath.

The chill in the air was unfriendly but gave me pep. The snowflakes continued to fall, with the tiniest ones landing on my eyelashes. I walked to the corner to Le Bergamot for some rich, creamy hot cocoa, but then I had a change of craving. I was thirty today but felt like a little girl. This little girl wanted a cupcake with sprinkles on her birthday. My spirit deserved it, after all I'd put it through. This was going to be a birthday exception, as I was sticking to my healthier lifestyle post-retreat. In a perfect diagonal path across the street, I headed to Billy's Bakery.

"Good morning. Happy Valentine's Day." The girl behind the counter was whipping smooth, fluffy butter-cream icing on cupcake after cupcake, making it seem so effortless. She pinched the baby pink sprinkles and dusted them over the hot pink sweet treat.

"Happy Valentine's Day," I said as I smiled back. I realized I would repeat this phrase throughout my entire day.

"So, what is your sweet tooth in the mood for this morning?"

"I will have exactly what you are creating right there, and a hot cocoa to go."

As I walked back home through the white streets, I savored every delicious bite, topping each one with a sip of cocoa.

It was almost 10:00 a.m., and I hurried home to get ready to meet Pia at the Peninsula Hotel for a champagne brunch and anti-aging spa day. Dinner was at 8:15 p.m. at David Burke & Donatella on the Upper East Side. We spent the day at the spa, as now that I had entered my thirties phase, anti-aging regimens were appropriate and a necessity. At 5:30, Pia and I headed up to Bergdorf's to change into our party attire before meeting the others at the Gramercy Park Hotel Rose Bar for martinis.

I found a black baby-doll dress by Alice + Olivia that had cap sleeves and a mixture of black and diamond jewels and beads from shoulder to shoulder. Paired with my four-inch Manolos and a tightly slicked-back ponytail, it was my perfect birthday suit. It was simple, but not simple enough.

Pia and I looked stunning as we walked through the entrance of the hotel and made our way to the bar. Alexa, Vito, Desi, and Bobby were already at the bar, and I could hear Bobby yelling at a rowdy group of people. At first, I could not tell if he was fighting with them, as he always talked about three octaves higher than the rest of human species. Getting closer, I saw that he was indeed fighting with this group of unfamiliar faces.

"And what do you think Ian's thoughts would be on this?" Bobby demanded.

"Who is Ian?" Pia asked.

"He is referring to Ian Schrager, I'm sure, and I don't even want to know why." If Bobby was dropping names, it only meant trouble.

The largest of the three men sitting at the bar stood up now, slanting his face toward Bobby's. "Who do you think you are?"

Bobby leaned toward the guy, who most likely was about to hurt my dear friend and his uncontrollable mouth. "I'm with the New York State Board of Health. Yep, that's right, a health inspector. It is against the law to be smoking in here. What are you going to do now? I'm going to call the police if you don't put out your cancer stick."

This was quickly turning into a scene and a couple of the hotel staff intervened. With the unnecessary chaos interrupted, Bobby saw me standing there in horror. "Now look what you have done. This is my friend's birthday, and I won't let you ruin it. She hates cigarette smoke." As Pia rolled her eyes, I gave Bobby a nod of approval for a job well done. His solutions were dramatic, but he only wanted me to be happy this evening, without a complaint in the world.

"Desi and Vito, let's go. I will not have this punk ruin Isabella's birthday!"

Desi and Vito sent confused looks in my direction and then stood up to leave. They knew the only smart thing to do was get out of there fast.

It didn't matter that the Rose Bar didn't work out. I had remembered Pia's mentioning it at my first Nobu crazypants breakdown, so I thought it would be the perfect place to start the celebration of my thirtieth, but I didn't care about where we went, just the people I went with.

Outside, the car was waiting. Before getting into the getaway car, I turned, needing reassurance from Bobby. "Um ... do you think the restaurant will be up to par for you, Mr. New York State health inspector? I will see you at the restaurant." Pia and I slid into the car and were off to the Upper East Side. I wanted to spend more quality time with Pia, as we had not spent as much time together as a result of my crazypants chaos.

The car pulled up in front of the restaurant. Linking arms, Pia and I walked in and took center seats at the bar for a glass of Dom Perignon, a tradition my father started on my sixteenth birthday. Pia and I shared a private toast between the two of us. "To you, Isabella, and your thirties. I love you," Pia whispered, teary-eyed.

"To us and our friendship. I love you, too."

We had barely clinked our glasses when the bartender interfered. "Excuse me, but I could not help but hear."

Pia quickly cut him off. "You mean eavesdrop?"

He chuckled. "No ..." he said, not making eye contact with her but locking eyes with me. "Is it your thirtieth birthday? Well, someone is no longer a spring chicken. Happy birthday."

My mouth dropped. "Excuse me?"

"I'm just teasing. Why are women so sensitive? You are beautiful and do not look a day over twenty-five. The drinks are on me, sweetheart."

Nothing was going to irritate me this evening. I could not help but grin when I heard twenty-five. Oh, no, I was really getting old. That's what older woman do—become flattered when someone assumes they are much younger.

"Thank you," Pia said. "Now, if you could keep your lovely compliments to yourself and just pour."

Everyone was being so protective of my feelings; they all wanted to protect my new state of mind and heart.

"Darling, you all are being very sweet, but I'm fine. Please stop fussing over every little thing. I don't want things to be perfect. I want everything and everyone to just be." I turned to the bartender. "Thank you for the birthday wishes and champagne," I said politely. Then I heard the entourage enter from behind.

"Isssaaabbbeeelllaaaa!"

"Happy birthday to you, happy birthday to you ..."

"You silly little people! Shhh" I said, but I giggled. I loved the attention. There was my New York family: Bobby, Alexa, Vito, and Desi.

"Earth to Isabella, hello?" Bobby said, clearing his throat as he was always attention-deprived. "What are you thinking about, old lady?"

"So sorry; I'm just so happy to be here with all of you."

One of the four servers winked at me while handing me a menu. "Good evening and happy birthday to you." I noticed that our party was a bit loud and grabbing the attention of the other diners. I did not mind so much, as it was not in an obnoxious way. I mean, my table had the biggest attention-seekers, which was actually quite dangerous, now that I thought about it. It was my birthday, so that meant that the others would have to lay low in my presence in order not to take away the spotlight. I stifled a giggled while burying my face in the menu.

Bobby looked like he was about to jump out of his skin; he was waiting for a moment to take a jab, I was sure. "Isabella, lookey here, it's warm rolls and buuttterrrrr."

In an awe-struck manner, I peeked my head around the right side of my menu. "Yeah! Pure carbs and saturated animal fat—my favorite." Well, it was and especially at this restaurant, as the rolls were served in mini metal baking dishes, and the butter was soft and silky, just the way I loved it. A perfect, smooth spread. Tonight was purely a special treat. I was going to enjoy my birthday dinner without overdoing it and without the guilt.

I began buttering and eating while assessing the menu. "I have a suggestion for dinner tonight. There are so many yummy items on the menu, so why don't we do sort of a family style and order several of these sides? It is my birthday dinner."

"Of course, darling." Bobby winked as he agreed. "Your wish is our command. Whatever you want, Isabella."

Vito was on board. "We must do that; how could we not?" Desi was always about trying everything on the menu so that she could discuss anything if someone were to ask, "Have you ever been to David Burke & Donatella?" Desi was famous for saying, "Oh, it's amazzzzzing! You must go there to try ..." this or that.

Pia interrupted, "Well, that's what we always do, Isabella."

I never combined my Pia dinner extravaganzas with any of my other friends and wondered how she would deal with the loss of menu power. We never discussed it, but she knew she had been right about my going to Italy. However, she did accept that the best thing that happened to me was my standing back up on my own after hitting the ground so hard.

"Guys ... guys, do you really think all of this food is necessary?" Alexa asked seeming incredulous. "Isabella will die—her body will reject all this stuff."

We all whipped our heads in her direction in unison, Bobby with a jaw-dropping mouth. "Honey, this is not your birthday. Do not cause Isabella to force us to a healthy, organic, juice-fasting dinner, tonight of all nights. She will have us all taking turns doing headstands or one of her new crazy yoga moves. I refuse to sweat in Gucci," Bobby said, rolling his eyes.

"Excuse me," Alexa said, squinting her eyes.

"Excuse me!" I said, clearing my throat. "This is my birthday. Please order your own courses, and I will order extra starters and sides for the table. If you don't like it, well, don't eat it. I will taste here and there. This is a special treat for everyone tonight, and I will be back to organic and yoga tomorrow."

We all began laughing hysterically as we noticed that the table on each side of us had overheard our entire insane conversation.

"Sweet Jesus, Isabella. You already finished your roll." Bobby, being the typical smart ass that he was, gently slid his leftover half in my small bread dish, as he said it was too early in the dinner to seem like both the fat girl and the birthday girl. A disgusted gasp came from the woman at the table next to us, as she took Bobby's comment seriously. We all knew Bobby and how he loved picking on me, but he still could not help himself. Looking at her now, he leaned over and loudly whispered, "Oh, she just loves butter. Just watch her devour it."

Rolling my eyes and realizing it was going to take a while for everyone to adapt to the new Isabella Reynolds, I went back to studying the menu.

"Madam, are you ready?"

"Yes, thank you. I will be ordering for the table. We are having a family-style dinner this evening and sharing everything. Let's do the PB & J foie gras with macadamia nut butter, strawberry vanilla jam, and toasted brioche, and the bacon-wrapped Muscovy duck with the roasted mission fig, celery root puree, and pomegranate jus. I would like to order the market salad with goat cheese, walnuts, Asian pear, and extra crispy bacon, and the parfait of yellow fin tuna and salmon tartare with extra American sturgeon caviar. Also, some sides for the table—the eggplant and tomato gratin, the grilled asparagus with truffle emulsion, and the creamed spinach.

"We must do the handmade cavatelli and braised short ribs with wild mushrooms. I read that it was a signature dish, no?" Desi politely interrupted.

"Yes, of course," I agreed. "It looks amazzzzing." Even Desi got a laugh out of that one.

"I would like to make a toast," I said, raising my flute of bubbles.

"Darlin', hold on and put that glass down," Bobby interrupted. "Sir! Sir! Yes, we need six Kettle 'tinis with a twist. Now, I need you to listen very carefully. There is a precise way that this needs to be made. It is her birthday, and as her best friend—sorry, one of her closest friends—she needs the perfect 'tini-face. Are we on the same page here, sir?"

"Of course," the amused waiter responded.

"Now, pour dry vermouth in a martini glass. Swirl it around, then dump it out. Take Kettle One vodka and fill it to the top of the glass. It is very important that you do not waste any space. Then, garnish with a fresh and perfectly cut lemon twist," he added, tilting his head to the side as he eagerly waited for a solid confirmation from our server.

"Yes, sir."

Four minutes later, our perfect 'tinis arrived.

"Isabella, please proceed, but we need to do your birthday toast with the perfect 'tini," Bobby said proudly, like he'd just prevented a crisis.

I looked at him passively, my face expressionless. I was not impressed.

He quickly responded, "What? Ya know I'm fabulous."

As we all raised our 'tinis, I said, "I want to thank you all for joining me tonight. I am looking so forward to this new phase of my life. I love you all and could not imagine spending this night any differently, with anyone other than all of you. To us." With that, I took a *tiny* sip of my 'tini and then pushed the drink behind my water glass.

27

DINNER WAS SCRUMPTIOUS AND, OF course, we devoured everything, even all the sides I had ordered. Alexa ended up not sharing and eating half of the tomato and eggplant gratin, but I didn't use my "I told you so" card.

The waiter began to hand out the dessert menu, but I interrupted. "That won't be necessary."

"We would like one of those cheesecake lollipop trees with an extra side of raspberries, but no bubblegum whipped cream." Ever since I'd had a childhood dental checkup with bubblegum fluoride, I could no longer tolerate its smell. The restaurant was known for serving this tree-like display with a variety of lollipops that were filled with different types of a cheesecake filling. "Also—my favorite and a must—the coconut layer cake with the passion fruit sauce and coconut anglaise."

"Coconut cake?" Bobby asked. "When do you like coconut cake, you chocolate whore?"

"Well, wait until you taste this coconut cake; it is ridiculously ridiculous!"

And there it was. The coconut cake coming down the aisle to our table topped off with thirty-one sparkling candles (as I knew Bobby would take every opportunity to add another one if he could). As much as I loved attention, I felt myself go red as all eyes were turned to our table. Everyone in the restaurant was celebrating that night; it was Valentine's Day. However, we were celebrating my rebirth.

The server placed the creamy white monster before me. It was perfectly covered with slivers of freshly shaved coconut and of course, the fireworks display of candles. I quickly began blowing them out. Everyone stared, and Vito stood up and took pictures. "Wait a minute, birthday girl," the server interrupted. "Now, take a moment and make a wish. This only happens once a year. Give me a minute to relight."

I turned to Vito. "Please stop taking a million pictures. It will seem like we have never been to a nice restaurant before!" I said with amusement, though I was somewhat serious.

"Oh, zip it, Isabella. It's your birthday. Do you really care, Reynolds?"

"You are so right; flash away. Now make sure you get one when I'm really blowing them all out. Get me making my wish!"

"Okay, birthday girl. They are all yours."

I took a deep breath and closed my eyes. The past year flashed through my mind and heart.

This past year had been the hardest year of my life, because I was broken. I'd had lessons that people go through all the time, but knowing this hadn't made it easier for me, because I had been a virgin to such real pain. My company was about a dream of success; about starting something and seeing it to the end, no matter the outcome. Santo, I now realized, was a desperate dream of love. I so wanted to be loved that I'd settled for having someone there, even though I was unhappy. Potato was that unconditional love for me. When I cried for Potato, I cried because I'd lost something I was responsible for, who depended on me, and upon whom I depended in return.

He was silly, bad, never listened, and made my life so difficult at times, but I never questioned my love for him. Unconditional love is when one loves with the heart and nothing can interfere—not the ego, not pride, not even one's own pain. It can't be touched. After his death, I promised I would never take anyone for granted, no matter what.

After last year, however, I'd taken myself for granted and for the first time, I could not even be there for myself. I could not hold it together. I was confused; I had a broken heart. And the innocent little girl that was supposed to protect my soul was gone.

I also felt free from the vicious B&P cycle. I was aware that it would be a struggle at times, but I was fully aware that I would fight every day for it to no longer be a part of my life. I was my focus—my health and happiness and not some ridiculous size that was tagged in my skinny jeans.

Feeling emotional, I could only unwind by giggling under my breath. My wish was to never forget this lesson; to hold it near my heart to remind me when I needed a little reminding.

Just as I opened my eyes, the 33J woman on my flight to Rome entered my mind. *"Your number is eight, my dear; just you wait and see,"* she had whispered to me months back. Quickly, things that had happened in "eights" were flipping through my mind. The eight online potentials, the eight flight attendants on my journey to find myself, the eight-letter name compliment, Mr. No. 8 T-shirt, even the eight pounds I gained from eating mozzarella and tomato (which I never admitted to anyone). These "eights" played a crucial role in my transformation.

And then it practically slapped me across the face. *"Your number is eight, my dear; just you wait and see."* Was it possible that Konstantino was my number eight? Mr. No. 8 was my eight. I may have seen my soul mate! Immediately, the familiar feeling flashed through my chest, the feeling that I experienced that day with him in the bookstore. I didn't know if meeting Mr. No. 8 was a sign or a coincidence, and I wasn't going to try to figure it out. What I did know was that my heart that day in the bookstore and my dream caused me to feel butterflies once again. This was a relief—a broken heart would be incapable of feeling. I was thankful to know that I would love.

Smiling and adding a chance to see him again to my wish list, I released my breath, taking out candle after candle.

"God! That looks amazing," Desi whispered.

"Doesn't he? He is the loveliest person that my eyes have witnessed."

"He?" she asked, as everyone looked at me, confused.

"I mean, I told you. The coconut cake was the way to go. Pass me one of those lollipops, please!"

Sitting here among my closest people, I felt connected. Connected to my mind, body, spirit, and to something even bigger than me, something bigger than even all of us sitting here.

After a lovely evening, I was relieved to enter my apartment and get into comfy clothes.

When I walked inside, I was greeted with the overwhelming scent of all the floral arrangements. Removing my Manolos and my Krugerrand, I sank into the couch and admired it all, even the childish balloons. I admired this sense of being comfortable and the weight of confidence I felt. The weight of self-value. The weight of my heart and not the gold coin, or the pressure of the deep, hollow pain. The weight that no matter what happened, I would remain grounded in my Manolos.

Then I noticed it—the letter stacked at the top of my mail placed at the edge of the coffee table. I had forgotten all about it, as I had been so occupied with my birthday agenda.

It was the business proposal from my previous project manager with my skin care company. She was thrilled to hear about my new business venture and eager to learn how I came up with starting a juice delivery business in Manhattan. Now that my business loan was approved, we were both ready to jump into work. We were ready to juice Manhattan and cleanse the city.

My transformation taught me that sometimes love happens backwards. Even though, I was the last one to love myself, I realized that I was the first person I needed to love before I could love anyone else or be loved myself.

I grabbed my retreat journal and put pen to paper.

Journal entry—February 14, Valentine's Day
Dear me,

Happy thirtieth birthday. My whole life is ahead of me. Always remember that at all times I have the strength to deal with anything and that each new day is another day for me to learn and live my very best. By exploring and reflecting on the past year, I have found pain, joy, love, frustration, excitement, fear, doubt, and even hope and survival—all these wonderfully empowering elements that make life so worth living.

I see the bigger picture of these lessons learned. I have inherited the greatest reward: self-value.

It was the test of surrendering to my destiny and embracing whatever comes my way, with love. Honestly and truthfully loving by jumping right in, wholeheartedly, and not caring how it would end. Whether it is my destiny or a lesson that I'm going to get crushed to bits and pieces, I will no longer fear rejection. It does not mean that I was not good enough, I didn't deserve it, or I failed. Absolutely not. It means it wasn't meant to be.

This spiritual opportunity allowed me to have a profound connection to myself. To reveal my truth. This is something some people dream of and can only hope for. I will never again, turn my back on life or love. Especially, the love for myself.

In my life, I will love wholeheartedly and love honestly. Whatever I do, I will do it beautifully.

Isabella Reynolds